Indian Immigrant

By

Biku Ghosh

Donated to friendly library

Biku Ghosh

1

'We looked for workers. We got people instead'

Max Frisch

To

Julie and Laura

Indian Immigrant

Indians have been travelling to and settling in Britain since the early 1600s, about as long as Britons have been sailing to India. Colonialism powerfully altered what being 'Indian' meant culturally and legally in Britain—a meaning that has been quite differently perceived in India and in the lived experience of Indians who ventured into Britain.

Contents

Glossary of Indian words

Adda – A gathering of friends for an informal chat

Almirah – A free-standing wardrobe

Anchal – The end of a sari

Baba – Father

Bangal – Someone from East Bengal with a thick accent

Begun bhaja – Deep-fried spiced aubergine

Beguni – Battered and deep-fried aubergine

Benarasi Sari - A sari made in Varanasi also known as Benaras. The saris made of finely woven silk and are decorated with intricate designs and worn by the brides in India during weddings.

Bindi – A coloured dot worn on the centre of the forehead

Boumoni – A term of endearment for one treated as a sister-in-law

Brahma Samaj – A Hindu reform movement during the Bengal Renaissance

Carrom – A South Asian 'strike-and-pocket' tabletop game

Chacha – A Muslim uncle

Chokari – A young girl

Dada – Elder brother (often friends and relatives of slightly older ages are also referred to by adding 'da' at the end of their names, e.g. Amitda)

Dadi – Grandma

Dadu – Grandad

Didi – Elder sister (often friends and relatives of slightly older ages are also referred to by adding 'di' to the end of their names, e.g. Aratidi)

Diwan – Administrator

Dupatta – Scarf

Fuchka – Indian snack

Ghat serang – An agent for the supply of Lascars

Ghugni – A chickpea snack

Jaggery – Cane sugar

Jhupris – Shacks

Kajal – An eye cosmetic
Kaji Nazrul – A Bengali poet, writer, and revolutionary
Kalikata – An earlier name of Calcutta / Kolkata
Khoka babu – Little boy
Kakima – Aunty
Lascars – Sailors from the Indian subcontinent
Luchi – Deep-fried Indian flatbread
Mehsub and mohan thal – Gujrati sweets
Mesomasay – Uncle
Namaz – Muslim prayer
Naxals – An ultra-left communist group in India
Nikah and ijab, qubul – Muslim wedding
Ojha – A person carrying out spells, incantations, and wizardry
Payesh – Indian rice pudding
Pranam – Paying respect, usually by touching feet
Sari – Commonly worn female garment in India
Shadi – Wedding
Shahid Minar – Column erected for the Martyrs
Shalwar kameez – Loose pyjama-like trousers and a long shirt or tunic
Shehnai – A musical instrument similar to an oboe
Sindur – Red pigment applied in the parting of the hair by married Hindu women
Sradha ceremony – A Hindu ritual performed after death
Subedar – Non Commissioned Officer
Zamindar – Landlord

Part One

1700 - First World War

In the first 300 years of Indian immigration, the majority of immigrants were seamen, servants, and, in the later part, some professionals. Many perished during the treacherous voyage and then in the harsh conditions they faced in a cold and inhospitable country. The alien population was somehow tolerated, but racial prejudices and injustices were frequent. Since the mid-nineteenth century, many professionals travelled, some for further education and many more as soldiers for the British army. Some of them successfully integrated into British society, albeit facing many difficulties in their personal lives along the way.

Chapter One

1710: Hooghly dock, Sutanuti, Bengal

Subal Das and five friends from his village, all in their early twenties, had walked several miles to the Hooghly dock by the Sutanuti village. This year, as well as the year before, there had been severe droughts in the country with very little work available in the fields with the local landlords. They had heard that some money could be made, albeit for just a few weeks, by loading and unloading from the foreign ships coming down the big river. Two Portuguese ships had just sailed away towards the sea as they arrived. They had since waited patiently for a few days for any sign of another ship. All of them were awestruck at the sight of the newly built Fort Williams, which was constructed by the British on the banks of the river only a few miles south of the port. Suddenly, in the early morning, there was excitement all around.

Pointing south in the river, an old docker said, 'There. A big ship is coming up the river.'

Still shivering from the early morning chill of the autumn and the gentle wind flowing by the river, they had all pulled their homespun cotton shawls tightly around themselves before running to the bank of the river. They strained their eyes hard only to find no sign of any ship in the dense morning fog and mist rising from the Hooghly River.

'Where is it?' asked several of them.

'It is coming. Believe me. You will see soon.'

Subal, always a dreamer, was mesmerised by the serene beauty of the mist rising from the gently flowing wide river. The sun had already risen lazily behind them for the last half an hour and its weak rays were still playing with the gentle waves of the river and the fog above it. He had always loved walking by the small stream next to his village during the sunrise. He found it almost hypnotizing to walk in the thick of the fresh smell rising from the green grass with the dewdrops still hanging on to their blades and gleaming with the delicate rays of the morning sun. The light fog hanging on to the narrow stream and early morning chatter of the birds, still unwilling to fly out of their comfy nests from almost ghostlike trees covered in patches with mist, always accentuated his bliss. But the elegance of this wide river with the other bank still imperceptible due to the haze was something else. Soon his daydream drifted to Shyama, his newly married wife of only a few months. Her beautiful face, as if carved out of dark stone, appeared in the misty horizon with her long flowing dark hair, not covered by the end of her sari like it usually was in front of others, but now like it was when she was alone with him.

His reverie was soon broken by someone calling out, 'Yes, I think I can now see the top of the mast.'

After only fifteen minutes, the large white sails of a ship were appearing through the fog, almost as if in a dream.

'Oh, there is another one coming behind it! No, there are two more!' someone shouted frantically.

It had taken more than an hour for the ships to arrive at the dock and still another hour for them to anchor. Already awed by the sight of the big ships with their tall masts and sails, Subal and his friends looked with open mouths at the men on board giving orders. They were not sure what they found most intriguing, the bright uniforms of the men or the colour of their red and white skin. It was like nothing they had ever seen in their lives.

All the men ashore, more than a hundred in total from the local villages, were given orders by the sahibs to come up to the ships and unload. Most of the more than eighty crewmen from each ship had gone ashore after their long voyage to rest and enjoy themselves. It was hard and back-breaking work for the next seven days, unloading heavy sacks containing mainly woollen and some metal goods. The ship's hold was only a quarter full coming up. Only a few sahibs who were present on the ship gave orders to the Bengalis. After unloading the cargo, they were asked to clean up the hull and the decks first, and then were supervised during some repair work around the ship and its sail. Subal and his friends had looked with nervousness at the several cannons mounted all around these large ships, each of which had three tall masts. They were told these guns were to protect the flotilla of ships from the pirates on the sea, mainly the Portuguese and Dutch ones.

Subal, who enjoyed climbing coconut trees to pick green coconuts, was thrilled when he was ordered to climb up the tall masts for maintenance work.

He shouted to his friends from near the top of the mast, 'I can see the whole of Sutanuti village from here, and further! Oh, on the other side I can see most of Kalikata!' Then, cupping his hands in front of his eyes, excitedly he said, 'I think I can just about make out the big Banyan tree outside our village.'

He was soon sternly ordered by the sahibs to finish his work up the mast and come down. They were paid their wages every evening after almost twelve hours of work. The money was definitely more than they earned after working all day in the fields for the zamindars in their villages. During this time, Subal learnt that twelve of the crew on this ship alone, and over forty between the three ships, had died on the long voyage from England due to some unknown illness. The captain was looking for any Bengalis to join the crew. None of the Bengalis, however, were keen on having to leave their families, possibly forever. They were ordered to load the ship, mainly with cotton, silk, calico, chintz, indigo dye, and molasses, as well as spices. After almost four weeks, the ships were loaded almost to their full capacities with the merchandise and were apparently due to sail the next day.

By the early evening, Subal and nine others were finishing with the last of the loading of water, fresh food, and vegetables in the hull when suddenly the door was shut from above. They started knocking at the locked door and then started shouting but there was no answer. After a long, hard day of work, all of them were bone tired and hungry, but now they were really scared.

'What is happening?'

'I think we are being taken as slaves,' someone said, shaking with fear.

After a few hours of shouting and trying to open the door from below in vain, some of them fell asleep on the floor. Subal, who had been married only six months back, could not sleep but only thought of his Shyama.

Several hours later, in the darkness of the hull, they were not sure if it was still night or early morning, but soon realised from the noises above deck and the movement of the boat that they were now sailing. Again, all of them started knocking loudly together at the locked door, but without any response. The place was slowly becoming damp with some water seeping through the bottom of the hull. Without food and water, in the darkness and damp, they were not sure how many days, perhaps two or three, had gone by before the door was opened from above and a sahib with a musket pointing towards them commanded everyone to come up.

Once up on the deck, they were all lined up with two sahibs pointing guns at them. They could see that the ships were now sailing on the open sea with no land to be seen on any side. Then they were all beaten up severely with whips by two other sahibs. Subal's friend Atul, who was taller than everyone else and more muscular, received more of a beating than anyone else. Soon they were marched down the hull and were ordered to clean up their vomit and excrement first before being sent back down there again. They were shown how to use the bilge pump to mop up the water from the seeping hull. Finally, they were given some water and thrown some scraps of bread, and the door was locked again.

'I will never see my widowed mother again now. She was very sick and begged me not to leave her. I didn't listen,' said one of them and began to cry, slapping his hand over his chest.

Most sobbed, whilst a few cried loudly. Subal could not cry. He just sat hunched over with his head between his legs, thinking of his beautiful young wife, Shyama, who had told only him before he had left, with some embarrassment, that she thought she might be pregnant.

The next morning, the hull door was opened and the men were ordered to come up and line up with guns pointed at them. Then they were all beaten up again with sticks, Atul more than the others. They were now allocated to work in different parts of the ship alongside the English sailors, mostly scrubbing and cleaning and using the bilge pumps. They were also shown how to furl and unfurl the sails. By the end of the day they were given water and some bread and sent down to the hull, but the door was left open. Soon the other sailors came down and made their beds in the drier part of the hull by the stacked goods, as far as possible from the cowering group of Bengalis huddled together in one corner.

The beatings continued every morning for the next three days, although they became less savage. Four of them, including Subal, were sent to help in the kitchen. The larder was stocked mostly with beef and pork, dried fish, flour and bread, cheese, butter, oatmeal, and dried peas. There were also gallons of fresh water and rum. Fresh vegetables and fruits were stocked separately to be consumed within the next few weeks. Subal and his friend learnt how to make loaves of bread from flour and to boil the meat before lunch and dinner.

'What are we going to eat? Only bread and oatmeal?' whispered his friend.

'Even if I starve to death, I am not going to touch any meat. I was born Hindu and will die Hindu,' replied Subal.

He need not have worried, as the Bengalis were given only some bread and water once a day during the voyage. They were grateful, as after a few days on the sea some old clothes and rugs were thrown at them, most likely having been used by the dead sailors on their journey to India from England.

One early morning, Ali, the youngest of the kidnapped group, was found by one of the sahib sailors praying on the deck facing away from the sunrise. He slumped on the deck after he was kicked repeatedly and then pulled up to be beaten mercilessly with a whip. Next, one of the abducted Bengalis was ordered to pull up a bucket

15

of fresh salty sea water which was poured over his raw, bleeding wounds.

While working in the kitchen, Subal managed to find and hide some lard under his clothes. He brought it down later and gently applied it over Ali's sore wounds. A few days later Ali was caught again, this time doing his Namaz inside the hull early in the evening. He was brought up to the deck and again whipped savagely before salty sea water was poured over his wounds. The same night, Subal found him creeping up to the deck quietly and, before he could stop him, Ali jumped out into the open sea. Subal kept his mouth shut before returning to his bed, crying in despair.

Punishment by beating and depriving of food and water for even the minutest of failings was now commonplace and almost accepted by the captured lascars. After a few weeks of sailing, they were all happy to see the ships sailing towards land.

Soon they found the sahibs pointing towards the land and shouting to each other, 'Mauritius!'

When all three ships anchored by the island, only the sahibs went by small boats to land onshore. Lining up by the deck, the Bengalis could make out Indian-looking men running to receive them no less than a hundred yards away. They became excited to see that also lining up by the decks of the other two ships were thirty other Bengalis who were working with them earlier in the Hooghly dock. They started shouting to each other in Bengali but soon were ordered by the sahibs to be quiet.

In the next few days, boatloads of sugar and dark wood were loaded into the ships. The Indians were amazed that most of the Mauritians looked like themselves but neither could speak nor understand each other's language. They were also completely taken aback by a few other men who had come aboard to load.

'They look like giants. Look at their skin. It's as dark as the wood which they are bringing up onboard,' whispered Subal.

'It's called ebony, I heard,' said one.

'And they are so big and strong. Any one of them can easily throw two of the sahibs over their shoulders, yet they are so subdued and never look any of the sahibs in their eyes,' said Subal.

One night, under the cover of darkness, two of the captured Bengalis from Subal's ship jumped into the sea, swam towards the shore away from the dock, and hid under the bushes. They found to their surprise that five other Bengalis from the two other ships were already hiding there.

After finally loading up with some fresh water, fruit, and vegetables a week later, the ships sailed again. So far, the only luck the Bengalis had had was sailing in the calm sea. The sailing now became very rough and an extremely cold wind was chilling them to the bone. They were now glad to have been given the rugs and clothes of the dead sailors. They were also happy to now be allowed, on alternate days, some boiled vegetables with their bread.

Two of the Bengalis, along with Subal, had been fighting a severe cough and fever for the last few days. Subal had somehow managed to carry on with his work with some help from his friends. But now, with the cold wind and rough sailing, in spite of the beatings, the other two were unable to get up to the dock. Most of the lascars had now gotten used to puking regularly with the large waves battering the ships. They learnt to clean up their vomit quickly to avoid further beatings. After a few more weeks of rough sailing, the ships came to another port. Again, the Bengalis were not allowed onshore. Most of the sahibs went ashore, leaving a few of them behind with guns guarding the decks.

'I heard them calling this place "Cape of Good Hope,"' said one of the Bengalis.

'I don't see any good hope for us,' sighed Atul.

This time, the ship was loaded with fresh water, fruit, and vegetables brought up by only the ebony-coloured giants. With the sahibs' guns pointing at them, they also carefully brought up a few wooden boxes which were taken straight to the captain's room. The Bengalis learnt much later that they contained gold and diamonds. In the nights, there was now always a sentry with a gun on the dock. After only a week at the port the ships sailed again, now going west towards constant high winds and cold. It wasn't long before the ships were facing a severe storm. Four men, including two of the Bengalis,

17

were lost in the sea during this storm. Subal and his mates were cowering, huddled together.

If they understood any English they would have heard the captain shouting to other sahibs, 'These Indians are like animals, completely useless and easily panicked! In a crisis they will not be worth saving.'

After almost a full day, the storm was replaced by only a strong cold wind. One of the Bengalis who had already been very sick and had been unable to get up died. The lascars were ordered to throw his body into the sea.

It took another eight weeks before the ship was sailing into much calmer waters with many other ships sailing on either side. From the excited talks of the sahibs, Subal and his friends learnt that they were coming close to London. After another day in the thick, freezing fog, the ships docked at the busy Port of London. It took them all almost ten days of working over fourteen hours a day to unload all the cargo from the ship and carry it to the nearby warehouses.

After all the cargo was unloaded and the ships were cleaned thoroughly, the Bengalis were paid their wages and ordered to leave the ship.

The Bengalis pleaded with the few English words they had picked up over the last few months in the ship, saying, 'Sahib. Please. We free work. Please, we go Bengal.'

They all begged and begged the big sahibs with tears running down their faces, but they were flatly refused and guns were pointed at them.

One of the officers said, 'We go to Venice next. Go away from our ship now.'

While the English sailors went to find their mates, families, and places to stay, all the Bengalis from the three ships huddled together on the port under a torn shade. The cold, drizzly rain falling from the sky with the thick covering of clouds of the British winter could only accentuate their misery. It turned out that ten more of the Bengalis had died on the voyage in total, either washed away from the deck during the storm or due to illness. There were still twenty-two of them left from the three ships, with two seriously ill and unable to even walk.

Little did the Bengalis know that the cargo they had loaded in Bengal and unloaded in London would make over 200 per cent profit in the English and European market! Also, they had no knowledge that the Honourable East India Company had asked for the English monarch's support with their trade in India by writing to Queen Anne only a few months earlier. After all, the company was already contributing several million pounds every year to the nation's revenue from its trade with India. Not even the masters of this company dreamed that in only forty-seven years, after the Battle of Plassey, the British merchants would take control of Bengal and would thus plant the seeds of establishing the largest and most profitable colony, its 'Crown Jewel' in India.

The cold and wretched newly arrived immigrants found some comfort in finding that more Indians were already working in the dock in miserable conditions, although as they came from different parts of India, neither spoke each other's language. In a way, they were not that different from the many other wretched, strange-looking people also working on the dock, who they later learnt were called the Chinese.

Abandoned by their abductors on a miserably cold foreign land in the harsh winter with no proper shelter or food, within a week both of the sick new immigrants perished. Forced into extreme poverty and close to starvation, the remaining miserable new aliens in the country tried to find whatever jobs they could in the port and around the streets of London. There was often stiff competition with the local stevedores, who looked in no better condition than the immigrants, for loading and unloading the arriving and departing ships at the dock. For the newly arrived Bengalis, with no education of spoken English, finding jobs even as street sweepers or loaders in the warehouses was tough due to the competition with the poor natives of London. A few tried to survive as beggars on the street.

19

Like most, Subal returned to the dockside as often as he could, not only to find scraps of menial jobs but also for any opportunity to get a return voyage home. In their first English winter, five more of the remaining twenty immigrants died on the streets of London.

Their miserable existence in the inhospitable weather and amongst unwelcoming locals, with no regular prospect of any work, continued relentlessly over the years. Subal had a recurring dream that Shyama had given birth to a beautiful baby girl. He tried to withstand all the hardship by imagining his daughter growing up at home. He named her Sukhi, 'the happy one'. Whenever things got really tough, he kept thinking of Sukhi and Shyama. Three years later, Atul was lucky enough not only to get a job as a street sweeper but also to take a destitute English girl as his wife after nominally converting to Christianity. He was christened as James. He tried several times at the dock to be allowed to bring his wife back to India with him. Over the last few years they had earned enough money between them to save for the passage, and he was also happy to work his way back as a lascar. But he was flatly refused by the captain, not because of their interracial marriage but on the grounds of safety.

'It would be completely unfitting for an English woman to be allowed on such a long voyage among so many unruly sailors,' he was told bluntly.

Some of the other Bengalis had moved to the surrounding towns outside London to find whatever meagre existence they could manage, and they had not been seen since. But Subal had been coming back to the dock area for the last few years whenever he could, looking for work to survive. His trips to the dock were also mostly to get a chance for a return passage home.

After almost six years, out of the thirty plus abducted Bengali lascars, he was the only lucky one to get a chance to return. Apparently, at the last minute, a few of the British crewmen of a ship were taken away by the police for a murder at the pub they were drinking at the night before their sail to India and the ship urgently required replacement crewmen.

Subal hardly noticed the arduous journey and hard work onboard, dazed at the thought of returning back to his family. Five months later, after arriving at the port in Kalikata, he was allowed offshore to unload and was told to come back in a few days to collect his wages, a total of five rupees for the return journey. He did not care that this was the only amount he had earned to show for his six years of hardship and labour in England. He only wanted to get back to his village and to his family as quickly as possible and decided to leave at the first opportunity, even without his pay. He was surprised at how much more the port had changed than he remembered. Two days later, as soon as he could slip away from the sahibs' guns, he left for his village without his wages.

Arriving at the village in the late morning, he was shocked to see from a distance that his mother was sitting outside their house wearing a widow's white sari. Seeing Subal coming over, she started crying loudly. Subal soon found out that his father had died two years back.

When he asked his widowed mother, 'Where is Shyama?' she just went on crying inconsolably, slapping her chest.

Subal soon found out from the gathered neighbours that a few months after he left his family looking for work at the port, Shyama had gone to her parents to give birth to their child. She had then died in childbirth from bleeding. Their newborn daughter had also died only a month later.

The next morning, Subal's body was found hanging from a tree next to their house.

Chapter Two

1810: Madras dock

No one in Telangana really knew or cared that more than half of the lascars going to Britain in the last century had died, either from jumping ship to avoid torture or in the harsh conditions in the cold and inhospitable voyage and then in the foreign land. Neither did they know that the great famine, lasting almost a decade in their world, had taken the lives of at least eleven million people in the country. Survivors had called it 'skull famine' as bones of the dead lay unburied or cremated, whitening the roads and the fields. This was followed only a decade after with another famine lasting a few years in the same region. Although it had been a few years since the last drought, finding work in the land was hard even now and it was hardly enough to sustain their families.

Groups of men from different parts of south India had travelled far and gathered over the months in the port of Madras with the hope of finding jobs as seamen in the merchant ships. A ghat serang, a fellow Indian who had apparently already been to England twice, appeared to have taken the role of the recruiting agent. His additional qualification was that he could speak and understand a smattering of English.

'We need a total of one hundred and eighty Lascars for the three ships which will be sailing in four weeks from here. All three ships will be going to London, which is in England,' shouted the serang to the gathering crowd.

Of more than 300 people already there, everybody rushed to gather around the man.

'My name is Athmanathan. You can call me Athma. I want you all to stand in three lines for me and then I will come around to choose the ones fit for the jobs,' he ordered.

Soon there were three lines of expectant men. People from the nearby villages queued on the same line so they could spend the long journey together.

The serang came along inspecting the lines and summarily dismissed the older and more frail-looking men first. Then he went to the office and came back with one of the sahibs for his final selection. Standing under the hot mid-morning equatorial sun of Madras, all the remaining men were now sweating profusely.

'Who do you have in the family?' asked the sahib, prodding one in the line with his stick. Athma interpreted for him.

'No one. Both of my parents died in the famine and I was their only child,' he replied.

The sahib nodded to his agent.

'Okay. Stand aside,' said Athma.

Soon it was apparent that they only wanted the men with the least family baggage. After about forty-five minutes, a total of 200 were selected and the rest were told to go.

'A final number of one hundred and eighty for the voyage will be decided after we see how well you all work in loading the ships!' shouted Athma.

Some of them still hung around with faint hope.

All the lascars gladly worked hard for the next three weeks to load their ships for the voyage. They happily ignored the occasional prodding to their stomachs with sticks by the sahibs and even by the ghat serang. Finally, the day before the ships were due to sail, twenty or so men were arbitrarily told that they were not strong enough for the journey.

The disappointed group of men gathered around Athma and asked, 'What about our wages for the last few weeks' work?'

When the serang found himself in a tight situation with the group of disgruntled men, he raised his hands, saying, 'All right, I will see what I can do. Come with me to the office.'

He went inside the port office and after a while came back with one of the sahibs who had a gun. 'I have managed to negotiate three rupees for each of you for your work for us. Come and collect them now, then leave this area.'

The defeated group of men had no choice and left after collecting their money, not knowing that the ghat serang had cheated each of them out of almost half of their wages.

Athma soon gathered the selected lascars and explained to the future seamen that for each month of their five- to six-month journey they would receive a salary of thirty-eight shillings, the equivalent of sixteen rupees a month. Also, when in England, they would get an allowance of seven shillings each week for maintenance pending their return passage to India. They would of course be required to work there as needed by the company. They were also told clearly that they must return back once a return passage to India had been found.

'But you have to work hard and wages will be deducted if you fail to do so or show any indiscipline,' added the serang.

The lascars happily signed up to a company bond in front of the port officials and two of the sahibs from the ship. Some of them tried to calculate with their friends how much money they would make in total for the journey. This was a lot more money than the prospective seamen would have made at home and everyone signed happily. They were also pleasantly surprised when all the lascars were given two coats and a blanket each, although some of them were old and already used.

Little did they know that the British seamen would be earning at least three times more than them on the same voyage and the British sailors had already been difficult to recruit as many of them were now drafted to the Royal Navy fighting in the Napoleonic War. Neither did they have any idea that Athma would be earning almost twice their salary on the ship.

24

In the first few days of sailing there was not much work for the lascars to do, but they were always kept on their toes by having to clean the decks and the rails and with repair jobs for the hull and the sails. They were also drafted in batches to help in the kitchen. Soon they were aggrieved to find out that the food ration they were getting on a daily basis was always much less than the British seamen and it was of inferior quality. When one of the lascars mentioned this to the serang, he was asked to stand aside and was then beaten savagely with a stick. Others watched silently. The complaining lascar was also told that his wages would be docked for one week. They realised that the Athma never did any work himself except when in the presence of the sahibs and always expected to be treated by the lascars as one of the sahibs. Soon they also learnt that he expected a quarter of their salary each month as his commission.

Rough treatment from the sahibs was common, often for no apparent reason, and it was then replicated by the serang. It got so unbearable at times that when the ships were due to land in a port in Africa for the purpose of getting fresh water and other supplies, a few of the lascars jumped overboard in the darkness and swam ashore to hide behind the trees, never to return.

With poor and unhealthy diets, a total of eight lascars in three ships died from severe diarrhoea and vomiting. In the five-and-a-half-month journey to England, a total of another thirty lascars from the three ships died due to the rough sea and ill health related to their poor living conditions. Their bodies were simply thrown overboard.

Two of the lascars who tried to earn favours from the ghat serang often used the tactics of spying against their fellow seamen. They soon learned from Athma that after this voyage he was hoping to return back home with enough money to buy some property before settling down to marry. However, he never mentioned to them that he was the person responsible for handing over the money due to the dead sailors to their relatives on his return to India.

'This will definitely be my last time going over to England to make money,' he confided to them one day.

Once the ships docked in London, the lascars were kept busy unloading the ships for the next few days. Then they were lined up by the dockside and were given their wages for the last few months. Shivering against the cold wind, none had any idea about English money and they did not know if they were being short-changed.

The ghat serang then told them, 'For your weekly maintenance payment, you will need to come and sign here in the port office. This will be only until a return passage to India has been found for you.'

'Where can we stay until then?' asked one of the lascars timidly.

'There are some lodges nearby. There is one called Gole's Depot not very far away and they can arrange transfer from here by cart. They will charge you but they are not very expensive. If you want, I can help you to find them.'

He did not feel the need to say that he would obviously expect a commission. Then he added, 'Do not get involved in any nuisances or create any trouble. You will end up in jail.'

'What about any work while we are here?' asked another lascar.

'You have to come back here at the dock and look for a job if you want one. You might also be lucky to find some job around the city from time to time,' Athma replied.

Soon most of the lascars left in small groups in search of places to stay. A few went straight to the local taverns in search of some proper food and drink. The newly arriving lascars, sitting in a group in the alehouses, soon found out that the only food available was bread, soup with potatoes, and boiled mutton. They all sighed and realised that rice with hot and spicy curry would only be in their dreams until their return.

With money in his pocket, Athma went to another tavern away from the dock which he had found during his previous trip. He ordered some beer and bread with soup. Three of his fellow British shipmates soon also entered the place. They had been jealous of the serang over the last few months, of a native enjoying all the privileges of a Brit from the officers on the ship. One of them went and whispered to the owner of the establishment.

As Athma was finishing his soup and bread and starting to drink his beer, he was soon joined at his table by a young woman in provocative clothes.

'Hello, sailor. Looking for a good time?' she asked with a broad smile on her face.

Athma spoke to her in a hushed voice. 'What's your name?'

'My name is Nelly. But you can call me whatever you want.'

'Do you have a place?'

'No. How can a girl like me have a place? Surely you can get a room in the back of this place if you ask.'

After finishing his drink, Athma went to the bar and quietly asked for a room. Soon he returned, jangling a set of keys and a bottle of wine in his hand.

'Let's go,' he told the woman.

As they left, the woman, who was following behind him, winked at the other sailors.

Once both were inside the small room at the back, Athma locked the door from the inside. He left his belongings and his blue coat inside a small cupboard in the room. Then, sitting on the end of the small bed, he indicated to the woman to join him. Soon they were kissing and the woman started taking off her clothes. In no time they were in a carnal embrace. After almost half an hour of sexual pleasure, Athma fell asleep, mostly due to exhaustion from his long voyage.

He woke up to the sound of the door being unlocked by the woman carrying his belongings. Outside the door were his fellow British shipmates. Wrapping the bedsheet around his waist, he chased them to the door, but two of the sailors hit him hard on his chest, almost knocking him out. Athma found the empty bottle near the door and attacked the sailors. One of them suffered a big cut on his face and started bleeding profusely. With all the commotion, the landlord soon arrived with a few other men. After checking on the injured sailor, he asked some of his men to restrain Athma and sent one of them to call for the police. By this time, the woman had already left with his money.

As soon as the police arrived, they put a handcuff on Athma. He tried to explain about the woman who had stolen his hard-earned money and was working in collusion with these sailors.

The lodge owner flatly denied the presence of any woman in his premises, saying, 'This is a reputable establishment. We never allow prostitutes here. You already know this, I am sure, officer.'

The police asked Athma to put on some clothes and then took him into custody. After spending several days and nights in miserable conditions in a police cell crowded with many other criminals, he was sent to the court before a judge with the charges of affray, violence, and bodily harm to a British sailor.

Athma tried to plead his case to the court in his broken English but avoided mentioning the prostitute involved as he was not sure whether that would bring further charges against him. He was sentenced to five years of hard labour in prison.

To add to the miserable conditions of the prison, he was often beaten up by other British criminals and the prison guards for no apparent reason. In the third year of his prison term, his health broke down badly and he was released on probation on compassionate grounds. Penniless, he returned to the dock office looking for any job to sustain himself but was denied any position because of his criminal record. There was of course no question of any further obligation to fund his maintenance payment or his return passage.

Neglected and destitute, he had no option but to resort to begging in the street. Already in poor health, in the winter months sleeping in the open air or beneath some paltry covering without any warm, decent clothing, Athma was found desperately ill on the streets outside the eastern dock. Luckily, he was spotted by a local social reformer and was taken to a hospital in a desperate condition. He recovered very slowly there and was well enough after almost six months to be sent to a workhouse.

Still in poor health while in the workhouse, he was spotted by a visiting priest as the only native in the place. The pastor advised him that if he converted to Christianity he might be able to help him in finding a return passage to his homeland.

In desperation, Athma agreed without much hesitation. Soon after, at the local church and in the presence of a few people from the community, he was baptised as William. Soon a job as a servant was found for him in a local landlord's house. The priest kept his promise by applying to the shipping company for a return passage for him, a fellow Christian.

By this time, Athma had fallen seriously ill again and was taken back to the hospital. While in hospital, he heard the news that a return passage had been secured for him on a ship due to sail in a month's time. Athma, now known as William, passed away in his hospital bed a week later. His body was buried in the local cemetery in a simple ceremony.

Chapter Three

There was some excitement in the poor village of Chaitpur in North Bihar. Three scouts, one rumoured to be from Calcutta, had come to the village looking for able-bodied people to sign up for jobs in the new tea gardens.

'We are looking for young families, even those with young children, for these jobs in the tea estates. This will mean that your men will not have go away, leaving the family behind for months on end. And both men and women can work and will be paid for their labour.'

'Where will the family stay?' someone asked.

'You will have your own place in the lines at the estate where there will also be other families. If more families from this village join up, you will have them as your neighbours.'

For the last few years, lives had been hard, not only in this village but for miles around. Three families from Chaitpur agreed to the allure of five years of security as indentured bonded labourers at the tea estate.

In 1833, when the British lost the monopoly of its tea trade with China, Assam, in the foot hills of the Himalayas, where the possibility of growing tea had already proven successful in the last two decades, became the focal point of the beginning of the tea industry in India. This state recently acquired from Burma, through forcefully implementing the Yandabo treaty by the Honourable East India Company, was soon added to the developing tea industry in the country. In 1840, the Assam Tea Company started commercial production of tea with the indentured servitude of labourers. Land was offered in North-Eastern India to any European who agreed to cultivate tea for export.

In spite of the British having their problems in their tea trade with China, they knew well about the Chinese expertise when it came to the skill and experience of working in tea gardens. Because of this, initially many Chinese workers were recruited in the tea gardens of Assam. But the Chinese workers were generally hard to control due to their protesting attitude. Because of this, with a long-term view, the company started to recruit local workers, mostly local Assamese initially and then people from the surrounding states of Bihar, North Orissa, Chattisgarh, Chotanagpur, and Bengal. They were paid lower wages than the Chinese workers.

Soon, the plantation owners realised that the indentured labourers far away from their homes were to be favoured over the local Assamese as they were less likely to leave to go to visit their families nearby. The owners preferred groups of families over individuals as they were more inclined to settle permanently in the estates. It also meant they could use the services of all family members, men, women, and children. In addition it reduced costs, as women were paid less and children were often paid nothing.

Sayeed and his wife Hasina, both in their late thirties, had come to work in the tea estate with their only daughter, sixteen-year-old Roshni. They had lost their second baby at only a few weeks old and their seven-year-old boy, Karim, had died only last year with a high fever.

Roshni was pointing excitedly at the sloping hills to the east. 'It is so beautiful here. Ma, you were sleeping in the morning and when the sun was rising over the hills breaking up the clouds, it was like magic!'

The tea gardens in the northern part of India flourished before long and were exporting hundreds of tonnes of tea to Britain from India, and the plantation owners were enjoying the most lavish lifestyle in their bungalows. Mr Kirkland, the owner of the tea estate who was from Scotland, had inherited some money as the only child after both his parents had died early. Now in his early thirties, he wanted to travel to India and acquiring the tea garden in Assam was not difficult. He named it 'Kirkwell Tea Estate'.

The Sayeed family lived in jhupris with another fifty or so families. Their walls were made of tree branches and mud, with sloping roofs consisting of branches and leaves. This was not too different than what they had in their own villages. A plantation worker's regular job, which started in May and went on almost until the end of November, involved men carrying out heavy work digging in the hard mountain soil and taking out the stones. Then they had to plant tea roots in rows. Women picked up tea leaves in large baskets tied to their backs. After plucking the buds and leaves, they needed to separate them, dry them, and finally store them. For the rest of the year, in the winter months, they had to look after the tea bushes, making sure there was adequate drainage and levelling the ground, which was harder because of the cold weather and occasional snow. In spite of the daily hard work from sunrise to evening, the Sayeeds were reasonably happy with at least guaranteed jobs and a regular, if meagre, income for all three of them.

One late afternoon, while Sayeed was carrying loaded baskets somewhere else, in the fading afternoon sun Hasina and Roshni were picking tea leaves. Mr Kirkland walked past them before stopping to look at the two women. He could not take his eyes off Roshni. Against the setting sun, which added to the natural beauty of the healthy teenager, her light brown skin was glowing. She had inherited her skin colour from her mother, who had very dark skin, and her father, who had very pale skin, almost like the sahibs. She also had long, soft dark hair which was now tied back, but her most striking feature was her beautiful face which was lit up with dark, almost black, eyes. Both mother and daughter were singing softly together but stopped upon seeing the sahib and his men walking by.

After stopping by them for several minutes, Mr Kirkland asked his diwan, 'Can you ask this family to come up to my bungalow this evening?'

The diwan saluted, saying, 'Yes, sir,' and then ordered Hasina accordingly.

At home, Roshni asked her mother afterwards, 'Do you think we are going to be punished for singing while working?'

Her mother did not reply but was definitely worried and started the open fire to cook for the family. Soon Sayeed came home looking exhausted. Hasina explained the afternoon's events to him.

After finishing their day's work, they were all hungry, but Sayeed said, 'We must go now. Wash yourself quickly and then let's go.'

Hasina put out the fire and got ready to go. In the sahib's large bungalow, made of bricks and with a tiled roof, a servant in a white uniform showed them into a warm, spacious room with sofas.

Mr Kirkland, who was sitting on a sofa reading a book, got up and looked at Sayeed. With the servant interpreting, he said, 'Is this your daughter?'

Standing close to the door, Sayeed replied, 'Yes, sir,' while staring at his own feet.

'I want her to work in my bungalow, in the kitchen, from next week,' said Mr Kirkland.

Hasina whispered something in her husband's ear.

Sayeed, still not looking up, replied, 'Sahib. She is only a sixteen-year-old unmarried girl. She cannot work in a house, even yours, where there are no other women. She will never ever get married after.'

Mr Kirkland walked a few steps towards the window before turning to face Hasina. 'Okay. I am looking for a cook anyway. You can work in the kitchen and she can help with the house,' he said, settling the matter as final.

From the week after, the mother and daughter left early in the morning for the bungalow while Sayeed went to work in the estate.

'I am Muslim. I cannot cook anything to do with pork,' Hasina explained in the beginning.

'No problem. We don't have a supply of pork here that often anyway. Ramlal, who cooks at the club, can come over here from time to time and help with that,' answered Mr Kirkland.

Hasina had to cook breakfast, lunch, and dinner every day for Mr Kirkland and his entourage of five personal servants, his diwan, and two guards. Roshni's job was to make up Mr Kirkland's bed, clean all five rooms in the bungalow and the veranda, make tea and bring snacks whenever Mr Kirkland wanted them, and tidy up the small garden around the bungalow. Hasina was allowed to bring some food for her family to have dinner together in the evening after their day's work. They felt lucky to be working in the shelter of the bungalow as servants, rather than working hard in the cold and rain of the tea plantation.

Also lucky were the few who worked in the clubhouse for the sahibs where every Saturday men and women came from the surrounding plantations, often travelling over fifty miles in their horse-drawn coaches to get there. Kirkwell Tea Estate was only ten miles from the clubhouse. Some sahibs and memsahibs even came over on Friday night and stayed in the luxurious rooms of the club for the weekend. The servants were mostly bearded Sikhs with white turbans, white outfits, shiny belts, and polished badges. They served drinks, lunch, and dinner with utter discretion and respect. The members played bridge and other games and danced to music. The club members were mostly married couples but there were also few bachelors, including John Kirkland. It only took a few months before rumours were flying in the club about John Kirkland and his young Indian maid.

'How is this young Indian lady living with you? We hear she is very good-looking. What's her name?' someone asked, winking at the others.

'Her name is Roshni. She does not live with me. She works for me with her mother and lives with her parents,' John replied sternly before leaving them to go outside the clubhouse in the garden with another drink.

Wild elephants often came and passed through the estate and usually the men and women would make noises by shouting together loudly and beating utensils and anything else they could find to divert them. But one early evening a herd of elephants came down and smashed through some of the jhupris on their track. Luckily, no one was hurt.

After hearing this, Mr Kirkland called the Sayeed family to his bungalow. 'Three of you can stay in the servants' quarters in the bungalow from now on. Sayeed, we need an extra hand here for the

34

storage depot. You will be working there from tomorrow. You don't need to work in the tea garden itself.'

Sayeed and his family, still scared from this evening's events with the wild elephants, were overwhelmed by the sahib's generosity.

John Kirkland, although clearly besotted with Roshni, had always behaved impeccably with her. He had never made her feel even slightly uncomfortable by being alone in the same room with her whenever he could avoid it. After a few months, sitting by the steps of the veranda overlooking the hills, he had started teaching simple English words to Roshni and her mother a few times a week. Roshni already had a secret crush on this handsome young man with good manners and charm, but there was no way could she share her feelings with anyone, let alone with her mother.

After his parents' deaths, John had fallen deeply in love with a local Scottish girl when he was in his late twenties. But after only eight months, she was married off by her parents against her wishes to a landed gentry with more wealth and higher family connections. Heartbroken, John had travelled for over a year in Europe before the opportunity to travel to India had come up.

For the last few weeks he had not gone to the club on the weekends; instead, he had taken daily walks by himself along the paths across the hills by his estate. After almost a month, he called Sayeed and Hasina to his sitting room. He insisted they also took seats on the sofas opposite. Very reluctantly, they sat on the edges of their sofas, expecting the worst.

John said, 'I have given it a lot of thought. I would like your permission for me to marry your daughter.'

Stunned, neither of the parents could speak for few minutes. Then Sayeed replied, 'Sahib. But we are Muslims and you are Christian.'

'Yes, I have thought about it too. She can be christened, if you agree.' Then, seeing the worried look on Sayeed and Hasina's faces, he added quickly, 'Otherwise I will be happy to convert to Islam before marrying Roshni.'

John had no doubt in his voice. Born a Protestant, he had never been a true churchgoer and since coming to India he had rarely been to one anyway.

Hasina, with a soft smile on her face, whispered to Sayeed, 'Go and ask Roshni to come over.'

When Sayeed went out to get Roshni, she turned to John, saying in her broken English, 'You will both be very happy, my heart knows.'

'Thank you,' said John.

Soon Roshni entered the room behind Sayeed.

'Please sit down here,' said John, indicating the sofa near his.

Roshni looked towards her mother, who nodded her approval.

Once she was sitting, John got up from his sofa and came close to her before asking, 'Roshni, I would like to marry you. Your parents have agreed. What do you say?'

She was speechless and her face glowed with her blushing. Roshni covered her face with the end of her shawl before nodding yes.

Sayeed's family, who were Sufi Muslim, arranged for their local Imam to come over to the Kirkwell estate a few days later. John Kirkland's simple two-testimonial declaration ceremony to the Islamic faith was followed by his and Roshni's nikah with ijab and qubul in the presence of two witnesses, chosen from his employees. As per tradition, John gave a gift of some money to Sayeed. A small feast was arranged on the day for all the workers of the estate, who were all given the day off for the wedding.

Next Saturday, John went with his wife to the club and announced their wedding to all present. Cakes and sweets were distributed but John refused to have any drinks. Everyone present was slightly taken aback with the announcement, but they were not totally surprised. British colonials marrying locals and even converting to local religions had not been unheard of over the decades, although this was becoming rare with the new wave of Victorian evangelism. Everyone congratulated the couple and wished them all the happiness for the future before John and Roshni left early for their home.

During the following months of their marital bliss, Roshni often asked, 'What is it like in your own country? Is it like they say in Delhi? Is it really cold there?'

John had tried to reply as truthfully as possible and had secretly hoped that one day soon he would travel back home and to parts of Europe with his wife.

He was overjoyed when Roshni announced she was pregnant within the year. He would have kept her wrapped up in cotton wool but need not have worried. Hasina looked after her daughter well and in time a beautiful baby girl was born. The baby, with dark skin inherited from her grandmother, was named Rabia after one of the founders of the Sufi school of divine love. John and Roshni could not get enough of their daughter growing up. Hasina and Sayeed were also in high spirits with their good fortune.

When Rabia was six months old, Sayeed came to John and asked, 'With your permission, I would like to take Hasina back to our village for few weeks.'

John readily agreed. A few days later, before leaving, Hasina held Rabia in her arms and could not stop crying. This made Roshni cry too.

'We will be back in less than two months,' said Sayeed.

'I know. But I will miss her so much,' replied Hasina.

Back in their own village, Sayeed and Hasina found that many of their neighbours had already left, seeking jobs in different parts of the country. An epidemic of smallpox was also going around. They were thinking of going back to their tea garden early when Hasina contracted the disease, followed soon after by Sayeed. The tragic news of their death reached John and Roshni a few weeks later. Roshni just sat by the window holding sleeping Rabia tightly in her arms with tears flowing down from her eyes. John came down to sit beside her and held her in a tight hug in silence.

37

When Rabia was over one year old and walking around the place holding her parents' hands, John asked Roshni, 'I was thinking of us going back to Britain. What do you think?'

'I have nothing to hold me back here anymore,' said Roshni with wet eyes. She then added, 'Do you think Rabia is too young for the long journey?'

They agreed to wait until their daughter was two years old before making the move. At the club, however, many of John's well-wishers warned him that because of the dark skin colour of both Roshni and Rabia, it may not be the best move. Although in the British Raj children of these mixed-race marriages were not uncommon, they were divided up and raised differently depending on their skin colour. Light-skinned, fair-haired, European-looking children were taken to England and educated there as Christians, while darker-skinned offspring were kept in India and raised as Hindus or Muslims. It was not uncommon for many such mixed-blooded children with fair skin to have been very successfully absorbed into the British establishment. Lord Liverpool, the early nineteenth century prime minister, was, after all, of Anglo-Indian descent. A lot, however, depended on their skin colour.

'Maybe you should wait until your second child is born, and if he is of lighter colour, then you can return home with him, leaving the coloured ones behind here?' someone suggested.

John returned back to his bungalow even more determined than before to go back to Britain. Finding a buyer for his estate was not difficult as it was now making large profits every year. Within six months, a date was set for their travel. To make the journey shorter and easier for his young family, he decided to travel from Calcutta by merchant ship to Alexandria in Egypt and then overland across to Port Suez. From there, with a journey by ship on the calmer waters of the Mediterranean to Naples in Italy, the whole voyage should take less than four months.

John got the first taste of colour discrimination when on the very first day of sailing the officers on board flatly refused to allow

Roshni and her daughter at the officers' dining table. John arranged to have their meals delivered to their cabin by paying extra money to the kitchen staff. He tried to ignore the occasional snide remarks about his dark-skinned family on the voyage. It was a relief for them to get off the boat and make the journey by land to Port Suez. The passage to Naples with the Italian crew, many of whom were somewhat dark-skinned due to the scorching hot sun over the Mediterranean, was a lot more welcoming for John's family

Roshni had never even been to a large city in India. After arriving in Naples, she was stunned by the city with its backdrop of Mount Vesuvius. 'The mountain is so beautiful!' she said.

John replied, 'A few hundred years back, the same beautiful mountain spewed out hot lava which buried a large city nearby.'

Roshni shivered before asking, 'Can it happen again?' and was then reassured by John.

They soon travelled to Rome and in the pleasant mid-summer weather Roshni truly marvelled at the grandeur of the new and old city.

John, looking at a group of Italian women, said, 'With your long dark hair and golden brown skin, you could easily pass as one of them here.'

Smiling, Roshni just said, 'Stop looking at other women.'

Both of them were pleased that the Italians generally loved children and no one batted an eyelid at Rabia's colour. However, the attitude towards Roshni and Rabia's skin colour started to change as they travelled to France via Switzerland before crossing the Channel to London. John tried to ignore this and tried to shield his family as much as possible. In London he was warned by several of his old acquaintances, many of whom he had helped with monetary support before, against the wisdom of bringing a dark-skinned family back to Britain.

Others wondered, 'Why did you have to bring your good-looking ayah from India with her child as well? You should have left the baby back there and brought only the ayah.'

39

Only once were they invited to stay with any of their families. An old friend of John's, who was his travel companion in Europe a few years back, had now settled down in London in his family home and had been doing well as a coal merchant.

Paul invited John, saying, 'You should come over and stay with us for a few days and we can talk about our old days.'

John agreed. The experience, however, was not altogether pleasant as Paul's wife, who was somehow connected to aristocracy, refused even to talk to Roshni once.

After a few days, John decided to take Roshni and Rabia to his family home in Scotland where his distant relatives were now living. His cousin's family had begged him for a place to stay before he had left for India as they had a growing family with very little money. They were informed about John's oncoming arrival. When John and Roshni with Rabia arrived in their coach from London on a late September afternoon, the whole family was waiting at the porch to receive them.

'Welcome home, John,' said James, John's cousin.

'Thank you,' said John, and then, looking at Rabia already sleeping on Roshni's shoulder, said, 'We'd better put her to bed first.'

'Sure. There will be a room for them in the basement,' replied James, and tried to instruct their maid accordingly.

John saw the shock on the faces of his welcoming family as he declared, 'She is my daughter, Rabia, and this is Roshni, my wife.'

Without saying anything more, James and his family followed John and Roshni inside the house. Later, dinner was organised with soup, boiled pork, and vegetables, and a bottle of old wine was opened.

John declared, 'We will not be eating pork nor drinking any wine as I have converted to Islam.'

James and his family tried hard to disguise their dismay.

Almost since their arrival in England, John had been suffering from a dry cough. Initially, he had put it down to arriving from a hot climate into the damp, cold weather of his native country. But in

40

spite of staying indoors next to the open fire most of the time, his cough started getting worse. After a few weeks, he decided to see the family doctor. He prescribed bed rest and rum with vinegar and liquorice.

'Sorry, doctor. I don't drink alcohol,' said John.

'Oh! In that case, you can try a balsam of sulphur, oil of vitriol, and syrup of coltsfoot,' said the doctor, and then also added some opium for night sedation. 'I will come and check up on you again in a week,' he said before leaving.

But in the next few days John's cough got worse, and Roshni was really scared when one evening he coughed out fresh blood. She sent for the doctor again.

'Unfortunately, I suspect this is consumption,' he said after examining John carefully.

'What do you advise for treatment, doctor?' asked John.

'Modern treatment, I believe, is rest, and ideally recovering in plentiful amounts of fresh, clean, cold mountain air and good nutrition. I understand that Switzerland has many such excellent facilities called sanatoriums.'

While making plans to go to Switzerland as soon as possible, a few days later John called his family solicitor and arranged to sell all his estates except for the family home. Then he asked his lawyer to prepare a will leaving his family home and all his cash inheritance to his wife and their child, with the provision for his cousin to stay in his house as long as both Roshni and their family agreed. In the next few days, however, John took a turn for the worse and one evening, after coughing out a large amount of blood, he died holding Roshni's hand.

Only a few days after John's death, his cousin called Roshni into the living room in the presence of the solicitor. He told her, 'I would like you and your child to leave my property as soon as possible. I am no longer able to put up with the gossip in the village, especially as I have got a young family myself.'

Looking at the stone-faced solicitor, Roshni asked, 'But what about the will?'

41

'The will never happened as John never got to sign it,' replied the solicitor, and then added, 'Even if he did, as a coloured Asian who is not a British citizen, you would have no legal rights anyway.'

'I know how John felt about you and I am willing to give you fifty pounds in cash, but you must leave soon,' John's cousin said.

Already devastated from John's death, Roshni had no choice. In Scotland she had not come across anyone she could call a friend, and the weather was always much too cold. She decided to move to London with Rabia in the next few days. After arriving in London, she went to John's friend Paul's house. Her knock on the door was answered by Paul's wife.

'What do you want?' she asked with a stony face.

Fortunately, Paul had also come to the door and invited Roshni and Rabia into the house. He was genuinely shocked after hearing the news of the death of his friend John. Afterwards, he heard Roshni's story with disbelief and offered for them stay in his house.

'I hope it's only temporary, otherwise I will be going back with our children to live with my parents,' Paul was told by his wife sternly as soon as they were alone.

'I will try to find some way to help her have a decent life here. I have seen how deeply John was in love with her,' he replied.

Paul tried his best through one of his lawyer friends to petition the court to restore Roshni's legal rights to John's inheritance. But he was soon told that as a coloured Asian, and with no written record of her marriage to John, there was no prospect of any legal recourse. Pestered daily by his wife at home to get rid of his guests, he finally managed to find employment for Roshni as an ayah to one of the families he knew well in London.

This aristocratic family in London was happy to have an Oriental maid in their household. Roshni, with her exotic-looking Indian attire, her slim body, and her honey-coloured skin, was something like a trophy they could show off to their esteemed guests, especially as she could speak some English with a quaint foreign accent. She was given the new name of 'Rosabel the East Asian' by them. When she was asked to bring refreshments, the guests mostly tried to hide their curious looks but never offended her.

Only once did a guest call out, 'Hello, Mary, and what is this freak?'

Working as an ayah, Roshni was responsible for cleaning the house, looking after two children apart from her own, and dressing the lady of the house. Still completely numb from John's death, the work was a welcome distraction for her. Rabia was growing up well and enjoyed playing with the two other children in the family.

Almost six months later, Paul visited Roshni one afternoon.

'I have been able to find a job for you as an ayah with an English family going to India for work in two months. It might be the best thing for you, under the circumstances,' he said. He was not sure if he could detect a glint of elation in Roshni's eyes with the news.

In the following week, while playing in the garden one afternoon, Rabia cut her hand on a rusty iron spike. Hearing her screaming, Roshni came out to the garden to find her bleeding. She brought all the children in and washed her daughter's hand thoroughly before carefully wrapping the wound with fresh lint. In the night, Rabia developed a high fever and her little body went into repeated contortions. Roshni wanted to give her a drink of water but her jaw was tightly locked in spasm. The family doctor was called in the night.

After examining the child, he shook his head before saying, 'The only advice I have for you is to sponge her with tepid water regularly. But I don't hold much hope.'

Little Rabia, after a final bout of violent convulsions, died in the early hours of the morning. In the next few days, Roshni did nothing but stay in her room clutching Rabia's old clothes. One evening three days after Rabia's death, she walked out of the house and went to the banks of the nearby River Thames. After standing by the banks for a while she looked up towards the clear sky and jumped into the cold water of the river. The next day her body, floating towards the east, was found by the fishing boats.

Chapter Four

Sakuntala had grown up listening to her parents' stories about the many achievements over the last few decades of the Brahma Samaj, of which her grandfather was a founder. She had heard with excitement stories of this Bengali Renaissance movement which started before the mid-nineteenth century and was associated with famous names such as Raja Rammohan, Dwarka Nath Tagore, Iswar Chandra Vidyasagar, and Swami Vivekananda.

Her parents not only told her stories from the past but also truly believed in its doctrines, which stated that the Samajis had no faith in any scripture as an authority and were fully against any caste system. She learned in her formative years that this movement was responsible for creating the atmosphere in which the British drew up rules against the sati system and child marriages in India. Her parents practiced and taught her the ideologies through all fields of social reform, including abolition of the caste system and of the dowry system, emancipation of women, and improving the educational system.

Sakuntala, who was an avid reader, was taught at home by both her parents as there was no schools for girls to attend nearby. At the age of fifteen she was admitted to the famous secular Bethune College of Calcutta. She thrived in her college and after two years she enrolled in Calcutta Medical College. Sakuntala had always wanted to study medicine and shined in the college. Her teachers there had recommended for this promising student to go to England for further training. They advised her to meet the Director of Public Instructions of Bengal, who was apparently keen to support suitable candidates with bursaries for this kind of training, as women's higher education in Bengal was falling behind many other states in India. She would be given a bursary of 150 pounds per year, as well as her passages to and from India.

45

As her degree from Calcutta Medical College was not recognised in England, Sakuntala had planned to take admission at the Royal Free Hospital School of Medicine for Women in London. While in India, she had already been inspired by the story of one of its famous alumni, Rukhmabai Bhikaji. In the 1880s, when Indian women hardly had any rights to speak of, this gutsy and determined lady did the impossible. Married at the age of eleven, child bride Rukhmabai contested her husband's claim to conjugal rights in a historic court case that later led to the passage of the Age of Consent Act in 1891. She went on to study medicine in London before returning to become India's first practising female doctor in 1894. Sakuntala vividly remembered her parents showing her two pieces of paper cuttings of her earlier writing with the pseudonym of 'A Hindu Lady' in *The Times of India*.

'The government advocated education and emancipation but when a woman refused to "be a slave" the government comes to break her spirit allowing its law to become an instrument for riveting her chains.'

'This wicked practice of child marriage has destroyed the happiness of my life. It comes between me and the things which I prize above all others—study and mental cultivation. Without the least fault of mine I am doomed to seclusion; every aspiration of mine to rise above my ignorant sisters is looked down upon with suspicion and is interpreted in the most uncharitable manner.'

She was Sakuntala's hero! She had carried copies of the above two pieces and had often used them in her debates in Bethune College. She dreamed of one day being someone like Rukhmabai, of challenging the unjust social practices against women.

Her parents wrote to a friend of theirs who had settled in England and was practicing law in London. Six months later, Sakuntala took a steamer from the Hooghly dock to the Indian Ocean where she boarded the large ship going to England. There were twenty other students travelling for further studies from Calcutta, three of them women. Most of the students were going to study law or civil service and only two other male students from her own college were going to study medicine. All of the three female students were going for teacher training. There was almost a college common room atmosphere in the steamer. This continued when they boarded the large ship for England, which was already carrying twenty jolly Australian and New Zealander students. Four of them were women. One Australian woman named Judy was going to study medicine in the same college as Sakuntala.

After almost five weeks the boat arrived in Southampton, where her parents' friend Mr K. L. Dutta was there to meet her. Mr and Mrs Dutta had been settled in London for nearly ten years. Mr Dutta practiced law in Middle Inn, also called 'Indian Inn' because of the number of Indians either training or practicing there. Although Mrs Dutta had been a graduate of Bethune College in Calcutta, she was now a full-time housewife with two young daughters, both in school. It was great for Sakuntala to live with a family for the first few weeks in this very new environment.

In the first week, with Mrs Dutta accompanying her, she marvelled at the famous sites of London such as Saint Paul's, Buckingham Palace, and the Palace of Westminster. She then decided to visit the Natural History Museum on her own for a full day. Gradually, she started exploring the city more on her own. Although the family offered for her to stay with them during her studies, she decided to find a women's hostel near her college. No hostel near her college could be found but she found a suitable one with only a two-mile walk to her college.

She wrote to her family about London's busy, noisy traffic and its wonderful transport system with trams, two-wheeled hansoms, and bicycles. She described the wonderful railway system in the city running overground and underground. She noted that the policemen in London were courteous and polite compared to the corrupt and aggressive European policemen in India.

She soon moved to the hostel, which housed almost twenty women with two sharing each room. There were two other Indian women in the hostel, both in their second year at teacher training college. She was glad to see that Judy, the Australian girl who she had met onboard, was still looking for a roommate. Judy helped Sakuntala to move in with her.

'Be careful of the madame. She is always prying on the residents; what they wear, when they go out and come back. And don't even think of mixing with male students or bringing them here,' warned Judy.

Sakuntala smiled and asked, 'When do we get locked up here in this prison at night then?'

Judy replied, 'The outside door is closed at nine thirty and lights go out by ten thirty.'

Sakuntala said, 'At least we don't need to be chaperoned to our classes like it used to be here only a few years back!'

She found the atmosphere in the college friendly and less formal. Having already done her MB in Calcutta, where she had come second in her final exam, she found the course relatively easy. However, she found it difficult to accept the seating arrangements in the class where whites and non-white students were segregated, although the English students themselves were eager to mingle freely with the Indians. Judy was happy to have her as roommate, as Sakuntala could help her with revision before the exams.

She wrote to her parents about the poverty she was surprised to find in England. She was also shocked about the deprivation and drunkenness of the working class, especially the women, being most vulnerable. She was appalled at the class system, with glaring inequalities between vast wealth and wretched poverty. She agreed with Krishnabhabini, a Bengali writer living in England, about the British foreign policy implication of such all-consuming greed that *'they have cast nets in all countries to gather money, and wherever they smell money they rush like carrion-loving adjutant. In making money they care not for virtue but vice...How much money have they spent and how much blood have they shed in order to force opium upon the unfortunate Chinese!'*

In her correspondences Sakuntala also observed the British character, lacking in family affection, as cold, cynical, and reserved. She was, however, full of admiration for British women. She commented on the main areas of equal status enjoyed by English women—no man or woman here married without their free will, and children were treated with greater care and affection. Finally, she advocated for female emancipation in India like the suffragette movement in England.

Sakuntala had tried to attend meetings at the recently established India House in one of the hostels, where Indian students met weekly, as many times as possible. They discussed and read *Indian Sociologist*, a monthly paper dedicated to the great English philosopher Herbert Spencer's ideas. *'Everyman is free to do what he wills, provided he infringes not the equal freedom of any other men.'* She was highly impressed by Madame Bhikaji Kama, the best-known Indian woman in European revolutionary circles, who stated that *'no people should be subject to any despotic or tyrannical government'* and demanded withdrawal of British rule from India.

She agreed with others that here in England, the British Empire was taken to demonstrate the superiority of British culture rather than its colonial aggression. Sakuntala herself even contributed a small piece for the revolutionary magazine *Bande Mataram*. She was also a regular attendee at the meeting of the Indo-Egyptian Association, set up to promote understanding with other oppressed nations. In these radical meetings, her friends made her aware of the Scotland Yard's surveillance of the Indian students. Sakuntala suspected that her own hostel superintendent, a German-born woman, was spying on her students and reporting to the Yard. Madame would sometimes come unannounced into their rooms and, in the pretext of having a conversation about their studies, would leaf through their books. Fortunately for Sakuntala, she was always found to be 'a good girl' in the hostel and was often found helping others with their homework.

One afternoon, as she was returning from college very happy with the results of her fourth year exams and thinking about whether she

49

should send a telegram or just write a letter to her parents, she felt her purse being snatched. She tried to chase this young boy in rugged, dirty clothes but with her long gown she could not move fast. A young Englishman, however, chased the boy and recovered the purse for her. Still shaken, Sakuntala looked at this young man and thanked him. Her heart was pumping, but she soon realised that it was more likely happening because for her, it was love at first sight.

The young man offered, 'I will walk you to your place.'

Sakuntala readily agreed as she was still feeling quite shaken. In conversation, it turned out that he was also a medical student, in his final year at nearby St Mary's Medical School. They agreed to meet the next day after class at Hyde Park Corner.

George Brown, the only child of his parents, was brought up in London where his father practised as a barrister. He was very keen to find out about India, a country which had always fascinated him, from Sakuntala. Their weekly rendezvous continued over the next few months. They frequented the London theatres as often as possible.

In one of her letters to a friend in Calcutta, Sakuntala said, 'Theatres in London are most impressive. Anyone who comes over here must visit them.'

On some weekends, George also showed her around the famous museums in London, or they simply walked its busy streets. Apart from being charmed with this Oriental young women's beauty, George was clearly impressed by her liberal-thinking mind. One weekend he invited her to meet his parents in their house.

Although apprehensive in the beginning, Sakuntala found his parents very welcoming and liberal-minded. George's mother, a passive supporter of the suffragette movement, had expected Sakuntala to be a helpless, degraded victim of religious custom and uncivilized practices, as this was how Indian women were usually represented. Instead, she was most impressed by this charming, free-thinking young woman with her strong personality.

The next day, Sakuntala wrote about George and his family in her letter to her parents.

Within a few weeks, George took his final exams and passed them with merit. He had mentioned to Sakuntala a few times already that he wanted to move away from the hustle and bustle of London to a provincial town to practise medicine. Soon he found a suitable position in a hospital in Liverpool to start in six months once he had finished his apprenticeship at St Mary's.

A day later, he proposed to Sakuntala, who was delighted to accept. George wanted to get married before he moved from London and a date was set in four months' time to allow Sakuntala's parents to come over for the wedding. She telegrammed her parents with the good news and the invitation. Her father replied with a telegram that her mother was very unwell and unfortunately they would not be able to make the long journey. They wished the couple all the best in their lives.

George's family was expecting a big wedding in a church. His uncle, who was a reverend, suggested that Sakuntala could be christened before the marriage.

Sakuntala, upon hearing this, said to George, 'I have grown up having no faith in any scripture as an authority. You have known my views over the months. I love you. But you have to accept me as I am or not at all.'

He replied, 'Although I have been conditioned into going to church all my life, I have always admired your views. I love you more than anything in the world and would love to get married to you, church wedding or not.'

A wedding in the registry office was planned. Both of them ignored the large notice displayed in the registry office which said, *'Interracial marriage between white and non-whites is risky.'* A week before the wedding, Sakuntala was over the moon to find one morning that both of her parents were at the door of her hostel. Apparently her mother had improved and both of them desperately wanted to come over for their most beloved daughter's wedding. They did not want to worry Sakuntala and, wanting to give her a surprise, had contacted Mr Dutta earlier, who had collected them from Southampton only yesterday. George and Sakuntala took them

51

to George's parents' house the next evening for a dinner. For the next few days, Sakuntala skipped her classes in the afternoon to take her parents sightseeing in London, including to a theatre show.

For the wedding in the registry office there were about twenty people including George's immediate family, Mr Dutta's family, and a few close friends of George and Sakuntala. She took George's family name, now to be called Sakuntala Roy Brown. She looked stunning in her red silk Benarasi sari, which her mother had brought over from Calcutta for the wedding. Her Australian friend Judy was struggling to keep on her sari, which she had borrowed from Sakuntala for the day. George's parents had organised a reception in the evening which was attended by more people, mainly their family and friends. As Sakuntala's parents were going to stay in England for only a month, the newlyweds agreed to have only a short honeymoon to Brighton.

Her parents soon after went back to India, it was also time for George to move to Liverpool to take up his new job. Sakuntala was glad that she now had to concentrate hard for her upcoming final exam and not think of anything else. She passed her exam with credit. She also obtained qualifications at Edinburgh and Glasgow before graduating in 1911.

Judy scraped through and, to say a big thank you to Sakuntala for her help with the exam, she took her out with a few other friends for a posh dinner. She had decided to go back to Australia the next month to look for opportunities to practise medicine.

Over the last few years, Sakuntala had been closely following the suffragette movement in England and had attended some of their demonstrations. She also attended the International Suffragette Fair at Chelsea Town Hall in 1912. However, she was irritated by the British feminists' preoccupation with imperial authority and how they looked at Indian women as their special imperial burden. They automatically assumed helplessness in Asian women and saw Indian women as a white women's burden. Sakuntala was also annoyed when in gatherings English women often spoke on behalf of the Indian women even though they were willing to speak themselves.

Soon after her exam results, when the suffragettes decided to arrange a procession with banners stating their cause for the King George coronation, she joined the march in her sari holding a poster.

While the costumes and jewellery of Oriental women attracted the attention of the crowd, there were occasional comments from the onlookers, such as, 'Why, here are some brownies!'

Sakuntala was keen to join George in Liverpool as soon as possible to start practising medicine. George had tried unsuccessfully so far to find a position in the local hospitals for his wife. After arriving in Liverpool, Sakuntala went door to door in all the hospitals in the town and even into neighbouring places for several months only to be politely rejected from all. Run entirely by male doctors, they used any loophole to bar any woman doctor. Soon she realised that even now in the early twentieth century, although women in Britain were more than ready to offer their services for medicine, the male-dominated society was not ready to receive the female doctors. The number of female doctors in the country was still miniscule compared to their male counterparts. For over 26,000 male doctors in the country, there were only 610 female doctors.

George, who was a member of the local British Medical Association, took Sakuntala to one of their meetings. She got an icy reception there and soon learnt that the BMA had barred women from joining their association until only recently.

At home, Sakuntala talked with George at length about her prospect of finding any hospital appointment. The struggle to become a doctor was hard enough but it had only been the first battle in her more enduring struggle to be able to practice what she had learnt. She knew that several of her English female friends from her college had moved to Europe and even to America to fulfil their dreams of practising medicine.

'I don't agree with any of this, as you know, but the society still sees married practising female doctors as deviant from the normal expectation of their perceived feminine role,' George said.

'Only to bear children and look after the family. And we are in an advanced country in the twentieth century!' Sakuntala replied angrily.

After a few more months of repeatedly being told 'even a poor person would not like to be seen by a coloured female doctor', Sakuntala was more than happy to find an unpaid part-time job in a charity hospital just outside Liverpool. The hospital was set up only a few years back by an unmarried female doctor who was due to retire. Although the hospital dealt mainly with women and children, many local male patients came to the clinics there as it was free. She started in the job with gusto and within a few months was very popular in the community, which was made up of mostly very poor and working-class people. Within a year she also set up weekly clinics close to the community. Both of them were now working full-time, George with a monthly salary and Sakuntala unpaid.

When the war broke in 1914, George was soon called to serve in the army's medical core. Only two weeks after he left, Sakuntala found herself pregnant. She telegrammed George. Fortunately, he had been posted in the Bristol War Hospital and managed to get a week's leave to come and meet his wife. Over the moon, he hugged and kissed her as he arrived.
'I don't have to tell you. But you know that you have to take it really slowly now,' he said to her.
'I know, I know. I will be careful.'
A week passed quickly before George had to go back.

A few months later, on her due date, Sakuntala gave birth to a healthy baby girl. George had not managed to get leave from his work, which was getting busier than ever before. Soon he was posted in a clearing hospital in France and it took him another two years to come home and see his family. When he returned home on a short break, his two-and-a-half-year-old daughter, Neeta, was running around the place.
After seeing George, she ran back to her mother and, holding her dress, said, 'Mummy, there is a man in the house.'

'Yes, darling. He is your daddy.'

It did not take long for Neeta and George to be playing hide and seek together. Sakuntala noticed that he was walking with a slight limp. It turned out that George had suffered an injury to his knee during the war, but he had not written to her in case she got too worried.

By now, Sakuntala had gone back to her regular work at the charity hospital and in her clinic. Soon, George also had to go back to join his hospital for the war wounded in Brighton.

When the war ended, George returned home happy to find that Neeta still remembered him and came running to him and jumping into his arms before calling out, 'Mummy, Daddy is here.'

In 1930, Sakuntala returned to Calcutta alone for a month after hearing about the death of her mother. Memories flooded back as the father and daughter wept together. She tried to convince her father to come back to England with her but he was not at all keen. Reluctantly, she returned back to Liverpool only to learn six months later that her father had also passed away. She was completely devastated.

By the time the Second World War broke out, Neeta had already qualified as a doctor and was training to be a surgeon in London. Although female doctors were not conscripted like their male counterparts, she decided to join the Royal Army Medical Corps Training College in Leeds. After her training she was posted in the army hospital in Essex. She found it difficult not to laugh when passing soldiers saluted her because of the captain's badge on her uniform. Already holding his title of Major from the First World War, George was also soon called to join a military hospital near London.

A few months later, Sakuntala heard the news on the radio that during the Blitz some of the hospitals in London were bombed by the Germans. She spent several sleepless nights and days in a stupor before receiving a telegram from George that he was okay, although his hospital was bombed. He soon also wrote a letter that a few days back the King and Queen had visited their hospital after the recent bombing. She could not stop crying when the war ended and Neeta came home, to be followed a few days later by George.

George retired from his job in 1952 but Sakuntala carried on working in her charity hospital and clinics until 1960. By this time, their mixed-race secular daughter had completed her training as a surgeon and was an assistant professor in surgery in one of the medical colleges in London. Sakuntala passed away peacefully in her sleep a year later.

Chapter Five

1914: A WW1 Soldier

It was not uncommon in this small village of Bajar Bar in Punjab to find families where, over the years, the men served as soldiers for the British army in its Indian colony. After all, the British glorified things by calling the Punjabis and the men from the North Western Province 'the martial race'. As a result, considering themselves superior to the other 'non-martial' races, men from these provinces enlisted with enthusiasm to the British army. Almost seventeen years old, Gurprit was thrilled when the Punjabi Subedar, who was recruiting, selected him along with five others from his village. His older brother, Hari, had already joined the army one year earlier. His younger brother, Balbir, who was not yet sixteen, was very jealous as he was not allowed to join.

In the training camp, they were taught only with the old type of rifles, as after the 1857 uprising against the British, Indian soldiers were not allowed to use modern weapons or man any artillery. After just three months of training, when Britain declared war on 4 August 1914, with eleven rupees per month of salary, Gurprit was onboard a ship from Surat with the Lahore Division to the Western Front, where apparently the battle was heating up. None of these soldiers were conscripts—soldiering was their profession. They were serving the very British Empire that was oppressing their own people back home.

After an exhausting sea voyage, his brigade, along with another from the Lahore Division, arrived in Marseilles in September 1914. As the Indian soldiers were marching down the road from the dock to their initial military camp, French women with their children lined up the streets on both sides. Some were holding banners in French to welcome them. Gurprit, like most Indians, did not understand what they said. Some of the women even ran to the column of soldiers to

57

hand over bunches of flowers with a smile. A few of the Indian soldiers started chanting in Hindi, and soon the whole column of them was singing Hindi marching songs, causing much hilarity amongst the welcoming French crowd.

In the new camp just outside Marseilles, Indian soldiers handed over their old-fashioned rifles to be given the modern versions. They were taught for the first time how to use machine guns and mortars. Gurprit was terrified when they were shown an exploding grenade and how to use them. Apparently, the battle was heating up on the front and after only two weeks they were put on trains to move up north. The British army had already been experiencing heavy losses and was in desperate need of replacements. After almost two days on the train, they were transported by large motor cars, the likes of which they had never seen in India.

Very soon, his brigade was at Flanders to defend Ypres. Coming from India, like the majority of his fellow Indian soldiers, Gurprit was completely unprepared for the muddy trench warfare in the early winter. Pitchforked into battle in unfamiliar lands, in harsh and cold climatic conditions, they were neither used to nor prepared for fighting an enemy of whom they had absolutely no knowledge. They were risking their lives every day for little more than pride and duty to their employer, the British Raj. Standing often knee-deep in mud, fighting only with rifles and bayonets in the atrocious conditions of trench warfare against the technically far superior German army, who had more machine guns than their unit, his battalion suffered heavy losses. This was also compounded by heavy shelling and aerial bombardment by the Germans. Three of the men from his own village, who had been in the same company as Gurprit, died within the first three weeks of battle in Flanders. Gurprit, like many of his fellow soldiers, was shocked when they were ordered that the bodies of their comrades were to be left alone on the field with no attempt at burial.

Within only a few months, just a week after his seventeenth birthday, he had his first experience of a gas attack which killed some of his British officers as well as several Indian soldiers. Like most Indian soldiers, he did not have a gas mask but was advised to use a simple flannel pad soaked in his own urine to hold over his mouth. Being on the far side of the trench, Gurprit was lucky to survive the attack. During retreats, he was courageous enough to help rescue several wounded British and Indian soldiers from the nearby trenches.

His commanding officer called him to his to billet the next day and said, 'Young man, you are very brave. I am going to recommend you for a merit award.'

Gurprit only saluted to attention.

A few weeks later, a mortar shell fell in his trench. For a few seconds, everything went black and silent around him. Soon he realised that he had a nasty flesh wound in his left thigh which was bleeding heavily. He was attended in the trench by the medical orderlies who stopped the bleeding by wrapping a bandage tightly around his thigh. Then he was carried on a stretcher to the clearing hospital close to the front where a medic, with the help of a nurse, cleaned his wound thoroughly of the mud. The bleeding had already stopped but he needed to be sent to hospital for the large area of his wound to heal. First, he was sent to Hardelot Base Hospital in France and within a few days was shipped over to Brighton Pavilion, which had been converted into a hospital only in the last few months to accommodate wounded Indian soldiers.

Gurprit was very pleased with the care and attention he got from the British nurses and doctors in Brighton Pavilion. One of the young nurses who has responsible for his daily dressing had found this tall, young, brave Punjabi soldier very attractive. One day, as she was dressing his wound and making jokes with him with a broad smile on her face, the matron arrived.

'Nurse. Can I see you in my office as soon as you have finished with this patient?' she ordered sternly.

In the matron's office, the nurse was told in no uncertain terms that a relationship between a white British woman and a native soldier would not be tolerated. Within two weeks, Gurprit was able to walk slowly and was allowed to sit by the gardens around the hospital. He was surprised to find that the place was surrounded by barbed wire.

'I did not expect to find enemy forces around here in England. Why the barbed wire and the high fence?' he asked another wounded Indian soldier who was resting next to him.

'To stop the native Indian soldiers forming any relationship with the white women in the town. We are not allowed to go out and mix in the community. Apparently, the army bosses think that the British women of all classes find us brave and attractive with a sort of idea of an Oriental warrior prince. The very prestige of the English womanhood may be at risk if they mingle with us,' he replied with a wry smile.

Within another week, Gurprit was walking more freely and wanted to go out in the town to have a walk by the beach nearby. He was surprised to be told that he must be escorted by one white male orderly, although now he could walk alone with aid.

The same Indian soldier he had known before told him that in the beginning of this hospital, only a few months back, when the Indian soldiers went to the town English women would often come and hug them to thank them, give them presents, and treat them as heroes and saviours. The British authority did not like this at all. They felt that English women needed to be protected at all cost from mixing with these natives.

'But when the Indian army arrived in France last year on the way to the front we were sometimes billeted in French homes. The French women welcomed us heartily. They treated us as if we were their own private guests in their homes,' said Gurprit.

'Ah! They are not British,' was the reply.

After another three weeks, he was sent back to the front. The battle had reached stalemate when daily casualties had become routine. After only a few weeks trying to take over another trench, he was caught in machine gun fire when a bullet pierced his left forearm, shattering his bone. Somehow, he managed to crawl back to his own trench and after a while he was sent back to Brockenhurst where a hotel had now been converted into a hospital for the wounded Indians. Gurprit again noticed the barbed wire fencing outside the hospital, which had become the norm to stop Indians mixing with the white woman.

By now, Gurprit had had enough of this vicious war and wanted to return back home to his family. But within three months, with his arm still in a sling, he was sent back to the front where the fighting had become fiercer and lives were lost in heaps every day. He soon realised from talking to others that Indian soldiers were more often sent back to war hastily patched up after injury than their British counterparts. An Indian soldier was unlikely to be sent back to India unless he became crippled or lost a limb.

By late 1916, as the daily grind of senseless war was wearing on him and a deep depression was taking over his young mind, his battalion was sent over to Mesopotamia. Although the warm desert sun was far more welcome than the climate of muddy trenches, the fight against the Turks was no less vicious. Gurprit was lucky to survive and returned to England with further injury, this time to his right leg and torso.

During his nearly six-month layover in hospital, he wrote to his family in Punjab. Two months later, a reply came from his parents, greatly relieved that he was still alive. They also wrote the sad news that his youngest brother, Balbir, who had also joined the British forces soon after Gurprit had left, was killed in Egypt. They had not heard from his older brother, Hari, since he left with the army around the same time as Gurprit, and he was presumably missing in action. Gurprit had also written in his last letter about his desire to return back to India as soon as the war was over. His parents replied to him saying that they were thoroughly relieved that he was alive. They also wrote that although they were missing him badly, he must know that the situation in India was now grim. With the recession following the war and consecutive crop failures in their own farm, the family was surviving almost hand to mouth. He also heard the news that he now had a baby sister called Baisakhi. After spending almost six months in the hospital, by the time Gurprit was considered to be fit to fight again, the war came to an end. Gurprit, like most of his fellow soldiers, still did not know why the war had started in the first place except that the British asked them to fight for them and that he ended up with a medal and a small pension for life.

In the First World War, India sent almost 1.4 million soldiers involved in active service into France and Belgium, Gallipoli and Salonika, East Africa, Egypt, Mesopotamia, the Persian Gulf, and Aden. Before this, the main role of the Indian army under the British was internal peacekeeping, although small contingents were sent to other British colonies in East Africa, the Middle East, and, during the Boxer Uprising, to China. In addition, since the beginning of the war, Indian labour corps were sent to the Western Front to load and unload ammunition and construct and repair roads and airfields. India also contributed medical personnel, field ambulances, and hospital ships, and supplied war materials, ammunitions, uniforms, boots, raw materials, and even food. The British administration in India raised around 30 million pounds for the war, over and above the 100 million pounds that were given to Britain by the Indians as a gift. By the time the war ended, Indian armed forces had lost 50,000 lives, almost 10 per cent of the total deaths by the British army. They won almost 13,000 military awards for bravery, including twelve VCs, six of them on the Western Front.

Gurprit wrote to his family that now that the war had been declared over, he would try to earn some money by finding a job in England for a couple of years before returning back home. At the end of 1918, he managed to find a job in the Tate sugar factory in East London. The job was moderately paid for back-breaking daily work. After the horrors of the war, this was somehow a relief for Gurprit. But the war had also heightened his sense of self-esteem, allowing him to see himself as equal to any white European. He had also seen that 'Christian' white men were capable of brutal savagery. Although the Germans first used gas attacks in the war, soon the British had replied with the same. No longer did he feel that non-Europeans could be classed as an inferior race by the white men. Here, however, he was impressed by the educational opportunities for all children, boys and girls, being compulsory in France and England.

In his letter home, he wrote about his baby sister: 'You must send Baisakhi to school as soon as she is five.' He also wrote to his family about equality of labour in Britain: 'Here road sweepers, factory workers, train drivers, and office workers are all treated the same. Hard labour is not a disgrace here but is appreciated. And also there is no caste system here to discriminate one against another.'

He had obviously not been long enough in the country to understand the aristocratic classes here.

Like most Indians, Gurprit had expected the British Raj to offer some form of self-government for the Indians by the end of the war. Instead, when the war ended in triumph for Britain, India was denied its promised reward. Instead of self-government, the British imposed the most repressive Rowlatt Act, which vested the viceroy's government with extraordinary powers to quell 'sedition' against the empire by silencing and censoring the press, detaining political activists without trial, and arresting (without a warrant) any individuals suspected of treason against the Empire. Public protests against this draconian legislation were quelled ruthlessly.

This culminated in the April 1919 Jallianawala Bagh massacre in Amritsar, Punjab. The British Indian Army, under the command of Colonel Dyer, fired into an unarmed crowd with a majority of Sikhs in a park. All the entrances to this walled park were blocked by tanks and then, on Dyer's orders, troops fired on the crowd for several minutes. The British government stated that there were 379 dead and 1,200 wounded, but most placed the number of dead at well over 1,000. Dyer was lauded by the conservative forces in Britain. He became a celebrated hero among most of the people connected to the British Empire, including the House of Lords. Nobel Prize winner Rudyard Kipling even described Dyer as 'the man who saved India' and started collections for his homecoming prizes. The House of Commons, however, protested against Dyer's actions. Completely stunned by this, Gurprit, although conditioned over generations to ignore atrocities by the army, felt ashamed to have ever served in the British army.

By now, in the summer of 1919, race riots amongst the working class had also become frequent in England. With the end of the war there was now surplus of white labour and Indians found their labour in a competitive market against the native British. There were reports of mass demonstrations as well as physical attacks against Asians and blacks in almost all major cities. At work in the factory, he also soon realised that he was treated not as an equal race but almost like a slave. Following a racial slur by his immediate superior, young Gurprit was almost ready to fight him. His co-workers stopped him in time, but the next day he left his job.

Gurprit decided like a few of his fellow Indians to seek self-employment as a peddler. Hawking in door-to-door business required a valid licence, but this was easily obtained for anyone over seventeen years of age and of certified good character. With some of the money he had saved, he bought an old bicycle and two suitcases. He started filling his suitcases with ready-made new shirts, trousers, dresses, socks, ties, and lingerie bought at a wholesale market before travelling door to door every day of the week selling his goods. Travelling up to sixty miles every week, he developed a small clientele in East London. But he soon realised that there was increasing competition with many fellow street vendors around the place. It was also becoming expensive to live in London.

After two years, he moved to Cardiff and found a cheap lodging place in Butetown. He had not heard that just over two years back there was a riot against the foreigners in the nearby town of Newport. However, his hawking business started going well in Wales. Gurprit found that here in the provincial town, his clients had more time for him, and they were able to have a chat and often even offered him drinks inside their homes.

This tall, young, handsome bearded Sikh with turban and light brown skin soon became popular amongst his clientele, who were mostly women. This was in spite of a white woman in Cardiff being stripped naked by the crowd for marrying an African only a few years back. After spending a few years in Europe, Gurprit could speak and understand reasonably good English, but he did have problems with reading and writing English. One of his clients, a kind lady called Dilys, had always welcomed him into her house to have a chat and a drink. She was a war widow with two unmarried daughters. Dilys offered to teach him to read and write in English. Every week she spent an hour teaching him to write and gave him homework in English writing to do as well. Some weeks, when she was busy, her older daughter Anwen, who was almost eighteen years old, helped him to study.

To expand his business, Gurprit started going to the nearby town of Newport on market day on Saturday to open a stall as a vendor. He soon realised that he could only make a limited amount of money from this hawking by working alone. He needed an assistant and also help with keeping his accounts. Dilys was happy for Anwen to take up the job and earn some money. Within a few months he opened a grocery store in Newport with Anwen working as a shop assistant. He could now afford to hire a van when he needed to go away to London to get supplies of cheap ready-made clothes, woollen goods, Indian spices and fragrances, and especially silk materials from the large Indian retail stores there. In his absence, Anwen ran the shop with the help of her mother and younger sister.

It was not long before Gurprit, after asking Dilys's permission first, proposed to Anwen. She had already fallen in love with this handsome young Indian. She happily accepted and left the shop to bring the news to her mother and sister immediately. During his next visit to London, Gurprit went to the Gurdwara in London only to be strictly told that marriage between a Sikh and non-Sikh would not be allowed there. He decided to ignore them and arrange for their marriage in a registry office. He wrote to his family about his engagement and wanted them to come to Britain for his wedding. His mother replied that his father was seriously ill and wanted him to come home as soon as possible if he wanted to see his father for the last time.

Gurprit left within a few days and reached his village five weeks later to find his father on his deathbed. After his father's death a few days later, Gurprit washed his father's body before being taken to the local Gurdwara to be placed in front of the Guru Granth Sahib and then for cremation. He sent a letter to Dilys and Anwen explaining the circumstances and also saying that it would take him longer than expected to return. As the only remaining son of the family now, he arranged to sell their property and land in the village before returning back to Britain with his elderly mother and twelve-year-old sister. He bought a large supply of silk materials, Indian clothes, perfumes, and spices to bring along for his shop. By the time they arrived in Cardiff, it was more than six months since he had left.

Anwen was thrilled to see Gurprit back and hugged him tightly and then, realising that he was a little bit shy in front of his mother and sister, who were probably not accustomed to girls hugging men, she pulled back before kissing him lightly on his cheek. Dilys and Gurprit's mother, Banee, both widows, soon got on very well. Dilys took the newcomer to the country under her wing. His sister Baisakhi and Dilys's youngest daughter, fourteen-year-old Delyth, also quickly got on very well. Gurprit wanted his sister to go to school as soon as possible after the disruption she had experienced with their father's death and moving to another country. Dilys took her to Delyth's school and met the headteacher. It was agreed that Baisakhi would start in a class lower than those of her age to allow her time to catch up with English and the new set-up. Dilys also took on teaching both Baisakhi and Banee some spoken English.

Six months later, Gurprit and Anwen got married in the registry office in Cardiff. Between Dilys and Banee they had organised a reception for nearly forty people including some of Gurprit's Indian friends and Anwen's family and friends. The guests loved the mixture of Indian food and traditional food, although smoking and drinking were not allowed as per Sikh tradition. Baisakhi and Delyth both dressed up in Indian costume and did a few Indian dances with some of their school friends. Gurprit and some his Sikh friends then tried Bhangra dancing, which was fun, but they appeared rusty and made people laugh more as they lacked any coordination.

Afterwards, on their way to a nearby pub, a few of the Welsh guests commented, 'Well, that was a great wedding, we must say.'

Soon Gurprit and Anwen bought a semi-detached house in Duffryn to be near their shop in Newport and moved in with Gurprit's mother and sister. Dilys made regular visits to Banee and the two of them, one in traditional European dress and the other in Indian salwar kurta, were now a regular sight in Cardiff as well as in Newport.

Seven years later, Banee died after a stroke. Dilys was devastated. By now, Anwen and Gurprit had a baby girl and were expecting another one soon. Soon after finishing her schooling, Baisakhi started training to be a teacher while Delyth took up a job as an office clerk in Cardiff. Gurprit's business was doing very well and he started a retail business next to his now enlarged grocery shop where two local-born young Sikhs and two Welsh men were employed.

Dilys passed away from cancer after a prolonged illness just before the war broke out again. Gurprit was relieved to find that he was now too old to be called to join as a soldier. During the war he joined the home guard, while Baisakhi and Delyth gave up their jobs to work in the Bridgend ammunition factory.

In January 1947, Gurprit had a massive heart attack and died surrounded by his beloved Welsh wife, his newly married sister with her Welsh husband, and his mixed-race children.

Part 2

'They left India at a young age with the specific aim of obtaining further qualifications and training—to complete a stage in their careers. Most migrant aspirants were disappointed with their experience of working and studying in this country. They ended up being tied to the UK and its public services, such as the NHS, because returning without fulfilling your aspirations was not an option. They always hoped that they would break out of the cycle and in the end they did not, but stayed on to make the most of it. They were indentured to the system.'

House of Lords, 1961

Lord Cohen of Birkenhead: *'The Health Service would have collapsed if it had not been for the enormous influx from junior doctors from such countries as India and Pakistan.'*

Lord Taylor of Harlow: *'They are here to provide pairs of hands in the rottenest, worst hospitals in the country because there is nobody else to do it.'*

Enoch Powell, April 1968

'As I look ahead, I am filled with foreboding; like the Roman, I seem to see "the River Tiber foaming with much blood."'

Chapter One

The British Viceroy Lord Curzon divided Bengal in two on an arbitrarily drawn line for the first time in 1905 for so-called administrative reasons. Outraged at yet another 'divide and rule' policy by the British, the Swadeshi movement, which included boycotting British goods and public institutions, protest meetings and processions, forming committees, propaganda through the press, and diplomatic pressure, started all over India but more so in Bengal. Although Bengal was reunited in 1911 due to the mass protests, the most significant impact of this division was the greater communal dissonance between the Hindus and Muslims of Bengal.

Khulna District, even with its larger percentage of Hindu population, had become part of East Bengal. Since 1905, tensions between the mainly Muslim population and smaller Hindu communities in East Bengal had been rising slowly. But on the whole, both communities had lived happily together, mostly in the same villages, sharing each other's festivities throughout the years. The children's favourite thing in both communities was the colourful procession of Muharram and lighting up the dark evening during Diwali. Muslims, who made up almost two thirds of the population in East Bengal, were mainly agriculture-based and were mostly poor farmers working for landlords, whereas Hindu families were anything from landlords, clerks, teachers, doctors, or tenant farmers working for landowners.

In 1921, Neel Kanta, the only child of Rajani Kanta and Durga, was born in a village a few miles from Khulna town by the Rupsa river in East Bengal. Rajani was a teacher in the local high school and his closest friend was Rahim, whom Neel called Chacha. Growing up, Neel loved Chacha coming to their house almost every week.

'How is khoka babu doing today?' Rahim said, before lifting him onto his shoulder and shouting towards the kitchen, 'Boumoni, have you made ghugni today?'

Durga came out from the kitchen putting the anchal of her sari over her head and saying, 'No, Dada. Only muri and beguni today. Do you want a glass of water first?'

'Boumoni, I brought this rohu fish for you. The fishermen caught it earlier today in our pond. Any chance of making us a cup of tea?'

'Sure, I will boil the water. Khoka, look at the size of this fish. And it's still moving its tail.'

Neel climbed down from Chacha's shoulder to poke at the fish, which was still wiggling. Durga was married off at the age of sixteen and was childless for several years. After praying to all the Hindu gods when nothing was happening, following Rahim's advice, she went to give her offerings to the famous Pir Baba shrine in the next Muslim neighbourhood. Neel was born only a year later.

'So, Ramadan starts next week. It's going to be tough for you all, fasting all day in this hot summer we are having,' said Rajani.

'No, it's not too much of a problem. We are used to it. And as you know, we gorge ourselves between the sunset and sunrise,' Rahim replied with a smile.

'Still, I don't understand how you can manage without even a drop of water in the whole day.'

Rahim looked after the small amount of agricultural land Rajani's family had as well as his own larger farm. When they were talking about the weather and farming, Neel went inside the house to bring his kite to show to Chacha. By the time he came out with his kite, which his father had made for him, Durga had brought Rahim and Rajani plates of freshly fried large crisp pieces of Rohu, turmeric-coated and lightly salted, along with muri and beguni.

'Can I have a piece of fried fish too, Ma?' called out Neel.

'Okay, wait. I am going to bring the tea in a minute. Would you have a cup too?' she looked at her husband.

'Why not?' replied Rajani.

Neel, carefully separating the bones from the fried fish with his finger, asked, 'When is Muharram, Chacha? I love the sword fighting.'

Rahim replied, 'I think it's two or three weeks before Durga Puja this year'.

Neel ran to climb the mango tree in the garden, happily shouting, 'Wow! We will have Muharram, then Durga Puja, and then Diwali!'

'Be careful on the tree and bring back any green mango you can find on the ground. I will make some pickles,' Durga shouted after him.

During Neel's middle school years, there was huge excitement during discussions in the family and between the teachers at school about the salt march led by Gandhi and the India-wide boycott of British goods.

'I have no doubt that the British have brought some good things for our country, such as the education system and the court system. But they have taken much more from us than we have gained from them,' said Rahim.

'I agree, and also, what rights do they have to rule us and treat us as second-class citizens in our own country?' replied Rajani.

'If we boycott their goods it will hurt them where they are most vulnerable—in their own country. When the money and goods coming from India dry up and they can't sell their goods here, the mighty British Raj will have to face its own people, above all those who thrive on these unequal businesses,' said another teacher who was visiting Rajani that afternoon after school.

'They buy our cotton at next to no price at all and then print the clothes in their textile factories in Liverpool and Manchester before selling to us at exuberant price,' said Rahim.

While he was in high school, Neel also remembered Chacha and his father having arguments about whose poetry was the best.

'I like Rabi Thakur more than anyone else in the world, and that's not just because he won the Nobel Prize for us,' said Rahim as he started reciting his favourite poem.

'I am not saying that I am not proud of Tagore. Any Bengali, and for that matter any Indian, would be, but Kaji Nazrul's poems are the closest to my heart,' said Rajani.

71

'Have you read the new poem "Banalata Sen" by Jibanananda Das in the last issue of the *Kavita* magazine?' asked Rahim.

'It has been a thousand years since I started trekking the earth.

A huge travel in night's darkness from the Ceylonese waters to the Malayan sea—Except for a few soothing moments with Natore's Banalata Sen,' recited Rajani.

Rahim continued, 'Her hair as if the dark night of long lost Vidisha—'

'Nothing remains but darkness to sit face to face with Banalata Sen,' Neel completed.

Looking towards them, Durga said, 'But I also like his mother Kusumkumari Das's "The Ideal Boy".' She then recited, 'Amader deshey hobey shei chhele kobey / Kothae na boro hoye kajey boro hobey?' (The child who achieves not in words but in deeds, when will this land know such a one?). Then, looking up at Neel, she said, 'You'd better go in and finish your English reading for the test exam tomorrow.'

Neel went inside to study Keats for his upcoming exam.

A week before his matriculation exam, Neel was struck down by bloody dysentery. He passed his matriculation from Khulna High School in 1938 with good marks but in the second division. The choice for his father to make was where Neel should go to college. Rajani and Durga always wanted him to become a doctor but his marks were not good enough to try for any medical or even engineering colleges. Rather than going to Dhaka, which was over 120 miles away, there was Calcutta, which was much nearer and offered more choices anyway. City College, established in 1881, was known to be one of the heritage institutions of Calcutta and had played a prominent social role in the wake of the Bengal Renaissance of the nineteenth century. It was also recommended by his teachers at school.

Neel enrolled in City College for a BA in history, economics, and Bengali. He found a hostel in Amherst Street close to his college and the Sealdah station. If he wanted to take a train from there back home to Khulna it was only few hours' journey. In the hostel he shared his room with three other boys, two from Burdwan and one from Hooghly district. He was teased constantly by his mates as 'Bangal' because of his thick regional accent and thriftiness. Most of the boys were strong supporters of Mohun Bagan football club in Calcutta, who were the only Indian side to have won the IFA Shield in 1911 by beating a European team.

Over the weekend, on the way to watch a football match in the Maidan, Neel, who was a devoted supporter of the East Bengal club in Kolkata, argued that the IFA shield won by Mohun Bagan had happened over twenty years back and since then even Mohameddan Sporting Club had won the FA cup last year with a double of winning the First Division league, which so far no other Indian team had done.

His friends argued, 'Why don't you support Mohameddan then?'

By then they had stopped by the vendor on the Maidan selling corn roasted on an open coal fire and served with some salt, pepper, and just a squeeze of lemon juice.

Munching his grilled corn, Neel replied, 'I think East Bengal is going to do well next year and they do not bring players from all over the country to win competitions like Mohameddan. Personally, I also think that Mohameddan are a bit pro-British.'

Conversation moved quickly to politics, with a discussion about who would be the best leader of the National Congress, Subhas Bose or Gandhi. All of them were in full support of Subhas Bose's bold steps over Gandhi's rather placid approach towards the British.

In 1941, Neel Kanta passed his BA with Honours. He wanted to do an MA in history from the prestigious Presidency College in Calcutta but wanted to discuss this with his parents first after giving them the good news of his examination results.

He came home to find his father seriously ill with TB. The local doctor said the only treatment was fresh air.

'Where can we have air fresher than in this village by the river?' commented Rahim, who was visiting him every day.

'I hear that they now have some new drugs for TB in England,' said the doctor.

'Like the new wonder-drug. What is it called?' asked Neel.

'Penicillin. No, but that does not work for TB. The new drug for TB is not available anywhere in India yet.'

A few weeks later, Rajani passed away. Neel, a young graduate now, was heartbroken and did not know how to console his mother and Rahim Chacha.

It was Rahim Chacha who brought the news a few months later. 'Some of the illiterates in the nearby villages are talking about taking revenge here for the riots against Muslims in Calcutta,' he said with concern.

Still grief-stricken after her husband's death, Durga asked, 'Dada, should we worry here?'

'As long as I am here I will not let anything happen to this family. But I am getting old. The new generation thinks Jinnah is the next prophet and will stop at nothing.'

'What do you advise, Chacha?' asked Neel.

'It is very, very sad, but I would suggest that you should seriously think of moving to West Bengal, maybe to Calcutta, if you can.'

'But we have everything here. We really don't know anyone in Calcutta. It's almost a different country,' said Durga.

It took almost a year before Rahim Chacha helped them to sell their land and property at a reasonable price before Neel with his mother moved to Calcutta.

They found a small property in Shobhabazar.

Not knowing anyone around Calcutta, his mother said to Neel, 'We are now migrants in our own country.' Then she added, 'Nothing is the same here. They call us "Bangal" and laugh at our accent. Everyone here thinks they are so much better than us.'

But very soon the communal riot in Noakhali, near Khulna, made them realise that they had done the right thing by taking Rahim Chacha's advice to move from East Bengal. Muslim mobs attacked the Hindus, seizing their properties and forcibly converting them to Islam. Five thousand Hindus died and around one million fled East Bengal to relief camps in West Bengal.

Neel started a small business selling books in the College Street area of the city near the Presidency College. Sadly, Neel's dream of doing an MA from this revered college was now changed to seeing the dreamy-eyed boys and girls going in and out of the college from his shop window. His business thrived though and soon he joined with a newly-formed publishing company.

Neel's mother had been settling down slowly into the new city life after leaving their village in Khulna. She soon came to be friends with a few other Bangal families who had also recently moved from East Bengal. Amongst them she found a pretty seventeen-year-old girl from a good family who could be a good match for Neel. Juthika had left with her family for West Bengal just before her matriculation exam in Khulna when the trouble had started.

'I went to the Ghosh family in the neighbourhood this afternoon. You know, the family who have also moved from the Khulna area because of the trouble?' said Durga while serving dinner.

Neel just looked up towards his mother.

'Their daughter, Juthika, is very pretty. Have you met her yet?'

'No, Ma. I have not met any of them. When do I have the time?'

'That's what I am worried about. You are always working so hard.'

Neel just continued with his dinner.

Durga brought some more rice and fish curry for Neel before saying, 'I think it's about time we found you a wife, Neel. I am also getting old. I could do with some help around the house myself.'

'But we already have two part-time maids here, one for the cleaning and the other for helping with the cooking.'

'I am not talking about that kind of help. Both of us could do with some company. After moving here I feel so lonely most of the time.'

Neel gazed toward his mother's feet and said, 'Ma, I have always respected your advice. You decide what is best for us. But this is a very small house, even for the two of us.'

'We still have some money from our property sale in Khulna and you are earning decent money from your business these days. We should look for a bigger house as well.'

A few months later they moved to a larger house in Bagbazar near to the Ganges, and three months afterwards, Neel was married to Juthika.

India became independent in 1947 but was partitioned arbitrarily by the British into two countries. The communal riot of 1948 followed in both the east and west of the country when millions were displaced and almost a million were killed.

Just over a year after their marriage, Juthika had her first son. Durga named him Jiten. While the whole family was basking in happiness following the birth of the new baby, news came from Khulna that Rahim Chacha has been accidentally killed by his own faith group, Muslims, while trying to protect a Hindu family from being massacred.

Durga was inconsolable and, burying her face in her hands, kept repeating, 'Why Dada, of all people?'

Life in Calcutta was never going to be like the one they had in their village but soon they got used to their busy lives here. In the next few years, Juthika gave birth to three daughters, Saroja, Geeta, and then, a few years later, Meera. While Jiten went to the all-boys Bagbazar High School, Saroja studied in the girls' school where Geeta was also admitted a few years later. Saroja did not really enjoy her school but Geeta, on the other hand, excelled there. They loved their grandmother Durga, who used to read and recite Bengali poetry with them. Both Saroja and Geeta learnt to sing Bengali songs on the harmonium from her. Saroja had a good voice but was not fond of regular practice, but Geeta was a keen learner. Soon she was a regular at most family occasions and school ceremonies, beautifully singing Tagore and Najrul's song.

Durga often said to her, hiding her grief, 'Your Dadu would have been so proud of you.'

Young Geeta, pointing to the picture of her grandfather, would ask, 'What was he like?' which would bring tears to Durga's eyes.

Like most families, they had a cook, Madanda, and also two other maids in their house. One of the maids, Aratidi, was also from

Khulna and had become a widow at a young age with her only son, Swapan.

Arati lost her husband in the riot and was lucky to have escaped with her son to West Bengal with their lives. Soon Arati found employment as a housemaid with Durga strongly favouring her over the others. Arati and her son were allowed to stay in the house. A few months later, Swapan developed polio and lost power in both his legs. Juthika's children had grown up watching this young boy dragging himself on the floor to move from one place to another. Geeta, who was only two years older than him, was particularly attached to him and loved to spend time sitting with him and playing or reading her books to him.

When Geeta was only twelve years old, Swapan died from malaria. She was devastated. For months, Geeta was often found sitting down with Aratidi somewhere quiet after coming back from school, sometimes holding her hand, both of them comforting each other in silence.

When Durga passed away after a short illness, along with Neel and Juthika, all the children were inconsolable for weeks. Soon Juthika's widowed mother, whom they called Dadi, came to live with them. She was always teasing the girls with funny stories and making them laugh. Saroja was not surprised when she failed her matriculation exam. She was quite happy when she was married off at the age of seventeen only a few months before her retake of the matriculation exam, which she was dreading.

In spite of the pressures of her school exams and some teasing from Dadi, Geeta, who was now almost fifteen, started a weekly music lesson on Saturday afternoons for the young children of the maids working in the neighbourhood. Aratidi was always found sitting quietly by the door, looking at her with pride.

Chapter Two

Rani screamed, 'No! No, I don't want to go to that Civil Hospital! Our baby will die in that dirty hospital. I would rather give birth here in our house; at least our baby will not catch some deadly disease from that filthy place. I don't care if I die myself.'

The birth of their first child was imminent. Labour pains had started almost five hours back. As deputy railway station master, Pradeep's father Birendra was well respected in Nairobi. He had helped to develop and maintain railway services between Kenya and Uganda, which multiplied British business manyfold from both countries. Pradeep himself was a doctor of great reputation with a thriving eye clinic in the city. His clients included not only the city's rich Africans and Asians but also many Europeans. But this meant nothing where admission to the modern King George Hospital was concerned, as it was strictly restricted to the white Europeans.

Pradeep, the only child of his parents, had lost his mother soon after his birth in Nairobi. He was brought up by Indian and African maidservants who he called 'Aunty'. At the age of eleven, he was sent back to Calcutta to live with his uncle and aunt to have a proper education. After successfully completing his schooling he was fortunate enough to be admitted to Campbell Medical School. He not only then qualified as a doctor but soon went on to train in the Medical College Eye Infirmary as an ophthalmic surgeon. After his training, following his father's advice, he returned to Nairobi to set up his eye practice.

When Rani had declared a few months earlier that she was pregnant, the distribution of sweets to their neighbours and new clothes for the servants had followed in the immediate euphoria. Soon, Pradeep and his father had to decide where the child was going to be born. Rani's mother, in spite of her poor health, had offered to come over and stay with her daughter for a few months. But this was soon considered not to be an option because of her own ill health and the long journey by ship from India that was involved. Neither Pradeep nor his father were very keen for Rani to go to India for a few months to have her child as they could not leave their work for that long.

Their guest room downstairs was cleared up. Pradeep was petrified but Rani held his hand tightly, saying, 'I trust you completely. Remember all the stories you used to tell me about assisting in the delivery room when you were a house surgeon in your medical college?'

After nearly seventeen hours of labour, when the time actually came, the birth was surprisingly easy.

On 12 April 1945, Pradeep held their son to exhausted Rani, saying, 'Look, he is so beautiful,' before expertly cutting the umbilical cord.

His grandfather named him Ashok after the greatest emperor India had ever had over 2,000 years back. The two maidservants, Mercy, a childless Kenyan, and Purnima, an Indian who had grown-up children back home, had made bringing up the baby really straightforward. In Nairobi there were many Indian families, mostly from Gujarat and Punjab. Most of them were businessmen. All of them held a British passport after 1920 when the British government finally officially declared Kenya as its colony. Apart from Birendra, Pradeep and Rani already held British passports. Soon, a British passport was issued for Ashok as well.

Pradeep was often discussed with his father, who was now retired, and his friends about moving the family back to India.

'Nairobi is no longer as it used to be. It is getting swamped with people moving in from the countryside every year. In the last ten years the population of Nairobi has nearly doubled. Now there are slums everywhere,' said Pradeep's Indian friend Harbhajan, who was a businessman.

79

'You can't blame them though. Kenyans, mostly Kikuyu people, are so often forced to work for extremely low pay by the British farmers in the highlands. Everyone wants better opportunities for their family and their children, just like us,' replied Pradeep.

While they were planning to move back to India, news came of the 1946 communal riots in Calcutta and then in Noakhali. Neither Pradeep nor Rani was keen to go back to such a volatile place, especially with their very young son.

On 13 August 1947, Birendra, at the age of seventy-nine, was admitted to the Civil Hospital with severe chest pains. Doctors soon diagnosed a massive heart attack and said there was not much they could do. On the BBC radio for the last few days announcements were being made in the news bulletin saying that newly formed Pakistan was to be given its freedom by the British on 14 August and that the next day India was going to earn its freedom. Birendra wanted to be taken back home to his own bed against the doctors' advice. Listening to the speech by Jawaharlal Nehru on the eve of India's freedom from the British colony on 15 August, he passed away peacefully.

The cremation took place before sunset the following day. After the brief sradha ceremony three weeks later, Pradeep told Rani that he had to go back to India soon with his father's ashes to spread them over the Ganges. The journey by ship to Bombay and then by train to Calcutta took nearly three weeks.

Once in Calcutta, he spread his father's ashes in the Ganges and prayed in the Kalighat temple before going back to his uncle's house. Pradeep was inspired by the euphoria and optimism everywhere in the new India. He could not but agree that returning to India would offer better opportunities, particularly for Ashok's education. Pradeep was also told that there would be no problem in successfully relocating his eye practice to Calcutta.

After returning to Nairobi, Pradeep discussed this with Rani, who jumped at the idea. She had never truly settled in Nairobi and the chance to return back to Calcutta was too good to miss. Kenya was also becoming more volatile, first with the militant actions of KASU, the Kenyan African Study Union, and now with the Mau Mau rebel group of the Kikuyu people.

Only a month before their proposed move back to India in 1948, news came of serious communal riots in Calcutta as well as more widely in the India-Pakistan border areas in both Bengal and Punjab. The decision to move was cancelled.

Ashok started his schooling at St Mary's, a Catholic school, at the age of four. His closest friends at school were Rajesh, the son of another Gujrati business family, and Sanjay, the son of a Punjabi businessman. Both families were originally from India and had been in Kenya for over twenty-five years.

Their Gujrati and Punjabi family friends decided to move to the nearby country of Uganda where the cotton business was now prospering more than in Kenya and the country was still very stable under the British rule. Ashok was in tears for days after his friends Rajesh and Sanjay left for Uganda with their parents. Soon the Agarwal family also left for India.

On 3 October 1952, Mau Mau rebels claimed their first European victim when they stabbed a white woman to death near her home in Thika. Six days later, Senior Chief Waruhiu, a strong British supporter, was shot dead in broad daylight in his car. The British government declared a state of emergency and British troops were sent to Kenya.

Kenya was no longer a safe place to live and by now India was not only stable but seemed to be prospering. Finally, in June 1953, Pradeep moved back to India with Rani and Ashok. They set up their house in Ballygunge in south Calcutta. It did not take Pradeep long to establish his private eye practice nearby as well as getting an honorary lecturer position in the eye infirmary in Calcutta Medical College, his own former training place.

Ashok was admitted to the nearby newly established South Point School in April 1954. The school was ideal for bringing out the best in Ashok as it had a devoted team of teachers with only twenty students in its first year. With support from enthusiastic teachers,

Ashok flourished in his school. Both Pradeep and Rani were also pleased to know that he wanted to follow his father into medicine. Ashok became popular in his school as a sportsman too, and especially as a cricketer.

To his parents' delight, in 1962 he passed the newly introduced Higher Secondary Examination in West Bengal in the first division. His marks were good but could have been better, as his marks in Bengali, in particular, were not so good. After passing in the first division with reasonable but not brilliant marks, Ashok was not so sure that he would get admission in any of the four well-known medical colleges which were all in Calcutta.

He applied to all four medical colleges in Calcutta and was surprised to find a few weeks later that he has been selected for interview by all of them. The interview for the more prestigious Calcutta Medical College was a few days before the other colleges. His heart sank when he realised that for just over 130 places in each of these medical colleges, ten times more students were called for interview.

However, his uncle encouraged him, saying, 'But you have been called for the interview. Think of the many thousands who applied and did not get a chance.'

Ashok's memory of the interview in the principal's office at Calcutta Medical College earlier on that day was still hazy when he came back nervously in the early evening to check the list of successful applicants. Craning over other students, he tried to read the handwritten list, which was luckily in an alphabetical order. With the surname Basu, it did not take him long to scroll the list. His heart almost jumped out of his chest to see that his name was actually there. He triple-checked it before taking the bus to his house.

After paying respect by touching her feet, Ashok asked his mother, 'When is Baba coming home?'

'I think he should be here any time now. Do you want something to eat?'

'No, I think I will wait until Baba is home.'

As soon as Pradeep was home, Ashok went to him and paid respect by touching his feet. Before his father could ask anything, Ashok stood next to him and said, 'Yes, Baba. In Calcutta Medical College.'

With tears rolling from their eyes, both his parents hugged him tightly. All kinds of sweets from the nearby Ganguram's followed the good news to their relatives' houses and were also distributed to the servants and the neighbours.

Ashok was thrilled to find out that for his pre-medical year he had been selected to go to Presidency College. He had heard so many stories of this famous college in Calcutta which was associated with the names of many famous alumni, including Swami Vivekananda and Netaji Subhash Chandra Bose. Even Rajendra Prasad, the first president of India, and the famous Bengali film director Satyajit Ray were students there.

The year in Presidency College went like a dream. He also spent many days with his friends from college playing table tennis and volleyball in the nearby Eden Hostel. How he wished he could have boarded in the hostel rather than commuting from his family home in Ballygunge. He passed his pre-medical exam in the first division to the delight of his parents.

In spite of the scary professor and the cadaver smell which hung to their clothes for weeks from dissecting, Ashok loved anatomy. Not so keen on organic chemistry, he soon learnt how to arrange proxies for himself in the class in lieu of helping out his fellow students who found anatomy daunting. After successfully completing his first two years at the college, it was now time to start in the wards and begin attending operating theatres for their teaching. Before long, two things were clear in his mind: that he was going to be a surgeon, and that he would go for higher training.

For the first two years, Ashok had commuted daily to the college from his family home in Ballygunge on packed buses, often hanging from the door handles. He realised how much he was missing out on the sports and other social activities by wasting at least two to three hours every day travelling to and from the college. It was not difficult to convince his parents that the bus journey was putting too much strain on him and he needed more time to study, as in the third year he would be starting his clinical studies in the wards, often with duties in the evenings. Admission to the college hostel opened up the world of late evening games of table tennis and Carrom in the common room, as well as being able to go to the cinemas in the night with his friends. He soon also joined the college volleyball and football teams, and hoped to join the cricket team when the season came.

One afternoon, as they were coming out of the college canteen, Ashok and his two friends noticed a big rally march going through the street outside the hospital gate. All three of them came outside to find the large protest march with banners such as 'Down with the US Imperialism' and 'Long live Vietnam'.

'Let's join them,' said Ashok to his friends.

One of them said, 'No, I don't want to get into trouble. The pathology exam is coming up soon,' as he left.

Ashok and his other friend followed the march on the footpath towards Calcutta University. All around the place was now a sea of young people carrying banners and shouting anti-American slogans. Ashok and his friends decided to bunk their afternoon classes and join the protest march. The rally of tens of thousands of people then moved through Central Avenue towards the USIS building near Chowringhee. By now, the establishment was surrounded by hundreds of police. As soon as the protest march reached the outside of the place, the police charged them with batons. Unable to stem the tide of thousands of protesters, the police soon started firing tear gas. It was nearly two hours before the rally finally broke up.

Emotionally exhausted and still rubbing his eyes, Ashok returned to his hostel. Some of the senior students in the canteen were talking about donating blood for Vietnam. Two days later, Ashok went to the blood bank and for the first time in his life donated blood for a small country fighting imperialism.

Ashok passed his MBBS exam with good results and after a year as an intern was glad to be working as a surgical house officer. A few of his friends had applied for an MS in the Calcutta Post Graduate Hospital, also known as PG, for their further surgical training. Two boys and a girl from his class had applied to take the ECFMG exam for going to America. For Ashok, it was clear in his mind for some time that to pursue training in surgery he would go to the best place—England. There was no question of going to America, which had been bombing the poor Vietnamese with napalm for the last few years anyway. At least Britain had not joined them!

Only last month, a senior ex-student of the college, whom they all called Dada, was on his holiday from England, where he was now a senior registrar in psychiatry. In the hospital canteen, he was talking about how much the hospitals in England were currently looking for good doctors from India. Ashok joined the table of several aspiring doctors gathering around Dada.

'They are looking for more doctors from outside for their expanding National Health Service. But I must warn you that getting a job in the main specialties is not going to be easy. Competition is tough. But you will definitely have a better life there,' he said.

Most of them at the table were thinking of going there for a few years to train as specialists before coming back to India anyway.

'What is the pay like there for the doctors?'

After converting pounds into rupees in their minds, all were completely taken aback.

'Unbelievable. So much more than we get here,' someone said.

'But it is hard work,' replied the senior.

Like many of his other classmates, Ashok applied to the General Medical Council UK in Hallam Street, London, for clinical attachment. A response came within three months. The letter stated that he was being offered a four-week clinical attachment in surgery in the Doncaster Royal Infirmary in England in six months' time. Successful completion of the attachment would allow him to obtain full registration with the GMC before applying for further training jobs.

'Royal Infirmary! Wow! It must be a special hospital to have the name "Royal!"' said his mother.

'Once you have full registration with the GMC it will mean that you can apply for any job in surgery there,' said his father.

A week later one evening after Ashok came home after work, after offering him a cup of tea and his favourite homemade ghugni, his parents asked him to sit down for a talk.

'We are both very proud of you, Ashok, you know that. Your mother and I were talking and we think you should get married before you go to England,' said his father.

Ashok nearly choked on his ghugni before his mother added, 'We are not getting any younger, you know. We want to see you married to a decent girl here.'

'But I will be leaving for England in less than six months,' Ashok tried to protest.

'We all know that. I have a friend who has found out that there is a good family here with an eligible girl,' said his father.

'She is studying a BA in Bethune College,' added his mother.

Although he was twenty-three years old, like most of his mates in college, Ashok had no time for girls, except as classmates. He had been too busy with his sports and politics. There were only a few of his classmates who had girlfriends, but everyone teased them and made jokes about them. Sure, he had looked at girls with interest when they were not looking his way, but never anything more than that.

Seeing Ashok keeping his head down, his father said, 'We don't want you to get pushed into marrying someone you don't like. We will arrange for you to meet the girl first and then you can decide.'

Ashok, blushing slightly, replied meekly, 'You do what you feel best.'

Chapter Three

1971: The prenup

She was probably the last person in the family to hear about it.

She was going to get married in two months' time. Even her younger sister, Meera, knew about this before her.

Meera came running and dancing to Geeta, shouting, 'Shadi! Shadi!'

'Whose wedding?' Asked Geeta with mild interest. She was stunned to hear that it was her wedding her sister was so excited about.

Geeta was eighteen and was considered to be a bright girl. After passing her matriculation in the first division, she got a place to study in the famous all-women's Lady Brabourne College in Calcutta. Initially, she had found the English-medium college a bit difficult after her all-girls Bengali school education. Although some of the girls with English-medium Catholic school backgrounds in her class were high-nosed, most of the teachers were kind and patient.

She had done very well so far, gaining good marks in the first year of her intermediate degree in arts. She was seriously thinking of talking to her elder brother about doing a BA Honours in history and maybe an MA after. She could hardly talk to her mother, who was not at all keen for her to go to a college in the first place, about this. She would have preferred for Geeta to have gotten married soon, like her elder sister. It was only her elder brother Jiten, who she called Dada and who was now studying an MA in economics at Calcutta University, who had fought for her to go to college. Not surprisingly, their father had agreed.

Soon Geeta was summoned to the sitting room where both her parents, Baba and Ma, were sitting. Jiten was standing next to their grandmother, Dadi. She was told that a good match has been found for her by sheer luck and the wedding would take place in about two months on an auspicious date. She stood with her eyes fixed to the ground next to her feet, not sure what all this meant. She was not even sure if she was excited or frightened. She was curious, of course, but no way could she be so forward to ask her elders about her own wedding! Soon their elder sister Saroja arrived with her four-year-old son, Arun.

After paying respect to the elders by touching their feet, Saroja, holding Geeta in a tight squeeze, asked, 'Well, how do you feel?'

Meera and Arun ran off to play in another room. Ma left for the kitchen, ordering the servants to get some water and sweets for the new arrivals. Their father soon left as well, saying he needed to be back at his office for business.

It was only then that Jiten and Saroja elaborated about Geeta's wedding arrangements. The marriage proposal was sent from another decent family in Kolkata a few weeks back. Saroja's brother-in-law was a business associate of the groom's uncle. The family was very well-to-do and had connections in Kenya and Uganda. The only son of the family, Ashok had qualified as a doctor from the famous Calcutta Medical College over two years back. He had been lucky to get a chance to go to England very soon for further training to be a surgeon. The family wanted him to get married before he went to a foreign country where the girls were said to sometimes be too forward. His family was not interested in a big dowry but wanted to have a daughter-in-law from an educated family who could understand and speak English well. Initial talks between the families had already gone well. As Ashok was due to leave for England in just over four months' time, it had been agreed that the wedding would take place on an auspicious date two months from now. Once Ashok had settled for a few months in England he would come back to take his wife to join him there.

Saroja winked and said, 'From the photo, I think he is a good-looking man like Dilip Kumar in the last film we saw.'

Jiten, who had already met Ashok once, said, 'He is a smart-looking boy, all right.'

Getting straight to the point as usual, Dadi teased, 'How many children do you think you are going to have?'

Geeta, who had inherited the dark complexion from her father's side, blushed and then blushed again but could hardly talk. She was not sure if she was nervous or happy for the travel to a foreign land. In her history books she had to read a lot about Britain. A couple of times with her family she had also been to see English cinemas. During the news reel before the film they had shown something about the wonderful looking Houses of Parliament. She was mesmerised. She did not even want to think about the marriage and inevitably leaving behind her family. She could hardly utter a word.

Later, the two sisters sat on her bed being gently warmed by the few rays of afternoon sun which had managed to find their way through the first-floor window with its old, partly-drawn green curtain. Here, Saroja dropped another bombshell on her. Apparently, it had been agreed between the parents that Ashok should meet Geeta before the wedding. Although this was not usual practice, the families had decided that after all this was modern India in the seventies, already an independent country for over twenty-three years. The boy and the girl should get a chance to talk between themselves before their big day.

Until she was about thirteen, Geeta had played often with the boys and girls in the neighbourhood. Mostly hide and seek, as well as ekka dokka, hopping and jumping over squares drawn with chalk on the pavement. Since the scary day when she bled, her mother had forbidden her from playing outside with the boys.
'You are a grown-up girl now; it's not proper for you to be with the boys. You should know,' she had said.
Her all-girls school and college education had also made sure of that. Having an older brother and sister meant that going out to places nearby was always with one or both of them. Only very few of her classmates in Brabourne College boasted of having a boyfriend, but no one took them seriously.

The last ten days had been a blur. She had been to her college every day as usual, but so far had felt too shy to tell any of her classmates about the coming event. This Friday afternoon she was due to meet Ashok for an hour or so. Obviously she would not be alone. Meera would be with them. Their family pride, the new grey Ambassador car, would take them to the medical college. Jiten would go back to his university after introducing her to Ashok, who would meet them there after his hospital duty was over.

She did not go to her college today. After lunch, most had gone for their usual nap except for Geeta and her two sisters. She was jealous of Meera, who had a beautiful red shalwar kameez chosen for her. Geeta loved to wear them as they felt more modern, but for today she was asked to wear a sari. Nonetheless, when Saroja opened the packet of a new sari she had purchased with their mother for her, Geeta was immediately very happy. In her blue printed silk sari with the new style of tight, short-sleeved matching blouse, she felt like one of the heroines in a Hindi film. She had to stop herself from looking back in the mirror.

Their mother woke up from her nap early and joined them. After giving a look of approval, she took out her bunch of keys and opened the large stainless steel almirah. Carefully, she took out a beautiful slender gold chain and a pair of golden bangles. She put the gold chain around Geeta's neck and then gave her a quick hug. She in turn touched her mother's feet fondly with her right hand and then touched her own forehead with it. Saroja took off her wristwatch, her own wedding present, and put it on the right wrist of Geeta with the golden bangles.

'I am letting you borrow it for your special day, for today only, remember,' she said.

Next, she helped to put a set of multi-coloured glass bangles, which had recently become very popular after the last Hindi film, onto her left wrist. Geeta's long dark hair was now brushed thoroughly and tied with a beautiful silk ribbon. A silver hair slide was then attached to one side. After her sister had applied a light brushing of scented powder to her face, highlighted her eyelashes with dark kajal, and put a bright red small bindi on the middle of her forehead, Geeta was ready.

After following a slow-moving tram for a while, their Ambassador car turned into the large gate of the Calcutta Medical College. Meera, who had been chattering all the way so far, was speechless now. Geeta and her sister looked with amazement at the tall pale white pillars with the large winding staircase of the main hospital building.

'It's like the beautiful pillars of Rome in my history books,' said Meera.

They all got out of the car. Now, in the late afternoon, hundreds of people were sitting on the majestic staircase.

Jiten said, 'They are all relatives waiting for the visiting time before they can go in and see their family members or friends who are patients in the wards.'

An ambulance was waiting near the building opposite, marked as the casualty block. Two people carried someone on a dark stretcher. Throngs of people were going in and out through the large open door.

'There he is,' Jiten walked towards the casualty entrance, shouting, 'Ashok! Ashok, we are here.'

Geeta cast a quick glance to find a tall man with glasses and a stethoscope hanging around his neck walking towards them. She just gripped her sister's hand.

'It has been a nightmare in the casualty today. Too many patients. There was a bus accident earlier on. Glad that I could get away on time,' said Ashok, and then, looking towards Geeta, he said, 'Hello.'

Geeta meekly replied, 'Hello,' without lifting her eyes from the ground.

Jiten wanted to get back to his uni and said to Ashok, 'Shall we leave the car for you?'

Ashok asked Geeta and Meera, 'Do you want me to show you around the college hospital first, and maybe then we can go to the coffee house in College Street or somewhere?'

Geeta just nodded and Meera said that she would love to see the college. It was agreed that the car would take Jiten back now and would wait for them outside the coffee house in about an hour.

Walking next to Ashok, still holding Meera's hand, Geeta sent only some sideways glances from time to time to notice that he must be several inches taller than her.

'This is the Eden block, for all the gynae cases and deliveries. That's the Prince of Wales block for surgery, where I mostly work. Oh, this building next to us is the anatomy hall, where we learnt to dissect dead bodies.'

Meera's face went pale. Even Geeta, who was so far almost dream-walking, clenched her sister's hand tighter.

They turned the corner and Ashok pointed to the beautiful red building with a clock tower, saying, 'This is the admin building and upstairs is the library.'

In the small oval ground in the front of the building, an outdoor volleyball match was going on. A few couples, boys and girls, were sitting close to each other, some even holding hands in other parts of the grounds.

Someone from the volleyball court called out to Ashok, 'Not playing today, then?'

Ashok just smiled at them. It was then that Geeta realised he had an athletic figure.

'Shall we go to the coffee house for a drink and something to eat? I am starving. The college canteen at this time of the day will be too crowded.'

Geeta just nodded and Meera said, 'I have never drunk coffee. What is it like?'

They left the hospital campus through another large gate and came to College Street, now overflowing with people going back home after work and college. The road itself was very busy with trams and buses overfilled with people hanging out from their doors. A few taxis were dangerously overtaking them from all sides.

'You'd better hold my hand crossing. It's a bit mad here,' said Ashok, offering his hand.

Trying not to show the fact that she was blushing, Geeta just held his hand with her left and Meera's with her right. As soon as they had crossed the road she let his hand go and straightened her sari. Weaving through thousands of people, they arrived in front of

Presidency College. Hundreds of old and new bookshops, as well as bookstalls, were overflowing onto the footpath. Trying not to look curious to check some of them out, Geeta just followed Ashok to the entrance of the coffee house.

'Baba's bookshop is in the next block,' said Meera.

After going up a spiral staircase, they were at the entrance of the coffee house. The place was buzzing with people. While they waited by the door, Ashok, with an expert eye, had already spotted a table where the waiter had brought back change and the people were ready to leave. He quickly guided them to the table.

'So many people!' Meera gasped.

Ashok replied, 'Yes, this is the place where many writers and artists come for their adda.'

The whole place was humming with voices and the impressive-looking waiters in their white outfits with shiny metal belts were going back and forth from the tables carrying plates. It was Geeta's first time ever in a place such as this, and she was trying hard to hide her amazement.

'What shall I order?' asked Ashok. 'They make great pakoras here.'

'I love pakoras; can I have some?' Meera replied quickly.

'Please!' Geeta looked at her sister.

'Sorry—please can I have some pakoras?' repeated Meera.

'Sure. And what do you want to have?' Ashok looked at Geeta.

'I will have the same, please.'

A waiter brought a few glasses of water to the table. Ashok ordered three plates of pakora and then asked Geeta, 'Do you want some coffee?'

Geeta had only once in her life drunk coffee with her friends outside her college and she had not liked the bitter taste.

'Yes, please,' she replied, trying to show that she was a grown-up girl.

Ashok pointed out some well-known writer with his friends sitting at the far table. 'Did you read his short story in the *Desh* magazine last month?'

Geeta was glad that her family were regular subscribers to the magazine and that she was an avid reader of anything outside of her course. 'Yes, I like his writing very much. I enjoyed his last novel too,' she replied.

The waiter soon put their food and coffee in front of them. The warm pakoras with hot chilli tomato sauce were the most delicious Geeta had ever tasted.

'They are so good!' said Meera.

'Shall I order another plate for both of you?' asked Ashok.

Meera looked eagerly for approval from her sister, who did not want to look too greedy and said, 'No, thank you.' She then tried a sip of her coffee and had to hide her face, which was looking contorted from the bitter taste.

Meera left the table to go to the toilet.

Ashok turned towards Geeta and asked earnestly, 'Are you happy about the marriage? Is there anything you wanted to say or ask me?'

Geeta pulled out her chair slightly and fiddled with the anchal of her sari for a few seconds. She then forced herself to look at Ashok. She immediately thought, 'He has dark eyes like me.'

She asked, 'Can I finish my BA when I go to England?' and then, after a moment, added, 'Do you really like me?'

Ashok reached out with his hand and gently put it on Geeta's hand, which was resting on the table, saying, 'Of course, you must finish your BA there, and yes, I like you very much.'

She just smiled as she put her free hand over theirs and asked, 'Can we go out again next week? Only the two of us?'

Two weeks later, as agreed, they met in the afternoon when Ashok had arranged one of his colleagues to cover him for a few hours at the hospital and Geeta skipped her class. She arrived by bus to find Ashok already waiting in front of the Metro cinema.

'Do you want to see a film? They are showing *Bullitt*. I understand it's a great action movie with Steve McQueen.'

'Can we just for a walk to the Eden Gardens instead?' said Geeta quickly, not keen on English action films.

They crossed the busy esplanade road, Geeta holding Ashok's hand all the way.

In front of the Shahid Meenar, only recently so renamed from its old moniker of Ochterlony Monument, Geeta said, 'They are selling fuchka there. Do you like fuchka?'

Ashok nodded and bought fuchka for both of them.

When they had reached the spot next to the wide boulevard of Red Road joining the governor's palace Raj Bhavan to the historical Fort William, Ashok held Geeta's hand again and said, 'We need to cross this road quickly. Cars come dashing from both sides. Run with me when I do.'

They could not stop laughing after crossing the road in a hurry. Soon they were at the beautiful park. Geeta had never been inside the Eden Gardens before. Ashok pointed out the large famous cricket stadium close by to Geeta, saying, 'I went there a few months back to watch Australia playing India. It was awesome and of course India lost.'

Geeta had no interest in cricket and just to keep the conversation going she asked, 'Oh, do you play cricket?'

Ashok replied proudly, 'I played for our college team. Now with the job and all that there is hardly any time for any games.'

Inside the Eden Gardens there were only a few other couples, as it was a weekday. They found an empty bench under the shade of some trees next to a small pond and sat side by side. Ashok was the one who did most of the talking. He asked about Geeta's college, her friends, and her likes and dislikes in music and novels. While watching the solitary Lilly and the gently floating fallen leaves on the pond, Geeta answered mostly with short answers or a nod.

'Sorry, I am doing all the talking. You have not really said much,' Ashok stopped.

After a while, she asked, 'Did you have any girlfriends in medical college?'

A little taken aback, Ashok replied, 'I will be very honest with you. I thought I fancied a girl in our class who was from Madras. I never had the courage to talk to her alone though.'

Geeta turned around with interest, asking, 'Where is she now?'

'She went back to Madras soon after our final exam because her father was in Calcutta on a temporary posting for a few years.'

'Do you miss her?'

'Strangely, no. When she left I realised that though I fancied her, it was what they call puppy love, and I was never actually going to ask her out. You are the first girl in my life I have been alone with.'

Then, after a while, he added, 'I am really happy that we are getting married. I really like you.'

Geeta just smiled.

'I can find a few hours next Wednesday if you want to meet up again.'

'I better let Dada know this time. Just in case someone finds out.'

'No problem if you want to tell Jiten. But why are you worried? We are going to get married in a few weeks anyway.'

'Shall we go to Victoria Memorial next time? I have not been there since I was a child.'

'Okay. Why not meet me at the hospital, and we can take a taxi from there?'

Chapter Four

1971: The wedding

Both families had already agreed that there were going to be no dowries. It was modern India, after all. Everybody knew that despite the dowry law which had been in existence in the country since 1961, hardly any marriage took place where there was no dowry expected by the groom's family.

Ashok squirmed when, during one of the pre-wedding meetings between the two families, his uncle said, 'No, we don't want anything at all from you, but if your family wants to give some gold ornaments, bridal beds, or Godrej steel almirah, amongst other things, as a gift to your daughter and son-in-law, that is up to you.'

But it would have been very rude for him to protest against one of his elders. It was also agreed that it would be a small wedding with no more than sixty people in the bridal party on the wedding night.

Geeta was taken by her mother and sister to buy her wedding Benarasi sari in Shyambazar in one of the shops where the family had done their Puja and other special shopping over the years. Saroja chose a pink-coloured one but Geeta was glad that her mother overruled and chose her a bright red Benarasi with a beautiful peacock design on its anchal for her special day. Three more ordinary silk saris for Geeta's going away and two silk saris for Saroja were also bought at the same time. For Geeta's mother-in-law's present, Juthika decided on an expensive cotton silk sari, and for her father-in-law a raw silk Punjabi and a cotton dhoti. Then she bought a handloom sari for each of the maidservants and dhoti and Punjabi for the male servants in both the families. It was agreed that Saroja and Geeta would soon take a trip to New Market to buy clothes for the children.

'But what about you, Ma?' asked Saroja.

'I already have too many saris,' she replied.

'No, you have to get something for yourself for Geeta's special day, and we did not buy anything for Baba either,' insisted Saroja.

Both the daughters were happy when she agreed to buy herself a beautiful cotton silk sari. Then they chose a raw silk Punjabi and a cotton dhoti for their father.

The routine of planning for the wedding was already somewhat established from Saroja's marriage nearly six years back. But compared to that, this wedding was going to be a much smaller affair. Instead of over 600 guests on the night, this time there was going to be a maximum of 300, including members from both families, friends, and neighbours. All the corridors and verandas in the family house were given a fresh white wash of paint. In the house, the only large open space where the wedding feast could take place was on the flat roof. This was soon covered by the decorators with tarpaulin. Their neighbour across the small street agreed for their downstairs sitting room and two other rooms to be used by the bridal party on the night of the wedding. Other neighbours also agreed for some of their rooms to be used for sleeping the bridal relatives, some whom were coming from outside Calcutta. Heated discussions took place between Jiten and Saroja regarding whether there would be shehnai as well as records playing via gramophone in front of the gate. Jiten was already against so much spending just for a wedding while there were millions in the country starving. His parents had been concerned for a while about whether he had secretly joined the Naxals in the university. In the end, their father intervened and the music was dropped.

Gaye holud was scheduled for two days before the wedding itself. A small procession from the groom's family, minus the groom, arrived with a special sari for the bride, saris for all the females, and dhotis for all the males in the wider family of the bride, as well as some simple golden jewellery for the bride, cosmetics, vanity bags, seven kinds of sweets, and other gifts. They also brought with them holud, the turmeric paste, fresh mustard oil, and fresh fish. Geeta was seated on a beautifully decorated dais in a white handloom sari with a wide red border. Then all the females in the family took turns to apply turmeric paste and oil over her body. The younger members went overboard by covering her whole face with the paste and then applying holud to each other. Sweets brought by the procession were then fed to Geeta by all present at the ceremony. Before going to have her shower, when no one was looking, Geeta took a quick look in the mirror and had to supress her smile in case someone noticed.

Geeta and her mother were fasting the whole day of the wedding, which was scheduled to take place at an auspicious time between eight thirty and ten in the evening. Saroja took charge of dressing up the bride. Geeta was first helped with putting on the special blood red Benarasi sari with the matching blouse, slightly low-cut at the back, as was the fashion these days. Her long dark hair was thoroughly brushed with a parting in the middle before a plait was made, intertwined with white rajanigandha, the fragrance of the night flower. After gently powdering her face, kajal was applied to highlight her dark brown eyes and long eyelashes. A dark bindi was placed on the centre of her forehead. Then her mother brought out the golden jewellery she had been saving for Geeta for this special day. A thick gold necklace with a pendant, matching long earrings, nak chaabi, a beautiful golden nose ring, and a gold tikli from her own wedding were then wreathed on Geeta. Finally, the delicate white mukut, a crown made from shola, a version of light cork, was adjusted over her head. A tupur, a more elaborate headset also made from shola, was kept for the groom.

All the women in the family except Geeta and her mother went outside excitedly when it was announced that the bridal party was arriving and greeted them by blowing conch shells and some doing ululation for Ashok's arrival. There was much laughter during subhadrishti when the bride, dressed in her full glory seated on a beautifully decorated wooden seat, was carried seven times around the groom. Then they looked at each other as if for the very first time. Geeta could hardly raise her head to look into Ashok's eyes in front of so many people. Soon the bride and the groom were asked to exchange beautiful garlands made of rajanigandha before being directed to sit in front of a priest praying for them before a holy fire. Afterwards, with Geeta's anchal now tied to a corner of the shawl on Ashok's shoulder, Geeta had to walk seven times behind him around the fire.

She was now officially his wife, and very hungry. Soon, Geeta's mother fed some sweets to Ashok, who had also been starving the whole day, before feeding Geeta as well. Then the feast for all the guests except Geeta's immediate family followed on the rooftop where only a hundred people could be seated in one sitting. By the time the guests were all fed, and it was time for Geeta's turn, sitting next to Ashok and with the rest of their immediate families, it was after midnight.

Downstairs, their living room had been decorated beautifully with flowers for the bride and groom for the special night. But they were not going to be alone there. Younger women from both families, Jiten, and a few close friends of Ashok's were there in the basor ghar too. The room soon turned out to be a place of banter between the young men and the women. At the basor ghar, the two sides got to know each other and there was a lot of chatting, flirting, and jokes. This was soon followed by requests for singing by anybody who could sing. After a few songs from women and men from both sides of the families, everyone turned towards Geeta. After refusing for only a short time, she sang one of her favourite Nazrul songs. Ashok clapped more than anyone else.

After managing only a couple of hours of sleep in the uncomfortable bed on the floor with so many people around, it was time for Geeta to get ready to go away with Ashok in the early morning at an auspicious hour. She was accompanied by her younger sister, Meera. Arriving at Ashok's house, she was received by Ashok's mother who, as per tradition, was the only person not to have attended the wedding itself. Both Geeta and Ashok were fed sweets by her before she welcomed them into the house. As usual, the honeymoon night was going to be two days after the wedding. As was also customary, for the first night in Ashok's house Geeta slept with Meera and Ashok slept on his own. All through the wedding period there had been innuendos and hints given to the bride and bridegroom about what happens during fullsojja, the first night the married couple sleeps together in a bed adorned with flowers. Dadi and some of Geeta's aunts had been pretty embarrassing, and her older sister and cousins had been equally crude and naughty, explaining how to go about the foreplay before the sexual consummation.

Ashok's bedroom had been decorated with garlands hanging everywhere and fresh flowers thrown on the bed. But by the time the feast of another 300 or so people in Ashok's family was over, it was way past midnight. Alone with Ashok at last, Geeta collapsed to sleep with him on their marital bed.

Chapter Five

1971: Ashok in the UK

It had taken Ashok almost two months and a few visits to a patient-cum-friend of his father who worked in the Writers' Building, the main government administrative office in Calcutta, before his passport came through. Even with the letter from the General Medical Council of Clinical Attachment, it was not easy going at the British High Commission. Ashok felt that in the first interview, the Indian employees at the High Commission were rather high and mighty, and he was asked to come back the next week with his father's bank statement, a tax office letter from the last year, and a signed notarised letter from his father that he would be responsible for the expenses in case of Ashok's death there. The interview in the week after was more pleasant, although Ashok had to ask several times for questions to be repeated from the British man with the thick Scottish accent.

Once the visa was granted, Ashok needed only to do two visits to the Reserve Bank of India office in Calcutta to get his foreign currency, a total of three pound notes, which was the limit imposed by the UK authorities on what an Indian could bring to the UK.

'That's only about a hundred rupees. How will you manage until you get a job there?'

'Don't worry, Ma, I am writing to Arun, my classmate and good friend who went to England last year. He can come and meet me at the airport and lend me some money.'

'Is it Arun Mukherjee? I know his father very well. He is a pathologist in Calcutta Medical College. I can pay him the money here in advance, if Arun agrees,' said Pradeep, his father.

Arun replied within four weeks agreeing to meet Ashok but suggesting that he should try to get a flight arriving on Sunday so that he could be off duty. He also asked Ashok to send him a telegram with the details as soon as the air tickets were purchased.

Ashok was advised to choose BOAC rather than an Aeroflot flight, although it was slightly more expensive, for his first trip to London.

'BOAC is definitely more reliable. It is a British company after all, and the British are famous for their punctuality,' his family had argued.

A telegram was sent to Arun in the UK with his flight details.

In Dumdum Airport in Calcutta there were at least thirty people to say goodbye to Ashok that evening. All family members from both sides of his family were there as he was the first person from either side to go to England for training. All his close friends, most from the medical college and two from his school days, ten of them in total, had also turned up. They were teasing him as usual about all the beautiful blondes he would meet in England and how likely it was that he would forget all about Calcutta soon. The younger members of the families were running around excitedly in the wide, clean departure area of Dumdum Airport. Although he had arrived almost two hours before the check-in time, there was hardly enough time to talk to all the adults.

His mother hugged him, crying and saying, 'Make sure to write to us as soon as you get there.'

His father said, 'No, as I said before, send us a telegram first.'

With so many people trying to find a few minutes of his time to say something before he left, he could not manage to find any time to be alone with Geeta before the time came to leave for the check-in area through the gate guarded by the police. He paid his pranam, touching the feet of all the people older than him.

Last of all, he paid his pranam to his mother and said, 'I will be going now.'

'Don't say "going". Say "going to come back soon,"' said his mother, putting her hands on his head and silently praying.

Then Ashok gathered all his friends together to say goodbye. It was only just before leaving for the check-in gate that he could get close to Geeta.

'I will write to you,' he said, looking at her before going to the check-in.

He looked back to see tears rolling down her cheeks. After the check-in, before going through passport and visa control, he had to come back close to the place where everybody was still waiting, albeit now separated by low railings.

Geeta was almost being crushed to the railings by all the other friends and families.

'I will miss you,' Ashok whispered to her before going in.

Nearly an hour and a half later, they had to walk to the plane from the boarding gate. Before boarding the plane, he waved goodbye to the people gathered on the roof of the airport building, as he thought he could make out Geeta's timid wave amongst others in the darkness of the early evening. Ashok was delighted to have been seated by the window. He had flown from Nairobi to Calcutta when he was very young and could hardly remember any of it. To him, this was like his first ever flight and his excitement was heightened when the plane took off and the lights of Calcutta were below them. Before he could try to locate the famous landmarks of the city, the plane had moved on and there was only darkness below.

He was woken up by the air hostess asking, 'Veg or non-veg?'

When he next woke after the meal, he was fascinated to find an icy mountain range below his window.

'Alps,' said the passenger sitting next to him as he leaned over Ashok to get a decent view himself. He was returning back to London. It turned out his family had business in Southall, near London Airport.

After about two hours or so later, the plane seemed to be circling for some time over dense cloud before it was announced on the tannoy, 'Sorry to announce that due to the heavy fog around London today, we will be trying to land in Preston. We will make further announcements before landing.'

'Where is Preston?' Ashok asked the passenger in the next seat.

'Not sure. I think it is in the north. I don't know how we are going to get back to London from there.'

After a long journey by coach from Preston through murky weather, most of which he spent dozing, they arrived in Heathrow only five and a half hours late. Ashok's main worry was if Arun would still be waiting for him, as otherwise he did not know what he would do with only three pounds in his pocket. Luckily, he was still there waiting for him as it was Sunday and he was off duty.

They took an underground train to King's Cross station. Arun bought the ticket for him for the next Doncaster train which was due to leave in twenty minutes. He also bought something called a sandwich with bread and chicken, as well as a couple of bananas and some orange juice for him for the journey.

Arun reminded him, 'You know that you are not going to have any money for the next few weeks as the clinical attachment is unpaid. Here is fifty pounds for you as you asked in your letter.'

Ashok, after shaking his hand, heartily, said, 'My father had already paid this to your father.'

He woke up just a few minutes before the train arrived in Doncaster. It was already very dark and raining outside.

'I thought they said they were having an Indian summer here this September. Why is it so cold?' thought Ashok to himself as he pulled on his woollen overcoat to find a taxi. One of the suitcase handles gave way as he was lifting it into the boot of the car. The taxi dropped him off near the gate outside the main reception of the hospital, which was empty. Tugging his two suitcases, he tried to find someone to help.

A man in a smart uniform who was passing by noticed him and asked, 'What are you looking for?'

Ashok explained that he was starting as a new doctor. The man, who turned out to be a porter, took him to the telephone operator who already had his key for his accommodation and some papers with his joining instructions.

'Wait here for five minutes. I have got to take some blood from the ward to the lab. I will then show you to your place,' the porter said, and disappeared quickly.

Even in his extremely tired state, Ashok was amazed by the clean, shiny floors leading to the long corridors of the hospital with clean white walls. He remembered the dark corridors of his hospital in Calcutta, the floors only scrubbed by a broom and the walls often marked red in places with spits of betel nut juice.

The telephone operator lady asked, 'Where have you come from now?'

'From Calcutta.'

'Wow! Isn't that in India? That must be thousands of miles away. Are you cold?'

'I am freezing,' said Ashok, shivering in his heavy, wet woollen coat.

'Do you a want a cup of coffee? I am going to have some.'

'Yes,' replied Ashok.

'You must be knackered. Wait—hello, operator. Sure, I will put you through.'

'It was really nice,' Ashok muttered to the busy operator after finishing his coffee and before leaving with the porter.

'Let me give you a hand with one of the cases,' said the porter.

The accommodation was on the second floor.

After putting his suitcases on the bed, Ashok asked, 'Where can I find some food?'

'Sorry, it's almost ten thirty. Everything is closed. The dining room opens at seven in the morning,' said the porter as he left.

Ashok took out the banana and half of the sandwich he had left over from earlier on to eat and then straight away collapsed on the bed, unchanged. After a deep sleep, he got up and looked at his watch. It was only four thirty in the morning.

He was absolutely starving and fully awake. 'It must be the jet lag, as they call it,' Ashok thought to himself.

He was the first person at the hospital canteen as its door was being opened. Toasts, omelettes, and something called sausage went

106

down quickly with some orange juice and a cup of coffee. It was still too early for the hospital personnel office to open and the weather outside was drizzly and cold. Ashok decided to take a tour of the hospital's ground floor by himself and was immediately impressed with the long, wide, shiny, clean corridors with clearly marked departments. 'Outpatients', 'Radiology', 'A&E', and 'Operation Theatre' were all known departments. He had read about 'ICU', 'Physiotherapy', 'Occupational Therapy', and 'Ultrasound', but to see these departments in the hospital he would be working in was beyond belief.

The lady in the medical personnel office was very pleasant but Ashok was finding it difficult to understand her accent and she was speaking too quickly. Several times, Ashok had to ask her to repeat what she was saying. The personnel officer telephoned the surgical ward for one of the senior house officers in surgery to come down and show Ashok around the hospital. Soon, the SHO arrived and introduced himself as Saleem. It turned out that he was from Pakistan and had been in the country for over three years.

'Let us go and find a white coat for you first. Then I will show you the departments. Mr Donaldson will be doing a ward round today at two p.m. It's his weekly ward round.'

Almost in a state of stupor, Ashok followed Saleem around the various departments and wards in the hospital. Everything was so clean and well-organised.

'Come back to the male surgical ward on the second floor after lunch. Don't be late.'

Ashok was in the ward fifteen minutes before the ward round. One registrar, two SHOs, two junior house officers, and three medical students gathered shortly after. Saleem introduced Ashok to everyone quickly. The ward sister and the two staff nurses joined them before two. Mr Bernard Albert Donaldson, the consultant surgeon, then arrived. He was led to the male ward by the ward sister and the registrar, followed by the SHOs, staff nurses, and the junior house officers. The medical students trailed behind, followed by Ashok. All the patients were lying in their beds covered up to their chests with bedsheets. Mr Donaldson stopped by one who was looking very unwell with intravenous fluids in his arm, a tube in his nose, a catheter on the side of the bed, and an oxygen mask on his face.

The registrar said, 'This is the one I telephoned you in the evening about. He had perforated diverticular disease in his sigmoid colon with a lot of faecal soiling. I have done a Hartmann for him.'

Mr Donaldson said, 'Well done,' and then looked at the patient's observation chart for a few seconds before calling, 'Mr McDonald, how are you feeling today?'

The patient looked vaguely towards him but did not respond.

'You better keep a close eye on him. And Sister, please ask your nurses to keep a proper fluid balance chart,' said Mr Donaldson before moving on to the next patient.

Sister looked sternly towards the staff nurses, who tried to avoid her eye contact.

After the one-and-half-hour ward round, everyone except the medical students gathered in Sister's office. It was a bit crowded with only Mr Donaldson, the ward sister, and the registrar sitting. Ashok was waiting hesitantly outside the door. The registrar nodded for him to come in. A tray of tea and biscuits was brought in by the staff nurses. Tea in china cups was served to Mr Donaldson and the ward sister. The rest had their tea in white hospital teacups.

Sipping his tea, Mr Donaldson looked towards Ashok and said, 'You must be the new clinical attaché from India.'

'Yes, sir,' Ashok replied meekly.

'What's your name?'

'Dr Ashok Basu, sir.'

'Ashhoo what?'

'Dr Ashok Basu, sir.'

'Ashhoo what again? No, it's too complicated for us. We will call you Ash,' said Mr Bernard Albert Donaldson.

From then on, Ashok became known as Ash to everyone in the hospital.

He wanted to telegram home to let them know about his safe arrival but every morning he had to be in the ward before eight and he usually finished after six in the evening. Lunchtime was mostly hurried and the post office was at least twenty minutes' walk away from the hospital.

On Saturday morning, he went to the post office and sent one telegram to his father which read, 'Arrived safe. Everything going well.' He wanted to say a few more words but every word of the telegram cost money. He bought three airmail letters, one for Geeta and one each for his and her parents.

Ashok loved his first experience of working in surgery in the country. Everything was so well-organised; all the modern investigations he had only read about in his textbooks in India were routinely being done here. And to top it all off, unbelievably, everything was absolutely free for everyone, rich or poor. He not only worked for Mr Donaldson but whenever he could find time he went to the outpatients' clinics and the operating sessions of the two other surgeons in the hospital. He had always been a good assistant during operations but was now really enthused by the small comments on his ability by the consultants. In his mind, he was now more than certain that he would like to be a surgeon like one of them.

As a young sportsperson, Ashok was always hungry. In the hospital dining room, breakfast was the meal he enjoyed most with toast, eggs, sausages, and bacon. But for lunch and dinner, which were always too early, he found the meals tasteless. Boiled meat and overcooked vegetables had no taste in spite of adding lots of ground pepper to them.

'Food is so tasteless here. Roast chicken is okay but they make them only once a week. But I love these chips. I could live on them,' he said to another Asian doctor from A&E who had joined him for lunch, as he added more pepper to them, then dipped their ends in ketchup before putting them happily in his mouth.

Sitting in the dining room, he learned something new from his colleague from A&E. In the past few weeks, he had wondered how some of the nurses who had skin pale as white paper, had almost brown legs. Being shy in nature, he had tried to avoid looking at them at work, but sitting in the dining room he had often ended up staring at those legs under their dining tables. He was fascinated to see one pair of legs today was even pure white, while the owner of the legs just had usual pale skin.

When he mentioned this to his fellow diner, he burst out laughing, saying, 'Ashok, you are so stupid. They are wearing what is called tights. Apart from not showing their bare legs, it also gives them some protection from the cold.'

Never seeing tights before in his life in Calcutta, Ashok was embarrassed, but glad that he had not mentioned this to any of the local doctors or nurses.

At the end of his first week, Ashok was setting up an intravenous drip for a patient in the ward. One of the staff nurses was helping him. Ashok looked at her and asked, 'Another needle and a bottle of five hundred millilitres of normal saline.'

The staff nurse just looked at him.

Ashok, thinking that the nurse didn't understand his accent, repeated slowly, 'Another needle and a bottle of five hundred millilitres of normal saline.'

The nurse walked off and returned with the needle and the bottle of saline and looked at him.

Ashok tried to take them from her but she just plonked them beside him and left, murmuring, 'So rude.'

During the first two weeks in the dining room after he had collected his meal, as well as in the wards while asking nurses for something, Ashok had often heard people murmuring behind him, 'So rude.' He was not sure what this was all about.

He was invited for a home cooked dinner by two of the seniors from Calcutta NRS Medical College, one a locum registrar in gynae obstetrics and the other an SHO in ENT. Both lived in the same doctors' accommodation as Ashok. He watched them cooking in the small attached kitchen and wondered how these two Bengali men ever learned to cook. It was wonderful having chicken curry and rice

110

after only bland, tasteless English food for the last few days. He declined the offer of beer and instead had a glass of water.

After dinner, while talking to them about jobs, Ashok mentioned, 'Often I hear people behind me saying, "So rude." What do you think it is about? I am always courteous to people, saying good morning each day.'

'Ah, that's simple. We all had that. Do you say, "Please may I?" when asking for anything, and "Thank you," after every time?'

'Well, not exactly with those words, but I am never rude,' he replied.

'In India we don't say please and thank you because it's considered too formal. Instead we give a polite nod and a smile. But that's not enough here,' said one of them.

'Even young children here are taught to say please and thank you. So double please and thank you each time and more from now on for anything and everything, Ashok,' said the other, winking at him.

Following Monday in the ward, Ashok was going to change the dressing of a patient in the treatment room. The same staff nurse was there.

Ashok said, 'Staff nurse, please may I have some help with changing her dressing?'

With an amused expression on her face, the nurse helped him.

At the end, Ashok said, 'Thank you very much.'

The nurse smiled and said, 'That's quite all right, Dr Ash.'

He checked for the next available date for the first part of the FRCS examination of the Royal College of Surgeons, which was only two months away. He knew that the pass rate of the first part of the FRCS was dreadful, usually around twenty to twenty-five per cent. He had already come across stories of many taking the exam two or three times before giving up. Some said he was being foolhardy, but he decided he would sit for the next exam anyway. He was confident about his anatomy and he was not too bad with pathology. Next, he went to the medical library, which he was happy to find was really well stocked. He borrowed all the books he needed and spent all the hours he was not working studying, mostly physiology.

The doctors' mess had a snooker table. Ashok had never played or seen snooker before, but he came down from time to time to take a break from his studies. He absolutely loved the game and soon met two Indian doctors, one named Manmeet from Amritsar and the other called Bobby from Bombay. Both were married and in their first year in the UK with their wives still in India.

'I am hoping my wife will join me here in the New Year but it's still nearly three months away. We got married only three months before I left India. I really miss her. It's so lonely here,' said Manmeet, who was an SHO in ophthalmology.

'I am not having my wife coming over here. I will be here three or four years at the most anyway and probably go back to Bombay a couple of times in the meantime,' said Bobby, who was an SHO in orthopaedics. Then he added with a wink, 'Lot more fun without having your wife here anyway.'

After the game, which Ashok lost again, Bobby asked, 'By the way, we are going out for a drink at the local pub. Do you want to come?'

'No, I'd better get back to my study,' replied Ashok, who had only once so far in his life tried alcohol since coming over, but had not enjoyed the taste. It was also true that his Primary FRCS was not very far away.

'Don't forget this Saturday is the Halloween party in the mess. Are you working?' asked Manmeet as they were leaving.

On Saturday in the mess common room, the Halloween party was in full swing. All the lights were dimmed and Jethro Tull's *Witch's Promise* was playing on the record player. A few were dancing, others drinking at the bar. Ashok got himself a glass of orange juice and sat down in an empty sofa in one corner. A few minutes later, a girl in tight black clothes and black high-heeled shoes came over with a glass of wine in her hand and sat next to him.

'Hello,' she said, smiling at him.

'Hello,' replied Ashok as he tried to remember where he had seen her before, in the surgical ward or in the dining room.

'What's your name?' asked the girl with a smile, kicking off her shoes to move in really close.

'I am Dr Basu.'

'Dr Basu, what's your first name?'

'Ashok. What's your name?'

'I am Gail. Do you want to dance, Ashok?'

She held his hands, putting down the glass of wine on the coffee table.

Feeling uncomfortable, Ashok said, 'I think I will be going back to my room soon.'

'Where do you live, Ashok?' asked Gail, still holding his hands.

'Two floors upstairs,' said Ashok as he got up from the chair.

'Oh, upstairs! Shall we go up to your room and get more comfortable?' said Gail as she also stood up and put her arms around him.

'Look, I am married.'

'So where is your wife then, Ashok?'

'She is in India.'

'So? I am engaged too. Look,' Gail spread her left hand in front of him to show an engagement ring. 'But he is working in London and your wife is many thousands of miles away. Shall we go up to your room and talk about our loneliness?' Gail tried again to wrap her arms around him.

Ashok moved away quickly. On his way to leave the empty glass at the bar before leaving the party and then back through the room, he noticed that Gail was now sitting on the lap of Bobby, his married friend from Bombay, and they were kissing.

The next day he sent an airmail to Geeta asking if she could sort out her passport and visa as soon as possible so that she could come over when he started his new job in a few months. He knew that unfortunately it could not be any sooner because he would not be able to get married accommodation before that even if he tried. Then he reluctantly opened his *Ganong's Book of Medical Physiology*.

He found that there was a possible SHO job in A&E available in his hospital three weeks after his clinical attachment term was due to finish. Mr Donaldson suggested that he should take up the job, especially as he needed at least six months of A&E training before he could sit for the final FRCS. His surgical jobs in Calcutta Medical College were eligible for the Royal College but in India there was no such specialty as A&E. Although it was no surprise, he was still relieved to hear that Mr Donaldson had written to the GMC that his clinical attachment was satisfactory. He soon had full GMC registration and, with his consultant's recommendation, also a six-month job in A&E in the same hospital to start in less than three weeks.

But he had very little money left. The hospital warden was kind enough to let him stay in the same room, which was free for all single residents, as he was due to start another job soon in the same hospital anyway. But he still needed money for his food. Also, he needed to buy some warm clothes. The medical personnel officer suggested that he look for unemployment benefit and gave him the address of their office in the town. Ashok had never heard of any such state benefit in India and was very impressed with the speed and efficiency of the benefit office in Doncaster. He went back happy to his room with fifteen pounds of benefit for three weeks of unemployment in his pocket.

The SHO job in A&E was in shifts of twelve hours. Luckily for Ashok, except for the Friday and Saturday evenings, it was not that busy most of the time. He brought his textbooks to work and kept them in a cupboard. Whenever there was time, he took out his books to read. Sometimes the staff nurses in the department brought him cups of coffee while other times they just laughed at him while frolicking with the other SHOs, some of whom Ashok knew were already married.

When the day came for Ashok to travel to London to sit for his Primary FRCS he was not sure how ready he was. He had heard too many horror stories of the Primary. Surprisingly, in the exam itself Ashok felt quite comfortable, although he was not absolutely sure, as the newly introduced written part involved negative marking for any incorrect answer. He was thrilled to be called for the viva part a few weeks later. Sitting to answer questions in front of two stern-looking examiners in each of the three tables for anatomy, physiology, and pathology was more than nerve-wracking. He was glad when it was all over. But he was over the moon when he found at the end of the evening that his name was in the list of the very few who had has passed their Primary that day.

The next morning, he sent a telegram to his father: 'Primary FRCS cleared.'

A reply telegram came the day after: 'We are very proud of you.'

Ashok had already done more than two years of surgical jobs in Calcutta. Now, having passed his Primary, he started applying every week for all the jobs advertised for registrars in surgery in the UK in the BMJ.

In the hospital dining room, Ashok sat at an empty table and started his lunch. He noticed that the Pre Registration doctor Chris from his farm had bought his lunch and was looking for somewhere to sit. Ashok waved to Chris but he completely ignored him and went to the other end of the dining room to sit by himself. Ashok since observed that almost all of the white doctors avoided being seated together with the non-whites even in the doctor's mess. He mentioned this to another doctor from Nigeria who was having lunch with him one day.

'That's usual. They may have to work with us, but they can't be seen to be socialising with the coloured people like us' he replied.

There was a buzz everywhere now with Christmas coming. Everyone at work was talking about their shopping, what presents they still had to buy, and what they were doing for Christmas. When he was asked by a local doctor if would not mind swapping his on-call with him for Christmas and Boxing Day, he readily agreed. He had heard and read a lot about the fantastic Christmas dinner people had in the UK. But being on call on Christmas Day, when he found time to go to the hospital canteen at lunch just before it was about to

115

close, he found that they were serving only some roast beef with gravy and boiled potatoes.

'I was hoping for Christmas dinner today,' he said to the dining room lady.

'Sorry, love. We served Christmas dinner for the staff three days back. You must have missed it. Today we only have a few staff in the kitchen and I am due to close and go home to my family for a proper Christmas dinner.'

'What about in the evening today?'

'No, love. Have you not seen the notice? We are closed after lunch today. You might like to buy some sandwiches to take with you for your dinner now. Everything is closed today.'

After serving him lunch, the dinner lady said, 'Have a nice Christmas, love.'

Ashok said, 'Merry Christmas to you too.'

He had heard people talking a lot excitedly about the 'Boxing Day', the day after Christmas. He had the evening off and went to the TV room in the mess expecting to see a good boxing match.

One of the English SHOs was there too. He said, 'It's just my bad luck to be working on Boxing Day. Luckily I had the day off yesterday to go home to have Christmas dinner with my parents.'

Pointing towards the TV, Ashok asked, 'When does the boxing match start?'

'What boxing match?' he asked.

'Today is the Boxing Day, isn't it?'

He burst out laughing and then explained to embarrassed Ashok that Boxing Day is when people here traditionally box their presents. 'Sorry, no boxing match on TV for you.'

He was invited for dinner to the house of a married Indian couple a few days later. Amit, who was now a registrar in geriatrics, knew Jiten, Geeta's brother, from his old school. His wife Madhabi had done her BA in Calcutta but was now the full-time mother of a four-year-old son. Two other friends of Amit, Tarun, an SHO in psychiatry and graduate from R. G. Kar Medical, and Deepak, an

116

SHO in A&E from AIIMS in Delhi, both working in Coventry, also joined them.

Soon the discussion turned to the situation about jobs in the NHS.

'You can forget wasting your time applying for jobs in surgery here,' said Amit.

'Whatever your experience in India is and the fact that you have passed your Primary FRCS so quickly, there is absolutely no chance of getting a job as a registrar unless of course you are British, Australian, or New Zealander with white skin,' said Tarun.

'Occasionally they will call you for an interview to make up the numbers, but you will never be offered any job as a registrar in surgery. That's the same situation in general medicine as well,' said Deepak.

Ashok tried to say, 'I know that BMJ advertisements for many GP jobs clearly say that only British graduates can apply, but for the hospital jobs it seems to be more open to all.'

'Tell me, how many applications for surgery jobs have you made so far?'

'Sixty plus, and it's not easy. For each job you have to beg and pay one of the secretaries to type the new application with your CV. The hospitals always want at least five copies. I really wish I knew how to type,' Ashok replied.

'Knowing how to type does not matter. You will have to still beg for a free typewriter from the secretary anyway,' said Tarun. Then he asked, 'So out of sixty applications, how many have shortlisted you so far?'

'Well, none so far. There are a few more ads in the BMJ this week. I will apply for those.'

'Ashok, don't fool yourself. I have known many in your situation over the last few years. My honest advice is to make a decision soon. Either go back home and start your own practice. It's great that you have done your Primary FRCS. If you can also manage to get the final before you go, that will be a real bonus. But don't waste too much time here. Or if you want to stay in this country, start looking for jobs in geriatrics or psychiatry, and if you are lucky you might even end up as a consultant in one of those specialties,' said Amit.

Two weeks later, Ashok was thrilled to get an interview for the post of Registrar in General Surgery in one of the well-known hospitals in London. In the interview, he thought he answered all the clinical questions very well.

Then he was stunned when one of the panel of interviewers said, 'You are in this country for less than a year. Just because you have passed your Primary quickly, you think you can get a registrar job in a prestigious hospital like ours?'

Stunned, Ashok thought to himself, 'Then why did you shortlist me for the job?'

He went back to his hospital, checking the BMJ for jobs again. He noticed that in one of the advertisements from a university hospital in Wales, it said that the candidates were encouraged to come and meet the head of the department. He called the number of the secretary to find out that he could go and meet the professor next week. Armed with six copies of his curriculum vitae and an application letter for the job, he went to Cardiff.

The professor was very pleasant and looked at Ashok's CV with interest. He then asked a few clinical questions which Ashok answered easily.

The professor then congratulated him, saying, 'Very well done by getting that nasty Primary exam out of the way so quickly. I really like your CV. Look, I will be very honest with you. You have only limited experience in this country in surgery. I will advise you to get some experience here and apply for this job next year when we advertise. We will definitely be interested in you.'

Very pleased with the prospect, but still with no job in the next few months, Ashok went back to make more applications, now for the registrar job as well as for SHO jobs in surgery. Little did he know at the time that when he would come back to the same professor for the same job next year, he would be told, 'Look, Ashok, I really like your CV. But I will be honest with you. You are a bit too experienced for this job. We are looking for someone less experienced. Good luck though.'

Giving up the idea of finding a registrar job for now, he was happy to be offered a six-month job as an SHO again in A&E in Bedford starting from February. He asked for married accommodation, then went on to write to Geeta that he would be coming soon to get her over to the UK. He managed to get ten days' holiday in his new job after his first month of working. He was very happy that the warden had found him a married accommodation before he left for India.

Chapter Six

1972: Geeta in the UK

Fortunately, Geeta, now Mrs Geeta Basu, had managed to get her passport and visa without too much of a problem. A few weeks later, in early January, Geeta went with Jiten to New Market where most foreigners and Anglo-Indians in Calcutta did their shopping. After a lot of searching, she had bought herself an expensive full-length woollen overcoat. It was winter in Calcutta and the temperature was dipping sometimes to a chilling ten to eleven degrees Centigrade in the night. But even in this cold weather, the coat had made her feel like she was boiling inside. She had felt prepared for whatever the foreign land had to throw at her in the next few weeks.

Seven days in Calcutta went too quickly for Ashok. Although he was staying at his parents' house with his wife, he had to spend most evenings invited for dinner in other relatives' houses along with Geeta. He only managed a couple of times to go to his old place of study and work for almost a decade, the Medical College Hospital.

One day, he managed to meet the consultant who trained him in Calcutta. He was very happy to see Ashok.

'Done that dreaded Primary on the first attempt! Wow! Not many here can claim that. Now get that final fellowship done as soon as you can, Ashok, and come back to India after you have done your training. We need people like you here,' said Dr Mitra, and then, looking at the entourage of trainees with him, he said, 'There is someone who you should follow in your career in surgery.'

In the canteen at lunchtime, Ashok met with some of his old friends who were still working there. They listened with interest to his views about the difficulty in getting a proper speciality job in the UK. Some of his junior colleagues also joined, asking him for his advice.

'The NHS is one of the best health systems I can think of. There, you are regularly doing things which we can only read about in textbooks here. And everything is free for everyone, rich or poor. The UK in general is not only a very advanced country, but the society is also fair to all,' said Ashok.

There were almost the same number of people at the airport to say goodbye to Ashok and Geeta as on his first trip to England. Geeta had been trying to hold back her tears amongst the tear-filled goodbyes from her families until now.

As she was going through the check-in gate behind Ashok, Meera shouted, 'Didi, I will miss you so much. Come back soon.'

Geeta's eyes were now flooded with tears as she presented her passport at the check-in desk and sobbed when she was asked to confirm her name. Later Geeta looked really scared as the plane was due to take off. Ashok, sitting next to her, held her hand tightly and tried to talk about the weather Geeta was going to face in early March in the UK to take her mind off it. Soon, Geeta was peering out of the window like a little girl and talking to Ashok about the floating clouds, hills, and the city below them.

They both woke up from their sleep with the announcement, 'We will be landing in Heathrow shortly. Please fasten your seatbelts and keep your seats upright.'

Looking out through the window, Geeta said excitedly, 'We are flying over London! Is that the Thames River below?'

Once out of the Heathrow terminal, in the only short walk to the National bus station, Geeta was glad that Ashok had brought her the windcheater which she was now wearing over her woollen overcoat.

Geeta liked their small but compact one-bedroom flat. Growing up she had always shared a large bed with her two sisters, and sometimes also with their mother, when relatives came to stay with them. Here, she was in charge. She soon started rearranging the furniture. While Ashok had gone to work, in the morning sunshine, she went outside in the adjacent hospital garden and saw some lovely yellow flowers. As she was about to pick some, the gardener, who was working nearby, came around and stopped her.

'Lady, you should know that you cannot pick flowers from the hospital garden,' he said.

Thoroughly flustered, Geeta said, 'I'm very sorry; I did not know. I am new here.'

Seeing Geeta so embarrassed, the gardener said, 'Don't worry too much,' and then picked a bunch of daffodils himself before giving them to Geeta.

'Thank you very much,' said Geeta before returning back to her flat.

When Ashok returned back from work, Geeta said to him, 'People here are really nice,' before telling him the story with the gardener earlier on.

Until Geeta had come, Ashok was having his meals in the hospital canteen, except for his breakfast. He had a toaster and a supply of bread and butter for that. Neither Ashok nor Geeta had any experience of ever cooking in India. Servants and cooks in the house took care of that. Only occasionally would their mothers cook something on special occasions. Geeta was regretting now that she did not learn some cooking from Madanda, their house cook, before coming over. Between them, they soon started experimenting. The first problem was cooking the rice. It was either undercooked or very soggy with water. Laughing at themselves, in the first few days they only had rice with boiled egg and mashed potatoes. But between them, within a couple of weeks, Ashok almost perfected cooking the rice while Geeta managed to produce decent dahl and vegetable curry.

'We should try some chicken curry as well,' said Geeta, producing her first ever egg curry for their dinner a few weeks later.

Before rushing off to the hospital early in the morning, Ashok had not really noticed that for the last few days Geeta was not keen to have her breakfast with him.

She came blushing one evening to him to ask, 'Do you think I may be pregnant?'

'What?' Ashok almost choked on his biscuit, although it had been dipped in his tea.

A few days later, the GP surgery confirmed the pregnancy and asked them to arrange another visit a few weeks later.

They had to make a choice between two options. Geeta could soon go back to her family in Calcutta to have her baby, or her mother could come over to England before the due date and stay with them for a few months, helping them with the new baby.

'I want you to be around when the baby is born. And the hospitals here are so advanced.'

'That's true, and it will definitely be safer here. Also, I don't think I will be able to manage to get leave twice, to take you home now and then again a few months later.'

A few weeks later, they decided to go to Birmingham for the weekend to the house of some friends who were also from Calcutta.

'The bus will be much cheaper than the train,' said Ashok.

The married couple had been in the UK for over five years. Subir, who was now a registrar in geriatrics, had also been a few years senior to Ashok in Calcutta Medical College. They knew each other in the college through sports. His wife, Kanika, was the full-time mother of a three-year-old son. Two other friends of theirs, Barun, an SHO in psychiatry, and Deepak, an SHO in A&E, both graduates from Calcutta working in Birmingham, also joined them for the dinner.

'This dahl is wonderful, Kanikadi,' said Barun during the dinner.

'I used fish head with it like we do at home,' said Kanika.

'Can you get freshwater fish here? I really hate the smell and taste of frozen sea fish in this country,' said Ashok.

'Tell me about it. You can't get rohu or katla here, but trout is a freshwater fish. I used trout's head for the dahl.'

'This chicken curry is also very good. You must get the recipes from her,' said Ashok to Geeta.

'Do you cook, Ashok?' asked Subir.

'Barely. I can boil the rice and make an omelette these days, but within only a few months Geeta has trained herself to be quite good.'

'I am still learning by experimenting on poor Ashok. We always had a cook at home, so never had to do any cooking.'

'Same here,' said Kanika.

123

The two women then went into the small kitchen to have some private talk. A few minutes later, they came out with bowls of payesh for everyone.

'Where do you find all your spices here?' Asked Geeta.

'I will pack some for you before you go tomorrow. There is an Asian shop not very far from here. The owner is from Pakistan but he's very helpful. You can get everything for Bengali cooking there. In fact, it's only ten minutes' drive from here. If you want, we can take you there tomorrow before you leave,' Kanika replied.

Geeta looked at Ashok, who said, 'Well, our bus tomorrow is not until three in the afternoon.'

Two weeks later, on a Saturday, Ashok went out in the morning to get some fresh trout. 'I asked them to cut the fish heads at the shop. You don't have to worry about it. But wait until I come back from watching the cricket match at the local club. It should be a good game. I should be back by six and then we can cook together. Unless you want to come and watch the game?' he said before leaving the fish in the kitchen.

'No, I am fine. I will try to finish the Bengali novel by Mahasweta Devi I borrowed from Kanikadi. You go ahead. Don't be too late.'

'I won't be.'

At about six thirty, Ashok opened the door, shouting timidly, 'Sorry I am a bit late! Our local team won by only five runs at the end. Geeta, where are you?'

Geeta came out of the bathroom and went straight to the bedroom.

Ashok went after her, saying, 'I am really sorry. We have plenty of time—' but then he stopped abruptly as he turned towards Geeta, who was looking pale and was shaking like a leaf.

Ashok went over to sit next to her and just looked at her worryingly.

Geeta said, 'I have started bleeding.'

'What do you mean, bleeding? Where did you cut yourself? Let me see.'

Geeta just said, 'It's the baby,' and started crying.

At the hospital, they said it was an incomplete abortion. She would need a D&C to stop the bleeding.

'What is D&C? Is the baby going to be all right?'

'Sorry, the baby is lost. We need to scrape out the lining of your womb to stop the bleeding,' said the doctor.

For the next few weeks they could hardly look at each other, let alone talk. Neither knew how to console the other and both wished that their families were here to give them support.

For the first time in their marriage, they did not know how to talk to each other, let alone comfort one another. Ashok felt guilty for probably being the more fortunate of the two, being busy with his one-in-two on-call. He was working alternate nights and weekends, on average 108 hours per week. He was also preparing for his final FRCS. When he came home after work, he did not know what to say to Geeta. Geeta hardly spoke and did not go out of their flat. She prepared their meals for them as usual but was hardly eating anything herself. She felt that she had lost some part of herself. How she wished that she was in Calcutta with her family.

They had earlier written to their families with the good news about the pregnancy. Another four weeks later, several days after the miscarriage, letters came from both the families in Calcutta happy with the great news, congratulating them and giving them some practical advice. This made both of them feel even more depressed.

After almost a month, while holding Geeta in his arms, Ashok said, 'Listen, it is not your fault. We can try again.'

She had been feeling as if she has deliberately left behind something of herself, something essential in a distant, forgotten place which had once been her home. Geeta only buried her face in his chest and started sobbing.

Ashok said, 'Let's go for a short walk.'

Without saying anything, Geeta got ready to go out. They walked slowly, holding hands, around the hospital garden without saying a word to each other. Soon it became their daily routine.

A few days later, on a Friday evening, Ashok came home and said, 'Something is arriving tomorrow.'

'What do you mean?' asked Geeta with only mild interest.

'You will have to wait and see.'

The next day, the TV rental company car came with a colour TV. Ashok cleared the table in the corner of the room and the rental man set it all up for them.

'You can get all the four channels now in these. Any problem and come and talk to us at the shop. Enjoy,' he said before leaving.

However, the novelty of their first ever TV lasted only a couple of weeks before Geeta said, 'I am going to try to finish my BA. I am going to the local college tomorrow to find out about it.'

But the next evening when Ashok came back from work, Geeta was sitting quietly on the sofa without the TV switched on.

'How did it go there? What did they say?'

'If I want to do the BA here, I have to start from the first year. And it's not cheap.'

'Money is not the issue now. I am earning a bit more as an SHO. But if you have to start from the beginning, why not look into the Open University course? Apparently, you can do it in your own pace and time from home.'

Geeta enjoyed the new challenges of the Open University routine. She was apprehensive after sending her first assignment well within the due time. Very favourable comments from her tutor, however, made her very happy. While she was in her third month of OU, she found out that there may be a summer school and she was keen to go. Ashok promptly agreed.

A month before the summer school, she found out that she was pregnant again.

'I am cancelling my summer school,' said Geeta.

'I think you are right. Do you have to let your tutor know anything?'

'No. I should be able to manage my assignment for now anyway.'

'Just take it easy.'

Geeta was reading one of her books from OU and sitting on the sofa. She felt something in her tummy moving. Unsure of what was going on, she waited, and a few minutes later she felt the same movement again.

Ashok had managed to squeeze a short time to come home for lunch and was in a bit of a hurry. He had not noticed the rare broad smile in Geeta's face. He went on to sort out their lunch quickly.

From her sofa, Geeta said, 'Come over here for a minute.'

'I must get back to hospital before two. There is a big operation I will have to assist.'

'Just sit beside me for a minute.'

As Ashok sat down, Geeta put his hand over her tummy and held it there.

'Wow! What was that? Is that the baby kicking inside?'

Geeta smiled and they hugged each other tightly.

From then on, from time to time they sat together with Ashok taking turns with Geeta feeling the baby's kicks.

At times, Ashok took out his stethoscope to listen to the baby's heartbeat. 'First of all, listen to your own heartbeat. Now listen carefully for the baby's,' he said, passing the stethoscope to Geeta.

'It's going so much faster than mine. Boom, boom, boom.'

'Yes, that's normal. It will be about the twice your rate.'

Geeta went on to lie with her head on Ashok's lap and her feet on the sofa. Ashok stroked her hair lovingly.

It was arranged that her parents would come over two weeks before her due date. Geeta's mother would then stay on for a few months to help with the new baby and her father would go back after a month. The next few months of her pregnancy went smoothly. At twenty-eight weeks, Geeta was actually relieved to write to her tutor that she would have to postpone her course until the baby was a few months old. She was already feeling very tired and having difficulty in keeping up with her assignments.

'Am I going into labour?' she asked one evening, breathing heavily between the bouts of pain.

'No, it's only thirty-three weeks. It must be Braxton Hicks.'

Screaming with pain, Geeta said, 'I don't know what that is, but it's getting worse. I can't bear it anymore.'

Ashok had to go back to the ward to see a patient's relative, but when he came back Geeta was still in pain and looked exhausted. He decided to take her to the labour ward just to be safe. She could barely manage to walk the hundred yards from their hospital flat to the ward. The labour ward was very busy on this Saturday afternoon. All the beds were full and midwives were rushing from bed to bed. While Geeta was waiting to be seen, two of the women, one after another, were wheeled to the labour room to have their babies.

The midwife came to check Geeta after a while. After checking her over briefly, she said, 'You are not in labour. You can go home.'

'I am still in pain and it's getting worse. I cannot go back to the flat. Please call Ashok.'

Ashok begged the labour ward sister to admit Geeta for observation overnight, especially as he was himself on call this weekend and there was no one to keep an eye on her if he was called to the hospital. She reluctantly agreed and Geeta was soon taken upstairs to the antenatal ward. She was put in a bed by the door in a six-bed ward.

The woman in the bed next to her was sitting in a chair by the bed looking very uncomfortable. 'How many weeks are you?' she asked.

'Thirty-three weeks,' muttered Geeta between bouts of pain.

'Oh, long way to go. I am overdue by almost two weeks now. They are thinking of doing a caesarean after the weekend if nothing happens in the meantime.'

The dinner trolley came around the ward and the elderly woman asked Geeta, 'What do you want, love? Baked potato or a sandwich?'

Still in pain, Geeta said, 'I don't want anything. Can you call the nurse for me?'

Twenty minutes later, the nurse came to find that Geeta was breathing heavily. The nurse listened to her tummy with a funnel and looked concerned.

'What is it?' asked terrified Geeta.

'Well, the baby's heart rate is a bit high. I will come back in ten minutes to check again.'

'Please call my husband for me. He has a bleep,' Geeta cried after her.

The nurse came back with the sister in charge fifteen minutes later and again listened in to her tummy.

'No, it's still one hundred and eighty beats per minute,' she looked towards the ward sister.

A call was sent out to the gynae SHO and to Ashok. The SHO examined Geeta with a blank face and hurriedly went out to call her registrar. Ten minutes later, the registrar explained to Ashok and Geeta that she needed a caesarean section urgently. It took another hour before she was wheeled to the operation theatre, Ashok holding her hand all the way.

After more than an hour, the exhausted-looking gynae registrar came out to meet Ashok in the relatives' room.

'It was difficult. We almost lost the baby. She is doing all right now though. The paed reg will talk to you later. Sorry, but I need to go; there is another obstructed labour.'

Ashok tried to mutter, 'Thank you.'

'We have a girl,' he thought to himself happily.

'When can I see our baby?' asked Geeta, waking up from anaesthesia.

'She is in the special care unit. I will take you there soon. You should have some rest now. Do you want a drink? You can only have water for now,' said the nurse.

'Yes, please,' said Geeta with a dry throat.

Later, she was wheeled to the special care unit where her daughter was in a glass box connected to all sorts of wires and tubes. She could only touch her tiny fingers with her hand through a hole in the box. She could not stop crying. Soon Ashok joined them.

'She is so small but so beautiful.'

'Yes,' replied Ashok, and then added, 'She will grow up quickly. How are you feeling?'

'I am okay, only a bit sore. Oh, look! She is wiggling her fingers!'

Soon Geeta was taken back to her ward for the doctors' ward round.

The busy paediatric registrar called Ashok to the doctor's office. Ashok had already met her in the doctor's common room a few times in the last few weeks.

She said, 'Look, Ash, her Apgar score to start with was only five. She is looking a lot better now though.'

'Thank you very much,' replied Ashok.

Twice daily, the nurse was using the breast pump to get milk from Geeta for the baby, but it was getting less and less every day. Then Geeta would go the special care unit and just sit watching her daughter until she was called back by the nurse for her meals or for the ward rounds. A week went by and her stitches were removed.

It made Geeta's day when the paediatric consultant said, 'She is making slow progress but probably will be out of the unit in another week.'

'Can we take her home then?'

'We will see how it goes. You live in the hospital campus, so it might be okay.'

When Ashok came in the afternoon, Geeta said excitedly, 'We will be taking her home in a week, the consultant said. You'd better buy the carry cot, the crib, some clothes, and everything for her today.'

'I can't today, and it's a bit late anyway. Also, I will ask the nurses for suggestions for her size and everything. She is still so tiny. Listen, tomorrow is Sunday. I have got the afternoon off on Monday. If you are feeling better maybe we can ask the ward sister to let you out for a few hours to come with me to do the baby shopping.'

A week later during the ward round, after checking on the baby, the consultant smiled at Geeta and said, 'You can take her home today.'

Geeta asked the ward sister to bleep Ashok, who came soon after.

'They said this morning that she is now one kilogram eight hundred grams. That's three hundred grams in just over two weeks.

It's a pity my milk has dried up completely now and I won't be able to feed her.'

'We have enough supply of formula baby milk at home. Let's take her home first. By the way, two telegrams came today, one from your parents and one from my parents.'

'I will write airmails to your parents once I am home. My parents are coming over in two weeks anyway. Even if I write to them today, they won't get it before they leave. Now, can you go and get the discharge letter from the nurse at the desk and give them this box of chocolates from us? Apparently you have to drop the discharge letter at the GP surgery soon. Also, when you come back to the hospital, find out about registering her birth,' said Geeta.

'She is going to be another British citizen in our family, like me,' said Ashok.

Geeta just smiled proudly. They named her Jayatri at the registrar's office next day. Soon, her name was shortened to Jaya. In the next few days, the health visitor came daily and even one of the paediatric ward nurses came down to their hospital flat one day. Ashok tried to sneak back to his flat as many times as he could during his duty hours in the hospital. Another Indian couple from near Agra had been living for a while in the accommodation next door to them. Akbar was working as an SHO in A&E and his wife, Ayesha, looked after their three-and-a-half-year-old daughter, Munna.

Ashok and Geeta had only known them enough to say 'Hello' and 'How are you?' and wave at Munna.

Ayesha, who was not a doctor, fully took over cooking for them, as well as helping Geeta with the baby every day. She did not speak much English but it was easy enough for Geeta to understand her Urdu and speak to her in Hindi as the languages were not so dissimilar. Munna loved sitting by the baby with her toys and singing nursery rhymes to her.

On the sixth night at home, Geeta called Ashok, who was watching the nine o'clock news on TV. 'Can you come here? She was not feeding and feels so cold. I don't think she is breathing right.'

They took Jaya back to the children's ward where the paediatric registrar told them she might have sepsis. She was put on oxygen and intravenous antibiotics. Both spent sleepless night with their daughter, but by the morning she was looking a lot better. After three days, they were told she could go home.

The same nurse who had visited them at home told them, smiling, 'Children are there only to worry us parents, you know!'

Two weeks later, Ashok went to meet Geeta's parents arriving at Heathrow. The BOAC flight was delayed by three hours. Both looked absolutely exhausted. On the journey to Bedford by bus, Juthika slept most of the way.

Neel, however, was awake and with his head plastered against the window of the bus, said, 'I never thought England was so green, and so many shades of green at that. And also, look at this wonderful road, so wide, and the cars moving so fast from either side.'

'It's the motorway. There are a few of them in the country joining big cities. We will be going to Bedford, which is a small county town by a river. I think you will like it there.'

'After our crowded roads with regular traffic trams, overflowing buses, and old cars in Calcutta, this is like a dream,' Neel replied.

The first thing Juthika said to her daughter after arriving at their flat was, 'You have lost so much weight. You almost look like the ghost of yourself.'

The baby was sleeping in her cot, nicely wrapped up in blankets. A little while later, Juthika picked up her granddaughter and said, 'She is so tiny but so beautiful.'

After giving her a few kisses, she asked Neel, 'Do you want to hold her?'

Awkwardly, Geeta's father held the baby for a minute before giving her back to Geeta.

In their single-bedroom married hospital accommodation, it was arranged that Geeta would sleep with her mother on the bed with the baby on the cot. In the living room, her father would sleep on the roll-over bed Ashok had borrowed from one of his friends, and

Ashok would sleep on the sofa. Geeta's father was going to stay for only four weeks anyway because of his business. But if possible, he wanted to see the Big Ben by the Houses of Parliament and the British Museum in London before going back.

Geeta's mother took over most of the cooking and now, after nearly a month, Geeta managed to get some decent sleep, mostly in the daytime as she was still getting used to getting up every three hours in the night, almost on the dot, to feed Jaya. Ayesha brought her home cooked food and snacks for the four of them most days as well.

For the four weeks of his stay, Neel walked the hospital campus at least twice daily in his full-length overcoat in late June and occasionally also ventured down the street to the nearby shops. Only a couple of times did he manage to go to the city centre, both times with Ashok by bus from the hospital stop. Juthika joined them on the second time when Ayesha came over and stayed with Geeta. After showing them the castle from outside, Ashok took his in-laws to the supermarket in the town. They were completely taken aback by the place, the likes of which they had never seen in their life.

'Normally, I can't stand shopping. But even shopping here seems so much fun,' said Neel. During dinner, he said, 'People are so polite here. Any people I pass by greet me with "Good morning," "Good afternoon," or whatever time of the day it is. Sometime people will even stop and ask me where I've come from. When I say I come from Calcutta, some will say, "Oh. Where is that?" and others will say, "I was stationed in Kanpur in India during the war," and some even say, "My father was in Calcutta before the war,"'

The evening before Neel was due to go back to Calcutta, Ayesha invited them for dinner in her flat next door.

'This lamb biriyani is out of this world. I have never tasted something so good in my life,' said Neel.

Akbar, looking towards Juthika, replied, 'But Ma ji, you have got to teach Ayesha while you are still here how to make the payesh you sent us the other day.'

Early in the morning the next day, Ashok went to London with Geeta's parents. They spent all of the Friday and Saturday morning visiting the London Bridge, Houses of Parliament, the Big Ben, the British Museum, and Buckingham Palace by Underground. Neel could not speak more highly of the wonderful places, as well as of the underground transport system.

In the early afternoon, Ashok took him to the airport to catch his flight to Calcutta.

Before leaving, his father-in-law said, 'Such a civilised and advanced country. We have so much to learn from them.'

At the six-week check-up, the health visitor said Jaya had put on another 500 grams, but she was slightly worried that she was very floppy. At the three-month check, the she said, 'She has put on another six hundred grams, but I think her muscle tone is still very poor.'

Geeta said, 'Sometimes she also goes into a kind of spasm for few seconds.'

The health visitor replied, 'I am going to make an appointment for her with the doctor next week.'

The GP examined the baby carefully and then, with a slightly worried expression on his face, looking at Ashok, said, 'With her history, I wonder if it is an early sign of cerebral palsy. I am going to make an urgent appointment with the paediatrician in the hospital.'

Ashok went pale.

Looking at him, Geeta asked, 'What does that mean?'

'I will explain to you later,' he replied meekly.

At home, Ashok, who was devastated, was completely at a loss as to how to explain to Geeta what the GP had said to them.

'I think we'd better wait for the specialist in the hospital to see her first.' He had always been honest with her and now struggled to explain what cerebral palsy meant for their own child.

The week after, the paediatrician examined their daughter for a long time and then, looking at both of them, said, 'I am very sorry. I think your GP is right. It is too early to say how severely she will be affected in the future.'

Geeta asked, 'Is it because they could not do my operation for over five hours?' 'It is difficult to say. It could be combination of so many things,' he replied.

'What is the treatment?' she asked.

'Sorry, but there is no treatment as such. We will have to see how she develops in the next few months or even years, and we have to provide support so that she can be looked after.'

'But she will be all right after?' Geeta asked.

'Sorry. With cerebral palsy she will need looking after all her life. Listen, I am already running late with my clinic today. We will make another appointment in three months for you,' he said.

The outpatient sister took them to a side room and sat with them quietly for a while as Geeta sobbed, holding her daughter.

'Do you want me to make both of you a cup of tea?'

'No, thank you,' said Ashok before leaving the clinic in a stupor.

Even at four months, Jaya's neck needed to be supported all the time. It was getting more and more difficult to feed her. Not only was she dribbling saliva most of the time, it also seemed that she was having difficulty swallowing. At times, she would have spasms for a few seconds which affected her face and her whole body. As the months went by she could not sit up even when supported. Because of her spasms, they needed to buy extra straps for her upper body while she was in the pram.

At the six-month appointment in the hospital, the consultant was away for a meeting. The same paediatric registrar who was present during the caesarean section was taking the clinic.

After examining Jaya for a while, she said, 'You obviously know by now that it is a case of moderately severe cerebral palsy.' Then, looking at Ashok, she said, 'I am telling you this in confidence, but you know that you can sue the hospital for damages? It will neither be easy nor cheap looking after her all her life.'

In December, Ashok had been looking at the BMJ for his next job in January as he would be finishing his six-month contract in general surgery at the hospital.

One afternoon, his consultant, who was now also the medical director of the hospital, called him to his office and said, 'Ashok, I have heard about your situation. It is very sad. I am going to offer you an extension of your job for another six months. That way, you wouldn't have to worry about your job as well as your child. But after the next six months it will be one year in this job and you must find another position.'

Grateful, Ashok almost broke into tears before saying, 'Thank you very much, sir.'

Geeta asked Ashok whether he had been able to find out anything about the compensation the paediatric registrar was talking about.

'They have been very kind extending my contract here. I don't think we can get into trouble with the hospital authority now. I definitely need the job for the sake of all of us.'

At their flat, Geeta's mother said, 'You know that in Kalighat there is an ojha who can get rid of any demons. Come back with Jaya to Calcutta. I will take her there to see the ojha and we will give Puja at Kalighat, Dakshineswar, everywhere. She will be all right.'

In a forlorn voice, Ashok replied, 'This is not a question of any demons. It is birth injury.'

Two weeks later, Geeta's mother went back home, accompanied by a colleague of Ashok's who was going to Calcutta on holiday.

Chapter Seven

1974: Geeta's charity

During one of her visits to the GP surgery, the practice nurse told Geeta, 'There are a couple of other parents registered in our practice with a similar situation to yours. If you want, I can introduce you to them so that you can get some idea of how they manage.'

'That will really help. Thank you very much,' replied Geeta.

The nurse arranged for her to meet up with Mary Griffith, a young, recently divorced mother who had a three-year-old son also with cerebral palsy. Joshua was her only child and soon after his first birthday her husband had left her, walking out with another woman.

'In the beginning, I thought somehow he would get better, at least to feed himself. Now I know that's probably never going to happen. But I cannot imagine my life without him. It's rare, but when he is happy and looks at me, I can almost sense he is smiling,' said Mary. 'He is so fragile. I am always scared that something is going to happen to him,' she added.

Geeta noticed that Mary was feeding Joshua with a drinking straw. 'Does he manage to drink well with that straw?' she asked.

'Otherwise he does not manage at all and the drink goes down the wrong way, making him cough and choke.'

Geeta also learned that Mary pureed all solid food and managed to feed her son with a spoon.

'It takes time but that's the only way I can get some proper food into him. After all, he needs to grow up.'

They arranged to meet up again the week after at the local supermarket and then, if possible, go to the local café.

As they were pushing their children in prams through the aisles of the supermarket, an old lady stopped by them and said to Mary, 'What's wrong with your child, dear?'

'Why?' Mary asked sharply.

'I don't want to be prying, dear, but I noticed that he was almost having a convulsion when you were chatting with this coloured friend of yours. Is he epileptic?'

'No. He has a birth injury. Let's go, Geeta.'

The old lady looked at Jaya in the pram and said, pointing towards Geeta, 'Is it the same with this coloured lady's child as well, dear?'

When none of them replied, she said, looking towards Geeta, 'Oh, poor you. And that for a girl. Poor angel.' As they pushed their prams quickly away from her, the lady was saying, 'Do you have another normal child?'

'This is what gets me most. The mock pity,' fumed Mary during their coffee.

'I have an idea. Why don't we put an ad in our local newspaper for mothers with children who need constant attention like ours to meet up? Maybe once a month?' said Geeta, and then added, 'I can ask Ashok to put the ad up this week.'

'I am not absolutely sure how it will work out, but at least we can find out from others how they are coping. Of course, only if any of the other parents turn up to start with,' replied Mary.

In their flat, Ashok was still sleeping after being on call the night before. Jaya had also fallen asleep in her pram. Geeta made coffee for both herself and Ashok and went to sit beside him. Looking at his tired face, she decided to wait until it was actually time for him to get up before getting ready for the night on call again. She busied herself sorting out the house and then started drafting the short advertisement for the paper.

'*Coffee morning for parents with children needing extra attention,*' read the headline. '*Please join us at the Regent Café, Mill Street on Thursday 10th July between 10:30–12:00 to share your experiences. Everyone welcome.*'

When Ashok woke up to his alarm clock, Geeta asked, 'Do you want another cup of coffee now? The coffee I made earlier for you has gone cold.'

'No. I am going to have a shower first.'

Geeta started sorting out his dinner before he was due to leave for his night on call. As Ashok was having his dinner, Geeta said, 'Mary and I have an idea.'

Before she could elaborate, Jaya was up and Geeta needed to change her and then feed her, which always took a long time.

Ashok was almost ready to leave and asked, 'What was the idea you were talking about earlier?'

'We will talk about it after you come back tomorrow morning. You'd better go now. You don't want be late.'

He kissed Jaya and Geeta before leaving, saying, 'Goodnight. See you in the morning.'

'Hope you are not as busy as last night,' replied Geeta.

After Jaya was fed and changed, Geeta rang Mary's number and told her about the draft she had written.

'We'd better talk to the manager of the café first. It may not be a big enough place if ten parents turn up with their children in their prams,' Mary said.

'You are right. Even the two of us with prams found it difficult getting in there. What about the library? In the outside hall there is enough space and there is a coffee machine inside.'

'Let's go there ourselves first and talk to the librarian in charge. Are you free the day after tomorrow in the morning?'

The librarian in charge, Mrs Bigham, was a woman in her fifties who listened with interest before saying, 'If it is on a weekday morning rather than on a Saturday, it should be fine with us. After all, the library is a place to support the whole community. If you want, we can put the notice on our main notice board when you are ready.' Then she had a look at the draft Geeta had made and said, '"Children who need extra attention" is quite vague. I would advise you to write clearly "Children with disabilities of any kind."'

'Isn't that too direct?' asked Mary.

'I gave birth to three children and lost my first one within a few hours of his birth. I was not even allowed to see him properly because they felt it would be too traumatic to a young woman like me. I regret every day of my life that neither I nor my husband pressed them hard enough to allow us to spend a few minutes with him.'

She took off her glasses and then got a handkerchief from her bag and wiped her tears.

It turned out that Mary had been good at arts in her school. With the help of Mrs Bigham, she produced a few copies of the beautifully handwritten notice: 'All parents with children of any disability are welcome to join us in the library hall on Thursday 10ᵗʰ July morning between 10:30 and 12:00. Let us share our stories.'

Over the weekend, Geeta showed Ashok a copy of the notice and asked if he could put it in the local weekly newspaper.

Ashok said, 'Excellent idea. The newspaper comes out every Friday. Today is Sunday. I would not be able to get there until the end of the week during their office hours. Why don't you go there yourself tomorrow? Then, if they agree, it would come out in this week's paper.'

The next day it was drizzling with rain. After putting the rain cover over Jaya's pram, Geeta walked to the office of the local newspaper in the town.

The young receptionist listened to her and was saying, 'I don't think we have any space for ad like that in the paper this week, unless of course you pay,' when a man in his sixties walked into the office from the street.

He was thoroughly soaked in the rain. After putting the folded umbrella in an umbrella stand, he looked at the receptionist and said, 'Can you please bring a pot of tea for me in my office, Annabel?' and then asked Geeta, 'How can we help you?'

Geeta introduced herself and then briefly explained.

'Two cups of tea for us, please, Annabel. Please come into the office with me, Geeta.'

With some difficulty, Geeta managed to bring the pram into the office and pulled away its rain cover. Jaya was still sleeping.

The editor listened with interest and then had a look at the notice Geeta had brought with her.

'I will make sure it goes out this week and the week after in the paper as the get-together is not until three weeks away. I might use some of my editorial amendments though. I know how difficult it must be for you. My youngest brother had what they called Mongolism those days. I think they call it Down's syndrome now. He died in his thirties.'

On Thursday 10 July, Geeta arrived early with Jaya at the library. Ashok wanted to come but could not manage to get away from his work that morning. Mary arrived soon with her son too. They were met by the librarian, who had already arranged some extra cups for tea and coffee and packets of biscuits for the meeting.

Geeta was expecting probably five or six mothers to turn up. She was surprised to find that twelve mothers with their children had come. There was only one father amongst the group. Mrs Bigham treated everyone to free cups of tea or coffee and biscuits. Everyone then briefly introduced themselves and their children. The children were between six months and ten years in age. Geeta learnt that there were five other children with cerebral palsy apart from Jaya in the group. This was the first time most of the mothers had met anyone else looking after a disabled child. Very soon they were all exchanging their everyday stories of having to cope bravely. Soon the awkward chats were replaced by funny stories and laughter.

The rain had stopped outside and the sun was coming out from behind the clouds. There was a photographer sent from the local newspaper who got everybody together with their children in the front of the library building for a group photograph. Time passed quickly and it was time for most to get back home with their children. They all agreed to meet up again in a month's time.

Mrs Bigham said, 'I will make sure that the library hall will be kept reserved for the get-together every month at the same time until the end of this year.'

By the time Ashok arrived, most of the parents and children had left.

'Sorry, I couldn't get away earlier. Just managed to sneak out for my lunch break early. How did it go?' he asked, looking at Geeta.

'Very well, we thought, for a first meeting,' said Geeta, and then introduced him to Mary and Mrs Bigham.

On the way back home, as Ashok pushed the pram, Geeta excitedly told him in more detail about the get-together and that they were going to meet every month.

'I will definitely try to come to the next meeting,' Ashok said.

The local newspaper printed a brief article on their inside page about the meeting with the picture and the date for next month's meeting.

At the next meeting there were a total of fifteen children and their parents. Three of the fathers, including Ashok, were there too. Geeta and Mrs Bigham tried to formalise the event a bit more this time by keeping a record of the meeting. All the parents wrote down their names, their children's names, and their medical diagnoses, as well as their own contact details. Geeta also encouraged everyone to come up with any big problem they were facing in their day-to-day life looking after their children. Accessing any local facilities with the pram was a common theme.

In their third meeting, after everyone had written down their personal details, Geeta asked all of them again about the problems in their day-to-day lives in managing with their children. Everyone talked about their difficulty in getting to places such as shops, cafés, and even to their doctors' surgeries with their children in the pram.

In most places, even at the pedestrian crossings, it was difficult to get to and from the footpath, which was almost three inches higher than the road. When Geeta asked about difficulties others faced at home, she was not surprised to find that everyone agreed that their child needed twenty-four-hour care without any respite. Three out of the fifteen mothers were single and only one of these three had her parents living nearby to help from time to time. Luckily, it turned out that one of the mothers had an uncle who was also a local county councillor. She promised to talk to him. Geeta heard soon after that he had also agreed to come to their next meeting.

Geeta spoke passionately in their next meeting not only about the daily problems the parents with disabled children experienced but also about the lack of any emotional support for the parents and their families. She also spoke about the absence of any real educational support for the disabled children.

She ended saying, 'We are made to feel like outcasts because our beloved children are disabled through no fault of their own.'

About two dozen parents with disabled children and several others who had attended the meeting applauded. The father of another ten-year-old boy with cerebral palsy started speaking but had to stop in the middle with his voice cracking and tears flooding his eyes. The councillor spoke briefly and agreed to make the issue an agenda item in the next council meeting. The local newspaper again highlighted the meeting and published Geeta's speech in full.

With the local council election coming within the next six months, they were keen to showcase a new project in the town. Within a few months, the zebra crossings from most of the footpaths and the schools and council offices were made suitable for disabled access.

One afternoon, after returning from her daily stroll with her daughter in the hospital gardens, Geeta noticed that Jaya was breathing very rapidly. She took Jaya's temperature to find that it was 103 degrees Fahrenheit. She tried to contact Ashok immediately but he was already on his way home from work. Ashok examined Jaya, whose breathing had now become shallow. They took her to the children's ward immediately where she was diagnosed with bronchopneumonia. In spite of treatment with antibiotics and oxygen, Jaya continued to deteriorate and passed away the next day.

Chapter Eight

1975: Geeta and Ashok

When Geeta found out she was pregnant again eight months later, she was in tears.

'I don't think I can go through this again.'

Ashok silently moved over to her and just held her tightly. He tried to cosset her the best he could for the next few months. Ignoring Geeta's protests, he arranged a house cleaner to come twice a week.

'If we were in India you would have no problem with having maids and servants in the house. She will come only twice a week to give you a break,' he said.

He tried to come back home almost every lunchtime, even for fifteen or twenty minutes. He took over most of the cooking during the weekend as well as on some weekday evenings. They had decided this time not to tell their families in Calcutta about her pregnancy until after the baby was born.

Ashok, after doing two six-month stints in the A&E, had worked as a locum SHO in general surgery for a year in Bedford. Unable to get further general surgery jobs, he then took up the gynae obstetrics job available in the same hospital. Ashok soon took his final FRCS exam. He felt lucky to have passed the exam on his first attempt. He returned home from London late in the night.

Geeta was asleep but soon woke up and, after hearing the news, jumped with joy and said, 'We must celebrate. Next weekend we are going to invite our friends like Kanikadi and Madhabidi to our house.'

Unable to find any regular job in the hospital after the end of his gynae obstetrics job, which was coming to its end, Ashok was glad when a job in general surgery for SHO, as well as one for registrar in surgery, came up in his old hospital. He went to meet his old boss,

Mr Donaldson, who was also the head of the department. Ashok enquired about the registrar post with him.

'Ash, you are a good candidate and we like you. By the way, congratulations for doing your fellowship. I will have to tell you honestly though that we already have another good candidate, a local graduate from the university hospital, who is waiting to take his final fellowship soon. Apparently he is very good and has been recommended by his professor.'

'What are my chances, sir?' asked Ashok.

'Frankly, I would say that we will guarantee you the job of SHO. But the registrar job will depend on how it goes on the day.'

Ashok thought for a second and remembering now that Geeta was pregnant again, said, 'I will take your advice, sir. I will apply for the SHO job.'

During their weekend celebration with mostly Indian friends, including Amit and Kanika from Birmingham and a few English doctors from his own hospital, Timothy, another SHO in gynae who worked with Ashok, asked, 'Ash, you must now be going to get the surgery registrar job in our hospital soon?'

Ashok did not reply and got himself busy helping everyone with their food and drinks.

After all the English doctors had left, Amit asked, 'Ashok, what is going on? Have you applied for the registrar job now that you have your fellowship?'

Ashok told them about his recent conversation with his boss. He also explained that he had already applied for over forty registrar posts advertised all over UK and was still waiting to be shortlisted for any of them.

'Nothing new, Ashok. Have you thought about going back to Calcutta and starting your own practice? And I am sure you will get a post in the medical college there soon as well.'

To change the subject, Ashok said, 'Do you know what winds me up most? If anyone hears that I am from Calcutta, they say, "Oh, it's the place of Mother Theresa. Isn't she wonderful?" as if Mother Theresa herself picked me up from the gutter to make whatever I am today.'

146

Everyone laughed and nodded their agreement.

Ashok and Geeta had not told any of them yet about Geeta's pregnancy. Geeta said, 'We have to think carefully about all the options in the next couple of weeks.'

After they had all left, Ashok made tea for both of them and said, 'Tell me honestly what you feel we should do.'

Geeta kept sipping her tea silently for a while before saying, 'I know how much you love surgery. You came here only because of that and against all the odds you have done your FRCS. I am more proud of you than you know.'

Then she continued, 'But we have to be realistic. Now that I am pregnant again, if we want to go back to Calcutta, we should go in the next couple of months at the latest, unless realistically you think there is any chance of becoming a surgical consultant here.'

'Even if I am lucky enough to find a registrar post here in the next few months, finding a senior registrar post a few years down the line and then being considered for a consultant position is way beyond the realm of possibility for an Indian graduate like me,' Ashok replied. He then added, 'That will also mean us moving every few months from place to place with a young child.'

'Shall we make plans to go back then?' asked Geeta.

After staying quiet for a while, Ashok said, 'Now that we are expecting a baby, I think we should stay here for your and the baby's sake. I also sincerely think our child will have a better future here.'

Geeta looked at him and said, 'It's getting late. Let's go to bed and we will think about it over the weekend.'

By Sunday evening, they had decided to stay in England whatever Ashok's prospect in surgery jobs was. Geeta herself felt somehow relieved as, like Ashok, she felt that their child would have better prospects in this country. And despite her past experience, she still had a lot of faith in the NHS. But she also felt guilty if Ashok was making a sacrifice for them. Ashok, however, made it abundantly clear that he was feeling happier being out of the impossible rat race where he had no chance of winning.

Near the end of his gynae obstetrics job, Ashok heard about a three-month locum job in a GP surgery nearby. By now he had sent about fifty applications for surgery registrar jobs without any luck. He had had enough of working as an SHO again and again. He went and met the senior GP in the practice, Dr Ahmed, and he was offered the post. No formal interview was needed.

He had never before worked outside hospital medicine and was initially sceptical about working as a GP. But soon the challenges of seeing a patient as a part of a wider family and the community and treating them as such struck a chord with him. Two months into his locum GP job, he was made aware by Dr Ahmed, that they would soon be advertising a GP post in their surgery.

Ashok had already taken to Dr Ahmed, who was originally from Patna in India and had gone through a similar situation with the NHS jobs more than a decade earlier, and he had a lot of respect for him. And above all, he was the only one in the practice who had a genuine interest in cricket! Ashok had seen how all the patients and the staff in their surgery held Dr Ahmed in such high esteem as a caring, committed doctor, as well as considering him as a good friend. A few times, when Ashok had sat with Dr Ahmed seeing a patient, he was impressed with how quickly he could make them feel at ease.

'It looks like once I finish my locum GP job in two months' time, there is a chance of a regular job in the practice. We wouldn't need to move all over the country to find a job and somewhere to stay,' Ashok said after coming back from surgery.

Geeta was delighted. 'We don't have to keep moving from place to place. And we would have to soon think of our child's schooling. The new comprehensive school here had such brilliant results this year. Did you see the newspaper the week before last?'

'We have to find a decent primary school for the child first, remember,' Ashok said laughing.

'I know, and when we look for our home to stay in permanently we need to make sure it has a good primary school nearby.'

Ashok was more than excited when Dr Ahmed invited him to come to Old Trafford in Manchester to watch the touring West Indies cricket team playing against England in 1976.

They both took the morning off from the surgery on the Saturday, the third day of the third test. On the one-hour journey, while keeping an eye on the road, Dr Ahmed, who was driving, asked, 'When was the last time you went to a test match?'

'Never in this country. I went to see India playing Australia at the Eden Gardens.'

'This is the first time I am going to see a test match live, although I have been to the county matches. I went to Gloucester and watched Zaheer Abbas scoring his century.'

'He is so natural and fluent. And batting with his glasses on!'

'I read that the English captain Tony Greig said a few days back, "We will make West Indies grovel."'

'He is a typical white South African now playing for England. I am glad that they have banned racist South Africa from all international sports.'

They talked about their favourite cricketers until they reached the test ground. Their day turned out to be something to remember for life. At first, they watched the fast bowler Michael Holding taking five wickets for seventeen runs as England folded for only seventy-one runs in their first innings. Then they were lucky enough to watch Roy Frederics and Viv Richards both scoring centuries for the West Indies.

During the lunch break, Dr Ahmed asked, 'Ashok, have you decided what you want to do after you finish your locum job with us?'

It took time for Ashok to form a reply.

Dr Ahmed said, 'Ashok, I have been in the same situation a few years back as you are today.'

Ashok looked towards him.

'My father was a doctor in Mombasa in Kenya. My parents had moved there when I was only eight years old, their only child.'

Ashok stopped munching his chips before saying, 'I was born in Nairobi. My father was an eye doctor there.'

'Very interesting,' said Dr Ahmed, before continuing. 'My parents were keen for me to also become a doctor. I was sent back to my family in Bihar in India when I was only fourteen years old. I then went to the Patna Medical School to become a doctor.'

'My proudest day was when both my parents came over from Kenya for my graduation. They then decided not to return back there due to increasing political tension,' Dr Ahmed continued. Then he added, 'When Health Minister Enoch Powell appealed for help to staff his massively expanding National Health Service a few years back, many thousands of doctors from the Indian subcontinent like myself responded full of hopes and ambitions for their own future.'

He continued, 'We came fresh from our medical colleges. Our dreams were quickly quashed when instead of getting posts in teaching hospitals or top medical specialties, the only doors open to us were in the "Cinderella" specialties like mental health, geriatrics, and accident and emergency, and that too only in the peripheral hospitals.'

'When you came over, what specialty did you have in mind?' interrupted Ashok.

'I wanted to be a cardiologist. After getting my MBBS with a gold medal in medicine, I was already trained for three years in my hospital before I came over here.'

He then added, 'There is, of course, the small matter of not being British. Unlike the Europeans, Aussies, or the South Africans, you can't just wear your suit and tie and no one will know the difference as long as you keep your mouth shut.'

Dr Ahmed then explained that after trying for a few years to get a job in general medicine, he soon had to accept that there was a clear pecking order. The only option for him in hospital medicine was choosing geriatrics. He had already had his family of a wife and two children move to England.

'Let's get back to the match. West Indian batting has some explosive characters. We can talk again during the drive back,' Dr Ahmed said.

On the drive back, they talked for a while about the carefree batting of Viv Richards. Then Dr Ahmed turned towards Ashok, saying, 'When we came over, we liked this country and wanted to live here. We felt the prospects for the future of our children were so much better here. Time and time again, most of us faced overt racism around the place and at work and had to make the best of the crumbs the British medical establishment offered us. The other option for me was to become a GP. The only opening even as a full-time GP was available in industrial urban areas, like in Wales or other deprived areas in the country like here.'

After a while, he asked, 'Ashok, have you given serious thought to the idea of joining our practice?'

'I know that the post is going to be advertised soon. I am sure there will be many applicants.'

'Discuss with your wife this weekend and let me know then if you are really interested.'

By the time Ashok got back home, Geeta was reading a book by Syed Mujtaba Ali.

'What are you reading? Oh, Mujtaba Ali. I especially like the stories about his travel through Europe between the wars.'

'Have you had your dinner yet?' asked Geeta. 'I was waiting to have dinner with you unless you were very late.'

During their dinner, Geeta asked, 'How was the match?'

Ashok replied, 'It was a fantastic day of cricket, unless of course you are an England supporter. On the way back, Dr Ahmed asked me if I would be interested in the GP job they are going to advertise soon.'

'What did you say?'

'He suggested for us to discuss this first.'

After clearing off the dinner plates, Ashok made tea for them and they sat together on the sofa.

'We have to decide soon if we want to get back to India or settle here permanently,' said Ashok.

'I miss Calcutta. I missed it even more when we had to go through everything with Jaya on our own. How I wished on so many days that I could speak to Didi or even to Ma. I miss the family. But to be entirely honest with you, with our new baby's future in mind, I would give up all that and make our lives here if you had a permanent job.'

She then added, 'Do you know what else I miss? I miss waking up to the Tagore's song in the morning on the radio. I miss listening to and trying to sing along to Tagore's and Najrul's song.'

'I loved your Najrul songs. Your voice really suited the style,' replied Ashok.

He got up and, watching through the window, said, 'We have to also think that both your and my parents are getting old. Being a doctor myself, I always think about their health and if one of them became unwell whether they can get the proper treatment there.'

'I know. That worries me too. Surely they don't have the best healthcare system in the world there. I heard from someone that nowadays you can book a call from Calcutta telephone exchange to call here. If someone was ill there and if they can call us, you can get the best advice for them from here.'

'That's not the same as being there if they need us. But I suppose it's a lot better than trying to keep in touch through airmail letters like before.'

On Monday, in the surgery, Ashok heard that Dr Ahmed had taken the day off as he was not feeling well. Ashok arranged with the receptionist to take over most of the appointments from Dr Ahmed's list and also picked up his home visits for the week.

Three days later, when Dr Ahmed came back, Ashok went to see him in his room.

'Are you feeling better? Is everything okay?'

'Hi, Ashok. No, everything is fine. I ended up going to the hospital on Sunday. They said it was diabetic ketoacidosis. It settled down quickly with insulin. They think we might be able to control it with tablets after a few weeks.' He smiled at Ashok before saying, 'I suppose the chocolate ice creams at the tea break during the match did not help! But we both had a great day, you must agree.'

Only three out of the five applications for the post in the GP surgery could be shortlisted according to their experience and qualifications. On the day of the interview, Ashok and only one other applicant turned up. The other doctor was originally from Sri Lanka. Dr Ahmed had invited one of his friends, Dr Bransom, from the nearby practice to help with the interview.

Ashok telephoned home immediately after the interview to share the news with Geeta that he was now going to be a full-time GP in the surgery. She was over the moon.

It was another three months before Ashok started as a full-time GP. On the first morning of his new job, Geeta brought out the silk tie she had bought for the day. But Ashok had already gone to the garage where for the last few days, he had kept his present for Geeta. He had gone away last weekend to Birmingham for a special shopping trip after telling Geeta that he was going to watch a cricket match. He carefully carried in a gramophone recorder and few vinyls of Tagore and Najrul songs.

Geeta could only smile broadly. She then put the tie on Ashok and gave him the tightest hug and a kiss.

As Ashok opened the door to call for his next patient, he could hear Mrs Johnson, a seventy-five-year-old lady he had just seen in his room, telling the receptionist, 'He is such a gentleman. So young but so caring.'

'Wednesday the fourteenth will be your next appointment. Three weeks from today. Will morning or afternoon be best for you?'

'Morning please, dear. I usually end up taking a nap after my lunch these days.'

'That's nice. Wish I could have a siesta after lunch! There you are, Wednesday fourteenth at ten thirty in the morning.'

'Thank you, dear. I hope it is with Dr Basu again.'

'Yes, it is. Bye for now, Mrs Johnson.'

Soon Ashok and Geeta got a mortgage for a three-bedroom house with a decent back garden within walking distance from Ashok's practice.

For the housewarming, Ashok invited Dr Ahmed and his family as well as both the surgery nurses and the receptionist with their husbands. He also invited two of his friends from the cricket club

153

with their wives, and Geeta invited Mrs Bigham, Mary, and few of her friends from her charity.

'Now you are properly settled in the country,' said Mrs Bigham.

'There is a saying amongst the Indians that when you stop converting every price tag in the shop into Indian rupees, only then are you beginning to settle in,' replied Ashok. Then, looking towards Geeta, he added, 'I think we are getting there.'

Everyone laughed.

Geeta's pregnancy was progressing smoothly. One evening during their walk, she said, 'I am terrified. Something awful is going to happen to us again.'

'No,' said Ashok, holding her hand tightly. 'We've had more than our share of bad luck already. I honestly feel that you and our baby will be fine.'

After Geeta's initial visits with the nurse in the GP surgery because of her history, when she was in her twenty-eighth week, she had an appointment with the obstetric consultant at the hospital. Two weeks later she also met the bubbly newly qualified midwife who introduced herself as Anna. Her biweekly follow-up with Anna was followed by another consultant appointment at thirty-two weeks. A careful examination was followed by an ultrasound examination this time. For the first time in her pregnancy, she was given a picture of her unborn child.

'Do you want to know it's a boy or girl?' asked the consultant.

Geeta looked towards Ashok, who said, 'No, thank you.'

As the consultant was due to go on his pre-retirement leave in a few weeks, an appointment was made with the new consultant to see her in two weeks. Back at their place, they could not stop looking at the picture again and again.

'You can clearly see this is going to be a beautiful baby,' said Ashok.

With tears rolling down her cheeks, Geeta only kept looking.

At the thirty-four-week check-up the new consultant examined her before saying, 'We would advise for you to have a planned caesarean section this time because of your history.'

Geeta had already taken a liking to this new female consultant. She just nodded her head in agreement.

Ashok asked, 'When are you planning for the CS?'

'Definitely around thirty-six weeks. My secretary will contact the midwife and she will contact you in the next few days. In the meantime, just take it easy,' she replied, before taking Geeta's hands in hers and saying, 'Both of you are going to be all right.'

The caesarean section with an injection in her back went well. The nurse brought the baby over the antiseptic green barrier of drapes to Geeta, saying, 'It's a beautiful boy.'

She cried as she held him to her chest. Then she looked at Ashok with a smile mixed with tears, and said, 'Do you want to hold him?'

In the next few days, while still in the hospital, Geeta held on to her son most of the time, praying that nothing would go wrong with him. Ashok came several times a day and just sat by the bed watching their son.

They named him Rajesh and were happy to be allowed to take him home only five days after the caesarean section. They had not mentioned this pregnancy at all so far to their families in India in their letters over the last nine months.

Now Ashok went to the post office and sent telegrams to both their parents saying, 'We have a beautiful boy. Baby and mother both are well.'

The next day, he took a photo of the baby with Geeta with his new Kodak Instamatic camera and sent it with letters to their families.

The day after a telegram reply came from India saying, 'We are all very happy and praying to God for you.'

They could not do enough to keep their son safe from everything around. But as a baby, Rajesh, whose name had since been shortened to Raju, bounced through his early months. In fact, he passed most of his milestones before the usual times. He started crawling when he was just over five months old, started saying a few words such as 'Ma' when he was only eleven months old, and was walking unsupported when he was only one-year-old. Although Geeta had her hands full with the toddler, especially as Ashok was very busy in his new job establishing himself to become a partner in his GP practice, she tried to keep up as much as possible with the disabled children and parents group.

She also wanted to resume her Open University degree and wrote to them. A reply came back from the OU that she could resume her degree, although she would now be assigned to a new tutor. Finding time to do her first TMA after a few years was the least of her problems but she realised there was almost a cobweb covering her brain when getting back into her subject. But within a few days she was busy doing her assignments in the evenings when Ashok was back home either playing with Raju or cooking for them. A few weeks later she was pleasantly surprised to get the marking score of seventy per cent on her assignment.

In the last ten months or so while she was pregnant and then busy with the new baby, the disabled children's care group had been stuttering along. Mary had a new partner and was thinking of moving up to York. Geeta was happy to find that Mrs Bigham was still there. Within a few months, the group was meeting regularly again.

Mrs Bigham suggested that to have long-term effects they should consider setting up their group's work as a charity.

'That way we might be able to attract more funding and other support from different sources and its finances will be above board.'

Soon Geeta managed to get everyone to agree to start the local town's first disabled children's charity. Then she managed to get the local mayor, who was due for re-election soon, to agree to become the honorary president of the society. A small committee of five members was formed and Geeta was voted unanimously as the honorary secretary and Mrs Bigham as the treasurer. Their first objective was to set up a day room for the children with disabilities. Mrs Bigham mentioned that next to the library one of the offices belonging to the county council had been kept locked since the office was moved to a new building two years back.

It took Geeta and others from the committee two unsuccessful visits to the county council estate department before they requested their committee president for help. The room, although in need of some repairs, was large with glass windows at the back, and was attached to a big toilets, a small kitchen, and a small enclosed lawn. The council estate team helped with the repairs and some modifications, especially making the entrance to the room and to its toilets larger.

The day centre opening day was advertised by the local chronicle. The committee members went door to door in the high street shops for raffle prizes. A small poster for the event printed by the local newspaper was pasted upon any possible space in the local shops, at the post office, and in the coffee shops. The day centre was opened by the local MP with a speech from the town's mayor. Apart from the several parents with disabled children, more than fifty others attended. Through selling homemade cakes and running the raffle, they raised over 300 pounds. Within a few months, there were several hundred pounds of donations from different sources. A fundraising day on a Saturday in the town's park was luckily a sunny day and was attended by many from the town, raising another 200 pounds.

The committee had decided that any money raised would be spent on supporting education for the children. In its minutes, it stated: 'Our charity strongly believes and will work on the principle that pupils with disabilities should be recognised as individuals, entitled to a dignified education of their own.'

Initially, the centre was opened for only two days every week. With the money raised from donations and with support from the local toy shop, the place was soon transformed into a large playroom for the attending children. A physiotherapist from the local hospital volunteered to come once a month and help teach the parents how to cope with their children's physical needs. A primary school teacher who had recently retired agreed to come weekly to help with teaching the older children. Coffee shops in the town agreed to take turns supplying soft drinks, tea, coffee, and snacks for the children, as well as for their parents. Although this provided some relief for the parents with disabled children, all of them were worried about the proper education and future of their children.

Geeta soon managed to arrange a meeting with the education department of the town council to discuss improving resources for the disabled children at the local schools. Geeta found out through one of Ashok's previous colleagues, who had by then moved to Birmingham Hospital in the children's department, about the Midland Spastic Association there. She contacted them by phone and was advised to visit them. She and two other committee members went by bus with their children. They ignored complaining looks aimed at their children from some of the fellow travellers.

It was exciting to see many other children were in the same situation as theirs but were still getting a proper education. They also visited the play centre for the younger children and were told about the youth club for the teenagers. On their journey back home, while the children slept happily in their buggies, they talked about the day. They soon agreed that although these special schools for the disabled children like in Birmingham, Edinburgh, and London were an excellent idea, it was not necessarily the best for everybody as their children would have to be resident in those places without their parents.

In their next annual general meeting, it was agreed that their society would push for integration of their children's education in their local schools rather than isolating them in separate 'institutions'. They also agreed to lobby wherever possible for the local schools to get better resources to care for the education of children with special needs.

Chapter Nine

1977: Ashok as a GP

With guidance from Dr Ahmed, Ashok found working as a GP relatively easy. He particularly enjoyed home visits. Although some of the calls were for trivial reasons, he began to understand more about the family structure in the country.

'I was surprised today to see an old lady of eighty-five years living by herself. Normally she does everything by herself and even maintains a small but lovely garden. Can you imagine this in India?'

'Has she got no family?' asked Geeta, setting out their dinner.

'She has a son and a daughter. Both married. Her daughter lives in another town and comes with the children during school holidays.'

'And her son?'

'He is married with children too. He lives only three miles from here. He comes around every weekend and also helps with mowing the lawn.'

'In India we are too spoiled by having servants for everything.'

'Only people who can afford them. Do you think servants in India have servants for themselves too?'

'True. That's why people here are so strong and independent-minded,' replied Geeta, taking away their finished plates.

Washing the dishes, Ashok said, 'But she must also be lonely a lot of the time. Having your family members close to you, especially young children, must help with that isolation.'

Ashok was on call for the night. As he settled down with Geeta to watch the *ITV News at Ten*, he got a call to see a patient at home. He left quickly with his bag. He found the patient was having a severe asthma attack and was almost breathless. He gave him an injection and then let him a take couple of puffs from the inhaler he had with him.

'Do we need to call the ambulance, doctor?' asked his wife.

'I don't want to go to the hospital,' replied the seventy-year-old.

'Let's give it another ten minutes and see how it goes,' replied Ashok.

'Shall I make you a cup of coffee, doctor?' asked the wife.

'No, thank you very much,' replied Ashok.

Within the next few minutes the patient was feeling a lot better and breathing almost normally.

'You better keep the inhaler with you and come to the surgery in the morning. I will do another prescription for you. And please stop the smoking, both of you. It's not helping your lungs. Call me if you have any further problem at night,' Ashok said as he collected his bag before leaving.

As he was leaving, he heard the patient saying to his wife, 'What would our NHS do without these coloured doctors?'

During his conversation with Dr Ahmed one day, Ashok said, 'I am thinking of preparing for the MRCGP exam. What do you think?'

'Why not? Of course, you don't need Royal College of General Practitioners membership for your job and you are already a full-time GP. But it will be another feather in your cap.'

At home, upon hearing the news, Geeta laughed and said, 'I am coming to the end of my Open University degree, Raju is in primary school, and you preparing for your exam. All three of us will be studying together.'

Ashok and Raju attended Geeta's Open University graduation ceremony. Ashok later sent copies of the photo of Geeta in her graduation robes to both the families in India. A large copy of the photo was also hung in their living room.

After three years, Ashok also got his MRCGP on his first attempt. He had heard that in his local hospital they were introducing a GP training scheme and they needed a recognised practice for the two-year training programme, which included one year of attachment in a GP surgery. Soon their practice became a training practice. By now, Dr Ahmed was thinking of taking early retirement. One of the trainee GPs who had grown up locally, Dr Nicola Adams, was keen to join the practice.

'It will be great to have a woman GP in the practice. Has she done her obstetrics and gynae job yet?' asked Dr Ahmed.

'I think she has. But I will check. She really is a good trainee,' replied Ashok.

In six months, Dr Adams joined the practice, and Dr Ahmed soon took early retirement because of his health. Ashok became the senior partner in the practice. Now with more time in hand, he became the organiser for the GP training programme in the area. He arranged regular GP seminars with the postgraduate centre in the hospital. Until now, the other GP practices in the locality had shown minimal interest in these seminars. But very soon they realised that to recruit new GPs, this would be to their advantage, and slowly got involved. Within five years, Ashok himself became an examiner for the Royal College of General Practitioners.

Geeta arranged a get-together to celebrate on the following Saturday evening, inviting some old friends. Dr and Mrs Ahmed, Subir, who was now a consultant in geriatrics, Kanikadi from Birmingham, Akbar, who was also now a GP in a nearby small town with his wife, Ayesha, as well as Barun, who was now a consultant psychiatrist, his wife, and Deepak, also a GP in Wales, and his wife attended. Ashok was delighted to meet his mentor as well as many old friends. After an elaborate dinner, the conversation turned to settling in the UK.

'We must actively try to integrate into the community, not just stick to the Asian community by every weekend going to each other's houses and comparing chicken curry, dahl, and where to find the best Indian shops,' said Ashok.

'True. But do you really think you can properly integrate with the British people? Let me ask you something. I know you always invite white friends from the hospital and the cricket club to your home for

Christmas parties, barbeques in the summer, and even to some of the children's birthday parties. When was the last time you were invited to any of their family functions?'

'Well, never myself nor Geeta, but Raju had been invited to their children's parties many times.'

'See, that's why they say "An Englishman's house is his castle." It's always protected from the outsiders.'

Everybody nodded and elaborated with their own experiences.

'This is modern England. You are supposed to pretend that you don't notice certain things, such as whites and Asians or blacks,' Barun added.

A few months later, a young man in his early thirties came to see Ashok at the surgery.

'I need a certificate from you, doc. I have hurt my back at work trying to lift some heavy stuff. I don't think I can work for at least a couple of months,' the young man said.

'Let me have a look at you properly first. Can you please take off your top clothes, then lie on the bed and turn around?'

'You really don't need to examine me, doc. My back hurts really bad,' said the patient, reluctantly getting onto the examining couch.

Ashok examined him carefully before saying, 'Your back is fine. You have a bit of muscle spasm only. I will write a prescription for some painkillers for you and you should be able to go back to your work after the weekend.'

After pleading with Ashok unsuccessfully for several minutes, the patient left abruptly, slamming the door behind him and shouting, 'Bloody Paki doctors!'

Mrs Johnson, who was waiting to see Ashok next, got up and said, 'Mind your language, young man! Where are your manners?'

Chapter Ten

1978: The train driver

Wasim had settled down in his job as train driver with British Rail quickly. He was always delighted to take his trains to different cities and towns in the country. Occasionally he also had the opportunity to stay in some of these places. Of all the cities he had visited so far, Edinburgh and London were his favourite places. He loved walking the streets in these places and trying to think about how lucky he was. After three years in the job, he went back to India and married a girl his parents had chosen from the next village. Amina, also a devout Muslim, was an English teacher in a secondary school in the local town.

His cousin Kamal couldn't take the day off to receive them at Heathrow Airport when Wasim returned to the UK with Amina. Instead, Kamal's wife Angie and their son Munar came to meet them. They travelled by bus to Angie and Kamal's house in Wolverhampton from the airport.

When they went to send a telegram to West Bengal the next day, Angie sincerely hoped that Amina would not notice the large painted slogan on a wall near the post office saying *'Keep Britain White'*.

Amina and Wasim stayed with them for three days. Every day, Angie took Amina to shop or just walk the streets to help her get used to the new atmosphere. As a devout Muslim, Amina wore hijab outside the family.

One afternoon, Amina and Angie came out of a coffee shop and were going to cross the street when some men from the other side called out, 'Go back to your Muslim shithole! We don't want you in our country, fucking Pakis.'

Another shouted, 'Are you on your bloody Masjid's payroll here to breed litters of Pakis?'

Amina was stunned and found that Angie had already crossed the road and was confronting the men, who just laughed before moving away.

Angie came back and, holding Amina's hand, said, 'I am ashamed of my country that it allows people like these to roam our streets.'

Still shaken, Amina held Angie's hand and said, 'But I am glad that there are more people like you here than them. Let's go home.'

Within six months, with some help from Angie, Amina managed to find a job in a primary school. She would have preferred to have worked in a secondary school but there was no vacancy around.

After a few months at school she met Geeta, who had come to their school with two other members of her charity for disabled children to promote their education in local schools. Amina was immediately taken by the work of this group. In her village and nearby towns in India she had seen disabled children forced to beg with no hope for any better future. After the talk was over she invited Geeta and her friends to their house, which was nearby, for tea. During their conversation, Geeta came to know that Amina was from Bengal as well.

'It is so lovely to speak in Bengali to someone after a few months,' said Amina.

'Same for me,' answered Geeta with a smile.

She agreed to come for lunch two weekends later in Geeta and Ashok's house. Wasim, Angie, Kamal, and their son Munar were invited too.

After lunch, Munar pointed to the chessboard in the room and asked Ashok, 'Do you know how to play this game? I have seen people playing before and it looks very interesting.'

'Do you want to have a go with me?' asked Ashok.

'I don't know the rules.'

'Don't worry, I will help you.'

'We better get back home soon. It's getting late,' said Angie after a while.

'Both of you must come to our house one day soon,' said Amina.

'And please bring the chess board with you,' Munar said, making everyone laugh.

Their friendship continued over the years when Geeta and Ashok learned more about Kamal and Wasim's families' journey from India to the UK.

Wasim was not the first person in his family from West Bengal to be going to Britain.

His family had lived in a village near the historical town of Murshidabad from well before the time of Nabab Sirajudullah. It is a well-known fact in history that Nabab's commander in chief, Mirjafar, was bribed by the British. This led to the defeat of Sirajudullah, the last independent ruler of Bengal, by Robert Clive in the Battle of Plassey in 1757. The capture of Calcutta by the British, and then all of Bengal, soon followed. This also started the process of British rule in India, which gradually became the jewel in the crown of the British Empire in the world. In every family in Bengal, Hindu or Muslim, calling someone 'Mirjafar', a traitor, is still the worst insult, even today.

Wasim's Chacha Kasim, one of the second cousins of his father, along with another distant relative from Sylhet in East Bengal had joined as lascars in the British merchant ships during the First World War. Like thousands of Indian seamen, they had braved the hazards of aerial bombings and U-boats. At least six and a half thousand Indian seamen lost their lives during the First World War. After working for more than three years in the ship, when the war was over they found the opportunity to stay in Portsmouth as assistant cooks in a local restaurant.

Within the next three years Kasim had moved to the east side of London where there was a thriving Indian community. He started a small Indian restaurant there and within another three years had

165

earned enough money to go back home and get married to a girl from a nearby village. Kasim's Indian restaurant now became more popular locally with his wife doing most of the cooking.

They settled well in East London and had four children, two girls and two boys. One of the girls died of pneumonia in the first year of her life. Both his sons joined the army in 1940 to fight in the war. Kasim was too old. One of the boys died in the war in France. During the Blitz, their house was turned into gravel and both Kasim's wife and their only daughter had died. Kasim survived as he was working in the restaurant at the time. After the war, his only surviving son, Kamal, joined British Rail as a ticket collector. In 1959, somewhat against his father's wishes, Kamal married a girl originally from Newcastle who was not a Muslim.

Until now, Kasim was just about managing to run his restaurant with hired cooks and waiters but was finding it increasingly difficult. Feeling old and frail, he soon sold his restaurant and was happy to be invited by his son and daughter-in-law to come and live with them in Wolverhampton. The only time he got out of the house these days was on Friday when he went for prayer at the nearby mosque. He now had only one wish: he wanted to go back to Murshidabad for one last time.

'You are not well enough to travel alone,' Kamal had said a few times over the months to his father.

His wife, Angie, a primary school teacher with a nine-year-old son, had been asking Kamal for a while if they could all visit India one day. She had been fascinated by the stories of India since she was a child. She also wanted to see the Taj Mahal with Kamal.

Kamal did not want to explain to her that as a non-Muslim woman going to his traditional Muslim family, it may not be the ideal experience she was hoping for.

After a few months of tiring talks from his old father, as well as from his own wife, Kamal agreed to take leave for a month and travel to the country of his father, which he had never visited himself.

It was arranged that the family would travel next year in 1970 in late January when the weather would not be so hot there. They would spend a few days with their family first before Kamal, Angie, and their son would go for a holiday of their own to Calcutta first and then by train to Delhi and Agra before returning home. Kasim would stay with his family for six to eight months, at which point Kamal would return there for a few days to bring him back home.

While he did not want to show this to Angie, Kamal himself was also very excited to be travelling to India. But he was also worried about how his family would accept Angie, who was brought up as a Christian. He knew that Angie and Munar were excited about the travel but he was not sure how she would feel faced with the society where women were still backward. His other worry was about language. He understood that most women in the family did not understand English.

Angie had learned only to say 'Sallam' and 'Alaikum Salaam'.
Munar, however, learned a few more Indian words and practiced on Angie and Wasim. He would say, 'Amar nam Munar. Ami bhalo achi. Apni kemon achen?'
Wasim smiled as he could speak Bengali reasonably well.
Angie asked, 'What does that mean?'
'My name is Munar. I am well. How are you?'
'I need to practice with you more,' said Angie, laughing.

Kamal should not have worried. In the family home in Murshidabad they were treated almost as royalty. Angie was soon a big hit with the women and was treated as one of their own. Most of the older women could not speak English, but there was always someone who could understand English and speak a little, although Angie had to learn to speak slowly as her Geordie accent was not easy to follow for most. Two of Kamal's second cousins, girls of about the same age as Angie, were always trying to be there to make sure she was having fun. One of them worked as a nurse in the district hospital while the other was a school teacher. Both had taken a week off from their work to spend time with Angie. Munar was always playing outside with the boys, cricket, volleyball, and even kabaddi.

'You know something, I have never tasted food so good in my life. And everyone is so kind to make sure we enjoy it here. I don't know what you have been worrying about!' Angie said to Kamal in the night.

'I agree. I am sorry that I had not come over to my family sooner,' replied Kamal.

The next day, the whole family, twelve adults and seven children, went out for a day trip, first to Hazarduari Palace, the palace with a thousand doors, in Murshidabad and then in the afternoon to Imambara, a Muslim congregation hall nearby. Kasim was not well enough and stayed at home to be looked after by the maidservants.

After visiting the palace in the morning, the family sat by the Bhagirathi River for their picnic lunch. The family had brought rice flour roti, thick chickpea dahl, and beautifully cooked bageri, a small, quail-like bird.

Wrapping a bageri with rice roti, Kamal crunched happily and, once finished, said, 'I think I am in paradise.'

'Have another one,' said one of his cousins, as she put more on his plate. 'There is still plenty there.'

Trying not to look at Angie, Kamal went for it happily. In the afternoon, they visited the nearby Imambara, one of the largest congregation halls for Muslims in India.

Next evening, a first cousin of Kamal's arrived from Jalpaiguri. He was working there for Indian Railways as a train driver for the last six years. After dinner, he asked Kamal about his prospect of finding a job in the UK. Unmarried, Wasim was keen to travel to see the other side of the world. Kamal explained to him that there was currently actually a shortage of experienced train drivers in UK. Many older drivers were taking early retirement and there was lack of interest among the younger generation to become train drivers. He agreed to find out more and write back to Wasim as soon as he got back to England.

Three day later, when it was time for them to leave for Calcutta, the whole family were in tears. The older women in the family hugged Angie and Munar tightly and said, wiping their tears with the anchals of their saris, 'Come back soon.'

Munar was in tears too.

Her own eyes also flooding with tears, Angie said, 'Most definitely we will.'

After falling asleep in the train from Murshidabad to Sealdah in Calcutta, Munar woke up mesmerised by the throngs of people covering every inch of the platforms outside. In Calcutta they stayed with the family of another cousin of Kamal's who was an engineer. Of all the places they visited, including the famous Victoria Memorial Hall, Nakhoda Masjid, and Chowronghee, Angie found the walk by the Ganges near the Eden Gardens to be her favourite.

Kamal had heard of the famous Sabir's restaurant in Chandni Chowk from many of his friends from Calcutta. One evening he invited his cousin's family to Sabir's for dinner. Following his cousin's suggestion, they ordered the famous mutton rezala with butter naan bread.

'This is food to die for,' said Angie after finishing her plate.

'Don't die until you have tried the firni, their famous dessert,' said the engineer cousin.

Munar enjoyed the one-and-a-half-day train journey from Howrah station to Delhi more than anyone else. He especially loved when at the stations on the way, the vendors were trying to sell varieties of food through the railed windows of their sleeper compartment.

Although they visited and enjoyed the famous historical Mughal sites in Delhi, both Kamal and Angie felt Calcutta was the bustling city to their liking. Initially, they were shocked by how dirty it was in Agra outside the Taj Mahal, but once they entered the place in the late afternoon they were stunned by its beauty. With the pink clouds of the evening, the palace had turned itself into a fairy castle. Soon, the Taj Mahal started to take on a faint golden yellow glow from the full moon in the sky above. The palace of love became truly magical for both, who sat quietly holding each other's hands, enjoying the most beautiful thing they had ever imagined in their lives.

Back in the UK, Kamal soon enquired about jobs as a train driver for his cousin. He was told that there may be job for Wasim as an apprentice and if he proved suitable he might even get a permanent job. Kamal had brought with him his cousin's CV and a signed blank paper for application. He filled out the application and submitted it with Wasim's CV the next day. A few weeks later he received the reply accepting his cousin as an apprentice with British Rail. He immediately telegrammed and sent the letter with his own sponsorship letter by registered post to his cousin. Wasim had already managed to get his passport ready by the time he got the letters from Kamal. It took him less than three months to get a visa before he sent a telegram to his cousin about his arrival date and time in the UK.

Kamal went to meet him at Heathrow. Back at their house, while Angie was preparing her own version of onion bhaji and tea for the guest from India, Kamal sat down with Wasim and asked about his own father.

'Wait. I have something for you,' replied his cousin.

He opened his suitcase and at first took out the presents for Munar, a set of blue and gold kurta pajama. They were slightly too big for Munar, but Angie assured him that he was growing so quickly these days it would only be a couple of months before they would be a perfect fit. Next, Wasim took out a beautiful red and green Kashmiri sari for Angie.

Looking at thrilled Angie, Kamal said, 'You know her taste in colour better than me.'

Wasim then took out an envelope and gave it to Kamal. It was a letter from his father. He had written that now in his age he did not want to make the long journey back to England. Although he missed his grandson very much, he would like to spend the rest of his life with the family in West Bengal. In the envelope there were separate letters for Munar and Angie too from many members of the family.

Two weeks later, Wasim joined as an apprentice train driver. He was the oldest of all the six apprentices but he was probably more experienced than some of the train drivers he was learning from. In the beginning, he was often ridiculed for his poor English and accent.

Wasim always brought his lunch in a box from home and ate alone.

'Why don't you join us in the canteen?' asked his supervisor.

'What special stuff is there in your lunchbox anyway?' asked another apprentice.

'It smells strong. Is it some sort of curry?' asked another.

Wasim only smiled. He also learned to ignore their teasing him for praying a few times a day during his work time, although he always made sure not to miss anything on his schedule and worked late to finish any work. In the yard, however, he soon earned the attention of the seniors and especially of his supervisor, a burly Irishman named Brendan, for his ability when there were any breakdowns.

During these few months, he stayed with Kamal's family. Angie and Kamal made sure to get halal meat for their guest, who was a devout Muslim. After four months, a job was advertised for a train driver and he applied for it. His supervisor interviewed him and announced later that day that Wasim had gotten the job. Wasim brought the news to Kamal and Angie in the evening with a packet of gifts for the family from the money he had saved from his apprenticeship pay.

At the end of his first day's work, his supervisor said, 'Let's all go out for a drink at the Railway Inn pub to celebrate.'

Wasim had to decline politely, explaining that he did not drink.

As he was leaving, someone muttered behind him, 'He does not drink, but imagine, he is allowed by his religion to have more wives than all of us combined!'

Wasim walked on. A few evenings later, he invited the supervisor and some of his colleagues for a dinner at an Indian restaurant nearby. Brendan and four others were waiting outside the restaurant while a couple of them were having their cigarettes. They were startled to see Wasim running frantically towards them.

Soon they realised he was being chased by a group of white young men shouting, 'Paki! Paki bastard! Go home!'

As soon as Wasim reached the restaurant, Brendan stood in front of him and shouted at the chasing group, 'Come up here, you shit, if you want a fight!'

The group stopped ten metres away and shouted towards Wasim, 'We will get you one day soon, and no fucking Irish will save you!'

Brendan and Wasim's colleagues gave them a chase but they ran away quickly towards the direction they had come from.

Later in the restaurant, even the tasty celebratory Indian meal could not save the dour mood hanging over them. By the end of the evening, as they were tasting some very sweet Indian gulab jamun with ice cream, a brick was thrown at the window of the restaurant from outside. Brendan joined the restaurant owner running out of the front door to chase them, but the assailants had already run away.

Before leaving the restaurant, after giving a squeeze on Wasim's shoulder, Brendan said, 'Don't let a few punks intimidate you. Stand up to them when you can. We face similar hatred around here, being Irish.'

Chapter Eleven

1980: Holiday in Calcutta

Geeta eagerly opened the airmail letter marked for urgent delivery from her father. Her youngest sister, Meera, was going to be married in three months' time. Since coming over to the UK nearly ten years back, neither Geeta nor Ashok had been back to India.

When Ashok returned home after his evening surgery, Geeta said, 'We are going to Calcutta. You have to take at least one month of holiday. It's Meera's wedding.'

Ashok read the letter before saying, 'We must go. I don't think I will able to get four weeks of holiday, but I will try. Maybe we can find some locum.'

Travelling with a bouncy young boy by long-haul flight was tiring. Both of them were exhausted by the time they reached Calcutta. But they soon perked up at the Dumdum Airport to find that not only Geeta's sister Meera but all the members from both sides of the family were there to meet Raju for the first time. Raju was happy to be swapped from one person to another. The star of the show, he took to his Indian family as if he had grown up there all his life.

As was the norm, they first went to Ashok's parents' house where they were welcomed with specially ordered out of season sandesh made from nolen gur, jaggery. Ashok was happy that his old room had not been changed much since they had last been there.

'Raju can sleep with us if he wants,' said Ashok's mother, with Raju hanging on to her lap.

'We will see how it goes,' replied Geeta, smiling.

However, both Ashok and Geeta were rather happy when, at around midnight, there was a knock on their door from Ashok's mother.

'Sorry, he wants you now,' she said as she handed over the half-awake child to them.

They did not have time to get over their jetlag properly as within the short period they would have to visit so many people, and of course the wedding was almost there. They left for Geeta's parents' house soon after breakfast the next morning.

Again, there were sweets, this time famous Bagbazar's sponge rassgulla. While Raju was being shown around by her mother like a rare, expensive Benarasi, Geeta went with Saroja to Meera's bedroom. A photograph of the groom was passed around to her. Geeta found out for the first time that this was not an arranged marriage, but the first 'love marriage' in the family!

'How did you two meet?'

'He was two years senior to me in my college. I was upset one day after my teacher had given out to me about my test exam results in front of the whole class. She said I was wasting my time doing a BA Honours. In the college canteen, I was sitting by myself in a table by the corner. I must have looked very upset.'

'And the prince came to the distressed princess and rescued her,' interjected Saroja.

'Didi?' Meera said shyly, as she gently tried to push Saroja away.

'Well that was almost two and a half years back. Of course, you know that Meera got first class in her honours degree. Lots of the credit goes to Manas, who had given her so much private tuition in that time,' said Saroja. 'We don't know what else he was giving her tuition for at the same time though!' she added with a wink.

Meera pushed Saroja hard as her cheeks and ears in her dark brown face went the colour of soft honey.

'Neither of you wrote to me about any of this,' Geeta complained while hiding a secret sigh about what she had been missing all this time being so far away from her own family.

Neither Saroja nor Meera had the heart to tell Geeta that it was because she had so much going on over there in her own life, not all good news either, since she went over to the UK.

Although the wedding was only four days away, their house was almost ready for the occasion. Geeta was surprised to find that although the wedding itself would take place in the family house, for the reception a hall only five minutes' walk away had been hired. Apparently, this was more common these days with weddings in Calcutta.

Lunch with everybody was at around two thirty in the afternoon, and her mother herself had prepared Geeta's all-time favourite, dahl with fish head.

After running around the place the whole day, Raju was half asleep when the three sisters went in their second new white Ambassador to pick up the matching blouse which was being altered to go with Meera's special wedding Benarasi. Going back to the same shop where her own wedding clothes were bought a few years ago brought back many sweet memories for Geeta.

Meera surprised both her elder sisters by suggesting they go to the College Street coffee house after. By this time, Raju had properly woken up and was mesmerised by the traffic of thousands of people with buses and cars honking through them. When they arrived outside the place, they were greeted by a young man in rimmed glasses with a broad smile on his face.

'You never told me Manas was going to be here,' said Saroja.

Meera introduced Manas to Geeta and Raju.

'Hello, Manas. How long have you been waiting here?' Geeta asked.

'Oh, not that long. Only forty-five minutes. I am used to waiting longer for Meera,' he replied as he turned towards her.

'Let me carry him upstairs,' said Manas as he lifted Raju up.

Once upstairs and taken to a table by the waiter, Manas sat Raju on a chair next to him before producing a wrapped up packet from his handloom cotton side bag.

'It's something small for him,' said Manas.

Meera helped Raju with the packet and took out a soft and cuddly toy tiger. Raju was mesmerised with the stripes of the animal.

'After all, he is a Bengali. So I got a small Royal Bengal tiger for him to remember the country,' said Manas.

It turned out that Manas had a younger sister called Arunima who was still in college. He himself was now working for the State Bank of India in its Vivekananda Road branch in Calcutta. He said to Geeta, 'My sister Arunima is very keen to meet you. We have all heard about your charity work in the UK from Meera.'

At the end of the evening, before saying goodbye to them, Manas said, 'I am a bit scared about the wedding in few days. What about you, Meera?'

'I am terrified. I wish we could just have a simple ceremony at the registrar's office,' replied Meera.

Both Saroja and Geeta reassured them and Geeta said, 'Just go along with what everyone asks you do. Remember that the wedding will not only be a great memory for you two but that the families want to celebrate too.'

After coming home, Geeta asked, 'Where are Aratidi and Madanda?'

While she was unwrapping some presents she had brought for both of them, she was told, 'Aratidi passed away two years back. Madanda still lives with us but is now too old to work.'

Geeta could not stop crying.

While the girls had been out by themselves with Raju, Ashok took himself to meet his friends in the medical college. He was greeted warmly by the canteen manager, who he had known since his college days. Even some of the waiters who were still there knew him well and asked him if he was still playing cricket and volleyball in England. He soon learned that most of his classmates who were working there before had either moved on to other hospitals or gone to full-time private practice. But he was happy to find soon that two of his classmates, one now the senior resident medical officer in surgery and the other a radiologist, were still working in the medical college. Soon, the three met for lunch.

'How are you getting on in England?' asked Sumon, the surgical RMO.

'You must be close to becoming a consultant in surgery there by now?' asked Bikash, the radiologist.

Ashok realised that his stories of upheaval in England had not reached his friends in the medical college. In some ways, he was relieved to share his personal stories of the last few years with his old classmates. Both listened carefully while lighting Charminar cigarettes for each other.

'Do you want one?'

'No. I still don't smoke. I think I have got my quota of nicotine for life through passive smoking while spending time with you all in my college days here.'

They both just laughed, deeply inhaling their smoke.

'I always thought you were going be one of the best surgeons from our college. All our professors said you had it in you. Do you miss surgery now that you are a full-time GP?'

Ashok thought for a moment before replying, 'Honestly, no. I thought I would when I could not get any full-time registrar job in surgery and then we had the situation around our child. But since I moved to becoming a GP, I have enjoyed every minute of it. There is so much more than doing an operation and hopefully sending them home better a few days later. There's so much more, and more afterwards, for the patient and the family to be cared for.'

'I need to get back for my afternoon list. If you are around, it would be nice to see you again in a few days. Usually on Wednesday morning I am free after the ward round,' Sumon said, leaving.

'I'd better get back as well,' said Bikash.

Ashok sat there alone reminiscing in the canteen, now almost empty after the lunch rush, and ordered another cup of tea.

'Oh, could I have it with no sugar, please?'

'They are all made with milk and sugar. I can make you a special one, but it will take time,' replied the waiter.

'Don't worry, I will have the usual one.'

The next three days before the wedding were hectic to say the least. The number of the bride groom's party this time was only forty and the total number of guests was going to be no more than two hundred and fifty at the most. The decorators had taken over the decorating of the reception hall as well as the inside of the family house where the wedding ceremony was due to take place. Although the three regular cooks usually hired for cooking at large family occasions were there, this time they were going to cook only the family meals leading up to the wedding and the day after. With all the near and distant family members arriving for the wedding, the number of meals to cook was going to be no less than forty each time for lunches as well as for dinners. In between the main meals they also had the task of producing varieties of snacks such as pakoras, samosas, and begunis.

The family storeroom next to the kitchen was now almost hazardously full. Sandesh, rasgullas, jilabis, and cooking ingredients such as mustard oil, flour, lentils, and spices were stored there, with Juthika holding the key wrapped in a knot around her anchal. She was called to open the store every so often but that was better than things going astray. Occasionally, when she was really busy with other things, Saroja or now Geeta could be trusted with the keys. Any new arrival was greeted with a glass of water and a plate of sweets from the storeroom, to be followed with snacks and a cup of tea or coffee as per their choice. Anyone arriving within two hours either side of lunch or dinner was automatically expected to stay for the full meal. The main dinner for the wedding night was going to be prepared and served by the caterers this time, with less of a hustle inside the house that way.

Geeta's father called her to an empty room on the second day of her arrival. He closed the door lightly before putting a hand on her shoulder and then started sobbing.

'There was nothing I could write in a letter that would have come anywhere near how I felt with all the tough times you had to go through over there. I felt so helpless.'

Geeta just held on to her father tightly with tears rolling down both their cheeks.

Someone pushed the door from outside and came in. It was her mother. Seeing them in such a state, she sat down next to Geeta and put her hands around her.

'I don't know how you went through all this over there by yourself. Since coming back, I have given Puja to all the gods. But sometimes I don't know if the gods really have time for people like us,' she said.

For the first time since her daughter had died, Geeta cried silently for a long time, holding on to her parents.

A few minutes later, Meera came in with Raju, who was looking for his mother now after his shower. Geeta and her mother wiped their faces with the anchals of their saris and her father took out a handkerchief to wipe his. Meera put on a new outfit the family had bought for Raju. It was a bit big for him but he looked delightful as ever. Both the grandparents could not take their eyes off him.

After giving Raju a hug, Geeta's father said, 'I'd better go and check what the decorators are up to,' as he left.

'We may have to order more rasgullas. I thought two hundred would have been enough for the family itself,' her mother said before getting up.

While Raju played with his toys, Meera sat facing Geeta for a few minutes before saying, 'Didi, I am so sorry.'

'Let's take Raju to the roof. He had never been up on an open roof,' said Geeta as she got up and gathered her son.

While they were on the roof, Meera took Raju, showing him people from other roofs flying kites. He was more intrigued by the drying saris of various colours hanging from the line.

Soon Jiten came up and said, 'I am dying for a cigarette. My room has been given to our eighty-year-old aunt from Bankura and her daughter, our cousin Purnima.'

'Purnima scares me. I know she is a headteacher in a girls' school but, she thinks we are in her class too' said Meera.

Jiten took Raju from Meera and put him on his shoulders.

'Be careful,' said Geeta as he smiled at them.

After a few minutes, Meera asked, 'Do you want me to bring you two a cup of tea here?'

'That sounds great, Meera, and some pakoras if you can,' replied Jiten.

Once she had left, Jiten turned towards Geeta with Raju still on his shoulder.

'When you and Ashok were going through such a difficult time on your own, I so wished I could actually talk to you.'

Geeta looked far away over the roof.

'Sending a letter which would arrive three weeks later was never enough. Man had landed on the moon a few years back. Isn't it stupid that you have a telephone line there and we have a telephone here in our house, but we still cannot talk to each other when we need to? We can make trunk calls to any city in India but outside the country we can only send telegrams!'

Geeta came over and held Jiten's hand before saying, 'I know, Dada. It's the isolation that gets you. You can learn to live a completely different way of life in another country, but when you really need your most loved ones they are thousands of miles away.'

Raju wanted to get down from Jiten's shoulder and run around the roof pushing the drying saris. Jiten started giving him chase. Soon they were both laughing, playing hide and seek behind the saris. A soft smile came over Geeta's face.

'Here is your tea and pakora. I have to go down now. The relatives who live in Asansol have come. I don't think I ever met them in my life,' said Meera before reluctantly trying to leave them.

'No, you did meet them. During Geeta's wedding. But you were too young to remember them all,' replied Jiten as he sipped his tea.

'I better go down to meet them as well. Are you okay with Raju for a while up here?' asked Geeta.

'Oh yes. We are going to carry on with our hide and seek behind the saris.'

Ashok came to the house to find that Geeta was busy paying her respects to the distant relatives. After paying his own respects to them, he asked Geeta, 'Where is Raju?'

'Oh, he is playing on the roof with Jiten.'

Ashok went up to find that Jiten and Raju had been joined by a few other boys and girls playing hide and seek.

Jiten left Raju playing with the other children and came over to Ashok.

'How are you, Ashok? I hear you are now a fully-fledged GP over there. Are you enjoying it?'

'Very much so. What about you? How is your job going at the college? I find from the newspaper headlines after coming back here that the political situation in West Bengal is so volatile.'

'We will have a proper chat another time. But yes, the leftist government here has let people down. I remember you were a supporter of the Naxal movement before you left. Are you still involved in politics in the UK now?'

'No, it's a very different situation there. No, Raju—don't pull the sari down, it will tear. Listen, we'd better go down now. Must find a proper time to talk to you about this. I really mean it. In the UK people talk about football, cricket, family, jobs, holidays, but political discussion, except during some big news on the TV, is usually frowned upon as a topic.'

In the next few days, Geeta hardly had time to think about anything else with the excitement about the wedding. She was in charge of doing the makeup for Meera on the day of the marriage ceremony. She took out the handbag full of cosmetics she had brought over for this special occasion.

The wedding ceremony itself went very smoothly. During the reception dinner, Geeta met Manas's sister, Arunima, who was keen to talk to her about her OU degree. It also turned out that she was involved in working as a volunteer in a refugee camp only forty kilometres outside Calcutta. Geeta was interested to visit the place with her after the seven-day wedding ceremony was over. Raju, who was asleep most of the time during the marriage ceremony, was in full form two days later when the bride's family and friends went for the reception of boubhat ceremony in the groom's house.

A few days later in the morning, Geeta and Arunima went for a few hours to visit the refugee camp. On the forty-kilometre journey, Geeta learned that Arunima went there once a week to do English teaching for the refugee children at the camp.

'I usually take the first bus to come here. The bus coming this way in the morning is almost empty. Takes me just over an hour. Then I go back by lunchtime before the late afternoon rush.'

They asked their driver to park their car away from the camp and wait there for them. From a distance, Geeta could see hundreds of sagging tents in rows. In the muddy roads between them, young children in ragged clothes, some of them younger than Raju, were running around. Arunima took her to the camp's office and introduced to one of the camp directors who himself was a volunteer at the place for over twelve years.

'I am glad you are here today, Aru. I know you are on leave this week because of your brother's wedding. By the way, sorry I could not get to Calcutta for the reception from here, but thanks for the invitation anyway. Are you able to spare a couple of hours now with the teaching? Rekha has not turned up today, I know her son was not so well. I hope it's nothing to do with that.'

Arunima looked towards Geeta.

'It's okay with me. Can I come with you?'

'Of course. You can help me.'

The classroom turned out to be a larger tent with several wooden benches with a table, a chair, and a blackboard at the other end.

'Today we will learn about how to make conversation in English. You can help me.'

Geeta nodded.

A bell was rung at 10 a.m. About fifty children aged between four and twelve years old rushed in, chattering to themselves, and took their seats on the benches. It was a bit dark inside the tent but became lighter when Arunima asked the older children to open the flaps of the tent.

She then introduced Geeta, saying, 'We have a new teacher for today.'

She called out the children's names and they said, 'Yes, Miss,' before coming over and collecting their notebooks.

'We keep the notebooks in the classroom. If they take them home, they often forget to bring them over for the class or they get soiled.'

'Now, Angur, can you tell us how you would ask for something in English, say, if you wanted a bunch of bananas in a shop?' she then asked.

182

The young, very slim girl of about eight years with faded and torn clothes stood up. 'I want some bananas.'

'Very good,' said Geeta. 'But in English, always try to add "please" when you ask for something.'

The girl looked at Arunima and then repeated, 'Can I have some bananas, please.'

'Very good. What about you, Aziz? How do you ask in English for a bus ticket to go to Calcutta?'

Skin and bone Aziz in his dirty shorts stood up and said, 'One ticket for Calcutta for me,' and then added, 'Oh, sorry, one ticket please.'

Then a story from a book about going on a holiday was read by Geeta to the class.

The class finished after about an hour. Some of the older children had been taking notes in their books, while the younger ones just listened. All the books were returned back. The children huddled around Arunima and Geeta.

'Do you want to come to our house?' asked one little boy of about the same age as Raju to Geeta.

She looked towards Arunima, who said, 'I suppose we have time to meet Naru's mother.'

Several children followed in a procession, Naru holding hands with Geeta and Arunima. Naru's mother was cooking outside her tent on an open mud stove burning with cow dung cakes and charcoal.

On seeing them approaching, she put the anchal of her sari over her head and said to Arunima, 'Namaskar, Didi.'

Naru introduced Geeta, saying, 'This is our new teacher.'

'Sorry I am here only for today,' replied Geeta.

'Namaskar. Do you want to come inside? The sun is so hot now after the rain yesterday. But at least we can dry up some clothes today and it will also dry up the mud outside.'

Two families lived in the tent. By the far end of the tent from Naru's family was an elderly man sitting on his haunches by the bed where a woman was lying under a ragged cloth.

'Kakima has not been well for some time. They think it may be TB or something. She is too unwell to go for an x-ray in the town hospital.'

She straightened the rag over her own mattress on the floor and motioned them to sit. After sitting on the bed, Geeta asked, 'What about her husband? He does not look too well either.'

'No, he is all right. Only he cannot move around much these days with his knees gone in his old age.'

'How long have they been in this camp?'

'I am not sure but I think they said they came over during the big riot in 1948 after the partition.'

'Do they have any children?'

'Not now. They had a daughter who was about twelve when we came here. Then one day she disappeared. They cried and cried. The police came over as well but she never come back. Maybe she was taken by someone to Sonagachi.'

Geeta had heard before about the cheap brothels of Sonagachi in Calcutta. She asked, 'How long have you been here?'

'We came over here when Pakistan and India were fighting. Must be over ten or fifteen years now.'

'That was in 1965,' Arunima reminded Geeta.

'I had my first baby born here. He died the same day. Naru was born after.'

'Where is your husband?'

'Oh, he goes out in the daytime to find some odd jobs. I think he is today working for a builder.'

'They cannot go out very far from the camp as they have no passport. If they are found by the police outside this place they may be arrested as illegal immigrants,' Arunima said.

'I have to go soon and collect my ration. It's always a big queue there. Do you want to see the place?' Naru's mother asked Geeta.

'No, we'd better get back. My son will be missing me.'

'How old is your son?'

'He will be seven in a few months.'

184

'That's nice. Same as my Naru. They are lovely in that age, aren't they? Always running from place to place and bringing all the dirt inside,' she replied with a tender smile towards her son.

'All the children look so malnourished,' Geeta said to Meera on the way back.

'The ration they get is never enough and the family can rarely afford anything like fresh milk, eggs, or meat. Only rarely they may get some dried milk,' replied Arunima.

They went back to the office to thank the camp director. Walking back to the car, Arunima asked Geeta, 'Are you okay? You look really down. I know it is quite grim over there.'

Geeta did not reply, just looked away.

Arunima took her hand and said, 'I heard from Meera about your first child. I am so sorry.'

The journey back took much longer because of the traffic which was stuck behind a protest march near a small jute mill which had apparently closed down suddenly only recently. Arunima explained that the refugee camp had almost 5,000 residents and over two-thirds of them were children under sixteen. Many of the children were born there and had not known life any other way. There were many who came over during the partition of Bengal for the second time into West Bengal and East Pakistan in 1947. Then many came during the 1948 riots and more after the Barisal riot in 1950.

'Did you know after the Barisal riot almost a quarter of the Calcutta population was made up of refugees from East Bengal?'

'Yes, I read about it in the newspaper. Also, the next big number came over during the war between India and Pakistan in 1965. I was in high school by then. I think the largest number went over to camps in Assam,' replied Geeta.

'During the Bangladesh war in 1971, over ten million came over to West Bengal to avoid the torture by the East Pakistani army. Most went back after Bangladesh was liberated but almost a million stayed,' Arunima said.

She added, 'Once from undivided India, now they are neither Indian nor Pakistani or Bangladeshi. They are just refugees. Every year some of them leave the camp and try to find some sort of a life working or begging in the streets of Calcutta or other towns. It's the children I feel deeply about. What kind of future do they have without going to any regular school?'

'And they are just refugees, not the real responsibility of any government,' Geeta said.

'Where do you want me to go first?' asked the driver.

'Oh, we are already back to Calcutta! Let us drop you at your place first,' said Geeta.

'No, no. You'd better go back to Raju now. I will take a tram or a bus from there.'

When Arunima was getting out of the car, Geeta said, 'Aru. Thank you so much for today. Are you sure you don't want to come with me to Ashok's house?'

'No, I'd better go. Geeta, I enjoyed the day a lot too. Thank you.'

In the same morning, Ashok had come over from his parents' to Geeta's house. As he was getting Raju ready to take him to their place, Jiten came down with his breakfast of luchi and begun bhaja on a plate.

'Are you leaving now?' he asked.

'Yes. Are you free this morning? Then you can come along to our house as well and we can finish what we were talking about the other day,' replied Ashok.

'I have to meet someone at five. I am free until then. Give me five minutes.'

Ashok's parents were delighted to have their grandson for the day and Ashok's mother took him straight on her lap, giving him a big cuddle.

'We have something in the room upstairs you will love. Let's go. Hello, Jiten. Do you want some coffee?'

'Don't worry about us, Ma. You two go ahead and play with him. I will ask Madhuridi to make some coffee for us,' replied Ashok.

After the housemaid brought them their coffee in the sitting room, Ashok said, 'Being so far away, I don't hear much about what is

186

happening here in the political scene. In the news I get there in the UK newspapers or on TV they don't even mention the Naxal movement. They have been all busy talking about the heroics of Americans in "saving" Vietnam, and now their retreat and the cold war.'

'I remember well that you supported the Naxals, finding medicines, bandages, and plasters for the comrades and even giving them shelter in your hostel. Because of the extreme police brutality, most of the party members have now gone underground or are dead.'

'Are you still involved?'

Jiten, without answering directly, said, 'Do you remember the guy who had been shot in his arm by the police while trying to escape the night raid by the army in Shobhabazar?'

'Yes, there was no way he could go to any hospital because he would have been arrested straightway. I went over to the hideout with instruments and dressings. Luckily, the bullet had gone through and was only lodged under the skin, not injuring any vessels or nerves. I also remember he was a star student at Presidency College.'

'Yes. He was killed three years back in another police raid.'

While they were talking, Ashok's parents had been busy playing with Raju in Ashok's room. He was then given a shower and had his favourite lunch of rice, omelette, and crispy besan phuluri followed by khir payesh. While Grandma was busy cleaning up Raju after lunch, Ashok's father came down and joined Jiten and Ashok.

Catching the drift of their conversation, he said, 'I am so sorry that so many of the bright and truly committed young people have died or are in jail. Such a waste. And what have we gained? The most corrupt people are still in power and, the only people who are successful are the ones who pander and bribe the politicians, who are even more corrupt than them.'

Ashok tried to reply by saying, 'But Baba, just cause is always just cause.'

'But have we got anywhere except the thousands of young people dying or still incarcerated?'

Jiten said, 'Mesomasay, you are probably right. Maybe it is now the time to think about what the best way of pushing the movement

187

in India forward is. The model which worked in China a few decades back may not be the one we need here in the eighties.'

Ashok's mother came down, saying, 'He has gone to sleep. I am asking them to get lunch ready for all of you. I will wait for Geeta,' and then asked, 'Jiten, do you want to have a shower before? What about you, Ashok?'

'I will show Jiten the shower. We won't be long, Ma.'

Geeta came back as the men were finishing their lunch.

'Do you want to have lunch first or a shower? Ma is waiting for you,' said Ashok.

'I will have a shower first. I am all sticky from the heat. Where is Raju?'

'He is having a nap in our room.'

Geeta went up to the room with Ashok and together they watched Raju sleeping peacefully with all four limbs splayed and his grandmother gently stroking his hair.

She said to Ashok, 'We are so lucky.'

After lunch, she explained to Ashok that there were around twenty refugee camps around the border with Bangladesh near Calcutta alone. She was visibly upset with the plight of the children in the refugee camp in particular.

'Even the disabled children get more attention and care from the society in the UK than these chronically malnourished boys and girls in the refugee camps. What future can they look forward to?' she said to them during her dinner.

A week later, the three of them returned back to the UK, a country they had now made their home.

Chapter Twelve

1985: Friends from Uganda

Prakash and Madhunath, two old friends, went to London together for the day with the idea to meet up with some common friends from Uganda who were apparently doing very well there.

In the late afternoon, while walking by a park near East Ham Station, they were chased by five skinheads shouting, 'You bloody Pakis—this is not your country! Go back home!'

The headline news of teenager Akhtar Ali Baig's murder by the skinheads, which had happened nearby only a few years back, was still fresh in their minds. Prakash and Madhunath tried to run away from them. One of the skinheads threw a beer bottle at them which caught Madhunath on the side of his head and he started bleeding. The chasing group moved away laughing. Prakash took Madhunath to the local A&E where he needed eight stiches in his head.

'We don't really fit in here; we never will,' said Madhunath, coming out of A&E with a bandage on his head.

'No, there will always be ignorant people like these anywhere in the world. We came here with nothing and now, within just over ten years, our families have built comfortable lives through helping each other. And more importantly, our children are doing very well here,' replied Prakash.

Cutting short their break in London, the next morning they took the train from St Pancras back to Leicester. Ashok got onto the same

189

train from Bedford to go to Leicester where he had a GP seminar the next day and, he was due to speak. His car had to be sent to the garage the day before and he had decided to take a train. He had plans to do some shopping in Leicester in the afternoon. In the late morning, the train was relatively empty and he found a small compartment with two elderly gentleman sitting by the window.

'Are these seats empty?' Ashok asked politely.

'Sure. Please take a seat, son,' said Prakash.

'Thank you,' said Ashok and then, looking at Madhunath, said, 'That's a big bandage on your head. Did you have an accident?'

'You could say that,' said Madhunath, and then asked, 'Are you an Indian?'

Ashok replied, 'I was born in Nairobi but grew up in Calcutta before coming over here.'

Soon they found out that he was the son of their old friend the eye surgeon Pradeep in Nairobi.

'How is Dr Basu? Is he also in the UK?' asked Prakash.

'No, he is in Calcutta. He is getting old but is very well.'

They asked him what he was doing in the UK and where he was going to on this train. After hearing that he was going to Leicester as well, both of them insisted that he to come and stay with them.

'You will meet your old friends Rajesh and Sanjay as both of them will be home later today.'

Ashok explained that he had a seminar all day the next day but would be delighted to spend time with them until tomorrow morning.

'It will be fantastic to see them both,' he added.

'You will also meet the other young ones. My daughter Devi is now a doctor like you, and Madunath's daughter Neela is a lawyer.'

Ashok had not arranged any place to stay in Leicester and was going to find a hotel after getting there. He agreed enthusiastically to stay as a guest in Madunath's house. Sanjay, Neela, and Kalpana were at home already. Soon, Rajesh and Milan arrived as well. Devi had gone to her hospital and a message was sent to her to come over as soon she could manage. Sumit was due to finish his duty at the police station in the late afternoon and would be back soon.

Sanjay, Rajesh, and Ashok could have hardly recognised each other until Sanjay's mother brought out an old album with photos of them playing together in the back garden, and also one of them in their school uniforms. After a couple of hours, the three old friends went for a walk down the streets of Leicester, just having fun talking to each other. Later in the evening, in the house, both the families were there to celebrate their reunion.

'I remember I used to love these mehsub and mohan thal when I used to come to your house in Nairobi,' Ashok said, having his snacks with coffee.

'I will pack some for you to take home tomorrow for your wife. You have got to bring her over here with your son one day soon,' said Madhunath's wife.

In the next few months, the old friends and their families met several times. Over this period, Ashok and Geeta came to learn about their traumatic exit from Uganda and their struggle to settle in England.

Ashok had been inconsolable when both his closest friends from school went away with their family to live in Uganda. Rajesh and Sanjay had been Ashok's playmates since before he could even walk. All three children were sent to the reputable English-medium St Mary's school which was run by the Catholic mission in Nairobi. When the political situation in Nairobi started to become unstable, Madhunath and Prakash decided to move to Uganda which had been one of the most stable British colonies in East Africa. The cotton industry there was also thriving more than in Kenya. Pradeep and Rani had listened to their friends' advice about moving with them to Kampala but were already settled in their minds about moving back to India when the time came.

Prakash and Madhunath's family had found settling in Kampala quite easy. They already had business contacts there and it did not take them long to prosper with their own businesses. Both Rajesh and Sanjay were sent to the famous missionary Mengo Senior School. Although Rajesh's father wanted him to be a doctor, Rajesh himself was inspired by the stories of James Mulwana. A famous alumnus of the school, a businessman and entrepreneur, who at the very young age of twenty-five had partnered with the reputable Chloride U.K. company to start his own battery manufacturer in Uganda. Following some protestations, his father agreed for him to take up business studies. After all, he would be the heir to his multi-million cotton business in the future. Once he finished his schooling, Rajesh enrolled in the newly established National College of Business Studies in Makerere. He got his diploma within three years and then earned his higher diploma in marketing after another two years.

His sister, Devi, had also been to Mengo School in the city. She would have preferred to go to the Toredo all-girls boarding school, but her parents would have nothing to do with this. For one thing, it was more than 150 miles outside Kampala. Devi passed her school leaving exams with flying colours and to her parents' delight she got admission to the Makerere Medical College. Their younger fifteen-year-old son, Milan, wanted to study arts. His parents hoped that when he was older he would change his mind.

Rajesh's friend Sanjay, unable to resist the pressure from his father, unwillingly had joined the Makerere Medical College. He struggled there from the very beginning and after failing his second year exams twice he decided to give up medicine. He soon joined his father's business, and his father was now happy to have someone who he could really trust in his ever-enlarging cotton empire.

His younger sister, Neela, passed her final exam from Mengo School with good marks. She then decided to join the newly established law school in Makerere University. The twelve-year-old son, Sumit, was still enjoying his football more than his routine school homework and their youngest daughter, eight-year-old Kalpana, was busy playing hide and seek with her friends.

Prakash's family had the chance to use their British passports for the first time when they went to London on holiday in 1969. While his father went around talking to his business partners in the UK, mainly around Manchester and Birmingham, Rajesh took his mother, sister, and brother sightseeing to all the famous sites in London. One day he went by himself to the world-renowned London School of Economics near the Royal Courts of Justice and dreamt of one day doing his master's there. He sought out the professor who was due to come to give the anniversary address in his college in Kampala in a few months' time. The professor was pleased to talk to him and accepted Rajesh's invitation to come to their family place in Kampala and stay with them. He had already been slightly worried about the hotel situation in the city there with the current uncertainty in the political scene.

On the same day, Devi went to visit the world-famous Guy's Medical School in London. During the day, she was fortunate enough to speak to some of the Indian and African doctors there.

She came back to the hotel in the evening and told her mother, 'I really hope that one day after I have finished my medical degree in Kampala I can come over here for training.'

With time in their hands, the four of them decided next to visit Leicester, where some of their distant relatives from India lived and one of their cousins from India had settled only recently. It was arranged that their father would also join them there after his visit to Birmingham.

A cousin of Rajesh's father was an engineer and had gotten a job with the Marconi radar company. They had moved to Leicester only two and a half years back from India. His wife was a housewife and the full-time mother of their one-year-old son. Their one-bedroom council flat with no carpet and no heating felt cold even in early June, although an electric heater was glowing on one side.

Rajesh and his family made the excuse that Prakash may be arriving late in the evening from Birmingham and went back to the hotel near the railway station where they had checked in earlier. The next day they met up with most of their other relatives from India who had settled in Leicester. They found that while a few of the men worked as train and bus drivers, some had started small businesses and were doing reasonably well.

The next day, the four of them went to visit the only tourist site in the town, the thousand-year-old Leicester Cathedral, while Prakash went to meet some of his relatives at their businesses. At lunch, the four reflected on how lucky they were with their lives back home in Uganda. They were already beginning to miss their large three-storey palatial house with five servants and two chauffeur-driven cars. All this on top of their resorts in their plantations in the provincial towns. But when they talked about this to Prakash in the evening during dinner, he reminded them that since the British colonial rule ended in 1961, under the leadership of Milton Obote, Uganda was moving into uncertain territory. Corruption was at its highest and in order to grab not only political power but also economic power, he was ruthlessly turning against the Asian businesses.

Coming back to London, they met another cousin of Prakash's from India, Amrit, who was the son of the only brother of his father. He was working in nearby Heathrow Airport as a ground engineer. In the last few years he had also started a small business in Southall outside London. Prakash's family was invited for dinner in the evening there but they had to decline as it would be late for them to get back to their hotel in central London in the night. Instead, the families were entertained for late afternoon Gujarati snacks and tea. Both Prakash and Rajesh were impressed by the thriving small businesses of the Asian community in Southall, while the women in Amrit's family hailed Devi, who was soon to become the first female doctor in their wider family.

Amrit suggested to Prakash that he should seriously consider buying a property in England. 'Although the properties around London are of a relatively high price, you could still easily find a three-bedroom house in outer London or in Leicester for between five and six thousand pounds.'

Rajesh's mother replied, 'We are settled Ugandans. We have a good life there. Occasionally we have discussed the idea of moving to India after Prakash retires. But not to England. It's too cold here most of the year to start with!'

But his father said, 'We should seriously consider this. It's not that much money to us anyway and if Rajesh and Devi want to come over here and study it will be useful. We will also have a base for travelling to England and Europe for my business.'

Rajesh and Devi both nodded.

Prakash asked his cousin to find out bit more about a decent property and keep him informed. Then Prakash would transfer the money through his bank. With his British passport, there should be no problem purchasing a house here.

Two days later they took their BOAC flight back to Kampala.

A few months later, the professor from LSE came to Kampala. He was met at the airport by Rajesh and he thoroughly enjoyed the Indian family's hospitality for the few days he spent in the city. Prakash organised a gala dinner in his honour, inviting all the big business leaders in Kampala.

Within six months, Prakash's family also became the owners of a property in England in outer London near Ealing.

In the summer of 1970, Rajesh moved to the UK to do his master's degree in business management at the London School of Economics. He was glad that their new family home in West London was only a small commute to his college. The year after, Milan came over to England as well. After passing his school exams, he wanted to study arts somewhere around London, but he could not find any placement except for one in Manchester. He started his course there while staying in a residential hall. The brothers kept in touch as much as they could by visiting each other over the weekends.

In the final year of his master's, Rajesh, with his uncle Amrit nearby in Southall, started a small business as an event organiser for the Asian weddings and other ceremonies. After only a few months the business took off in a market with a growing number of prospering Asian families around, and with Amrit's family contacts.

During one of the weekend wedding events, Rajesh came across one of his relatives he had met in Leicester earlier, who had come with the groom's party.

He was really pleased to see Rajesh doing well in his business and suggested, 'You should consider extending this business into Leicester where, as you know, there are also many Asians.'

'I must finish my master's first this year before thinking of expanding our business any further. But if you have time, I can come over to Leicester on a weekend in the meantime and explore this with you,' replied Rajesh.

Two months later he went to Leicester with Milan and furthered his business idea with some of his relatives there.

In Kampala, Devi passed her medical exam with a gold medal in paediatrics. A big celebration with the family and friends followed. During her pre-registration house job she wrote to Rajesh to try to find out about her prospect of getting any training jobs in London hospitals, her preference being in paediatrics.

In England, meanwhile, both Rajesh and Milan were aware of the ongoing anti-immigration fever whipped up by Enoch Powell and by the activities of the National Front. Rajesh had read in the local newspaper in November 1971 about Enoch Powell declaring in a meeting in nearby Southall that 'Asian immigration was more dangerous than Black Power.'

Madhunath's family took a holiday in India in January 1971. They arrived in Bombay before travelling by train to Ahmedabad, the capital of Gujrat. They were all impressed not only by how well their families were doing, but also with the general confidence of India as an independent nation. The women were most impressed by the opportunities Indian women had compared to what they faced in Eastern Africa. Most of their relatives had businesses in India as well as in other countries, including in Europe, North America, and Africa. Gujrat had been the hub of the textile industry in India for a long time but now the industries were flourishing in many other new areas such as agricultural as well as chemical engineering and producing a variety of processed food products for export. Sanjay and his father established many more business connections, mostly with the members of their extended families.

The week before they were due to leave India, the news arrived that Colonel Idi Amin had taken over power from Milton Obote in a bloodless coup.

From Uganda's independence from Great Britain in 1961 to early 1971, Obote's regime had terrorised, harassed, and tortured people. Frequent food shortages had blasted food prices through the roof. Obote's persecution of Indian traders also contributed to this. During his regime, flagrant and widespread corruption had emerged. In the beginning, people believed that Idi Amin's military government would stamp out bureaucracy and corruption. But looting and indiscriminate jailing of Asian traders increased.

On 4 August 1972, Idi Amin announced his decision to rid the country of the 'bloodsucking' Asians who he declared were sabotaging the country's economy and taking away African jobs. His intention to rid the country of what he called the 'British Asians' sent shockwaves not only around Uganda but around the world. Amin gave the Asians ninety days to leave the country. He ordered the army to seize their property, homes, and businesses. Women feared for their safety after regular news of military indecently assaulting them at checkpoints and not infrequently detaining them, leading to rape and murder.

In the same summer of 1972 in London, Rajesh had taken his master's exams and was reasonably happy with how they had gone. Waiting for the results, he was planning to go back home to Uganda for a few weeks when he heard the news on BBC of Idi Amin's decree to expel all Asians. He telegrammed his family and was advised strongly against making any travel plan back there.

When Prakash and Madhunath's family met one evening over dinner to talk about the decree by General Amin, the general consensus between the families was that with their British passports they would be better off going to the UK. Madhunath and his wife were suggesting that moving to India may be the better option, especially after their experience there not so long back.

'But in the UK, I will have better prospects of finding a decent training, hopefully in paediatrics,' said Devi.

Neela added, 'The same goes with my law degree and training. And we all know the UK is a far more advanced country.'

Prakash said, 'True. We also know that after all, the UK is a fair country. Our children will have more opportunities there in building their lives.'

Madhunath and his family also agreed. Then they discussed whether Leicester would be the best place for them to go initially in the UK, as many of their friends and relatives from Gujarat were already living there.

'Luckily, we already have a house near London, as you know,' said Prakash. Then he added, 'It's not a big house, but if needed, you should know that you all have a place there to stay to start with.'

'Thank you,' said Madhunath.

Sanjay said, 'Has anyone seen the advertisement in the *Uganda Argus* today from Leicester City Council?'

'No, what does it say?' asked his father.

Sanjay brought the newspaper from the living room and showed it to everyone.

'It is virtually advising people against moving to that city from Uganda. They are saying that thousands of families are waiting for housing, hundreds of children are waiting for school places, and social and health services there are stretched to the limit.'

'Also, the news channels from the UK are talking on a daily basis about rallies by the British National Party all around the country against the immigration of Asians to Britain,' said Neela.

'But we all have British passports and we have no choice but to leave this country anyway,' said Madhunath.

'Idi Amin has already ordered the seizing of assets of all the Indian companies here,' agreed Prakash.

Prakash's seventy-two-year-old aunt, whom the children called Nana, had been living with them for many years since her husband died. She was distraught more than anyone else at the thought of moving from Uganda. She had lived most of her life in this country where her husband had died a decade back.

While checking and collecting everyone's passports, Prakash found out that although Nana had a British passport, it should have been renewed the year before. Devi went with Nana the next morning to the British Consulate only to find that there was almost a mile-long queue to the gate. They stood in line in the hot, baking sun for hours, but by the time they reached the front of the embassy, it was 3 p.m. and the gate was closed. The next morning, they came well before sunrise and joined a smaller line in front of them. Fortunately, once inside it took just over two hours for Nana's passport to be renewed. The same day they received a telegram from Rajesh that he has passed his master's in business studies with distinction. The family sent a reply telegram back congratulating him but had to withhold their celebration until they were all together in England.

Prakash's family gave away most of their belongings, except the gold ornaments and jewellery, to the Ugandan neighbours, friends, and their own long-serving servants. They also gave away their cars to their neighbour friends. They hired only one small truck to take mainly their personal belongings and blankets—Prakash's wife had not forgotten the cold in England!

They were one of the few lucky families to be able to book a flight to the UK soon after Amin's three-month expulsion notice. On the journey to the airport there were several army checkpoints where their luggage was searched and some of the expensive clothes were looted. Prakash was glad that his wife and daughter had hidden all the family jewellery under their clothes. Only the thin golden necklaces they were wearing on their necks were ripped off by one of the commanders. Luckily, at the next army checkpoint, one of the officers recognised Prakash, who had given him a loan for his son's education only two years back. His son was in the same college as Rajesh.

'I will come with you to the airport, Mr Prakash, to avoid any more harassment,' he declared, and followed them to the safety of the airport in his army truck.

At the airport, although they had booked tickets, they had to pay bribes to the official before finally boarding the plane for the UK. They were all already emotionally drained and slept well on most of their nine-hour flight. After arriving in Heathrow, there was more than an hour of delay before they were allowed to come out of the aeroplane. No explanation was given.

'At least it's a sunny day here,' said Prakash's wife, still shivering in her warm clothes.

Nana, who did not speak English, muttered her agreement in Hindi, saying, 'Meri Huddee kampna hai'

At the immigration desk, the family were asked how they would sustain themselves in the UK. Copies of the ownership of the house in Ealing and their latest bank statement from Lloyds Bank seemed to finally satisfy the officer. They were finally asked if they wanted help with resettlement in the country. A resettlement centre was mentioned, if they needed it.

'No, thank you. We already have the property outside London,' replied Prakash.

They were truly relieved when after almost an hour and a half at the immigration desk they were finally allowed to go thorough. Rajesh and Milan, who were waiting to meet them, were beginning to worry outside the exit door as it was almost three hours since the plane had landed.

In mid-September of 1972, the family finally immigrated to the country of their citizenship.

The next day, Milan accompanied Devi in her search for a job in the Guy's Hospital. At the personnel department, a snobby middle-aged English woman asked, 'Do you have any experience in this country, and do you have referees here?'

When Devi tried to explain her circumstances, she was curtly dismissed. After having a similar experience in the nearby King's

College Hospital, she then decided to go to the library there and find the last few weeks of the BMJ. She scoured through them for any advertisements for paediatrics training posts, which usually started in February. But now, in September, there was none. She did, however, find a locum post to start as soon as possible for three months in Leicester, as well as a similar one in Nottingham.

Once outside the library, she found one of London's famous red telephone booths and rang the personnel department in Leicester explaining her circumstances. After a few minutes waiting on the line she was told that the post was still vacant and was asked to urgently send six copies of her CV by post. She next telephoned Nottingham Hospital to find out that the post had now been filled. Devi had already brought several copies of her CV which had been typed by her father's secretary in Kampala. She wrote her application for the job in her neat handwriting on blank paper and sent it with copies of her CV by first-class post from London to Leicester.

On the same day, Rajesh took his parents to buy some warm clothes for all of them in the town. Nana decided to stay home by the electric fire. The same evening, Amrit came over to pay respect to the elders and invited them all for a dinner with his family the following evening.

The next day they were all first taken to the local temple in Southall where everyone prayed, Nana for longer than anyone else. Amrit's house was in the back alley of the main street of Southall. Once welcomed into the house, Nana and Ma went to the kitchen with Amrit's wife. Devi and Amrit's teenage daughter reluctantly followed the women. Amrit sat with Prakash, Rajesh, and Milan in the living room. His twelve-year-old son came and sat by his father. Soon plates of samosa and khandvi were brought up by the women.

Amrit's daughter asked shyly, 'Do you want to have tea now with this? Dinner will be in over an hour.'

Prakash replied, 'Tea would be nice, chokari.'

After their snacks, Prakash said, 'What about taking a short stroll on the street? There seem to be so many Indian shops.'

Devi came out with the men for the walk. She was dazzled by the rows of Indian shops selling jewellery, saris, and sweets, nothing like she had seen in Kampala.

'I wish Ma and Nana were with us now. I want to check out some of these shops,' she said.

'It's too cold in the evening for them. I will bring them over one day soon during daytime,' Rajesh replied.

During dinner, Devi said, 'While we were making our arrangements for our move we heard a lot on the radio about some nationalist parties in this country strongly protesting against Asians coming over to the UK to live.'

Amrit replied, 'Yes, it's true. But this is not something new. When we first came over here nearly eight years back, white people would not rent their houses to us as lodgers. So it was a very difficult time in that sense too. Here in Southall, there was what you can call a white exodus, with them starting to move out as many of us started moving in.'

His wife said, 'It was routine to hear racial abuses on the street. So much so that we pretended we did not understand English. You gradually learn to live with it. Mostly, it's not a problem though.'

Rajesh and Amrit then talked with Prakash about the progress of their joint business. Rajesh soon broke the news that since his master's he had been headhunted by a reputable business firm in Birmingham for an assistant business manager post with a very good salary. They already had international trading but were hoping to expand further. Rajesh had not confirmed his response yet, waiting until he had the family come over to discuss it with them first.

He said, 'I am a bit worried about our business though. Who will run it if I am not there, especially now that it is starting to take off?'

Milan, who was due to finish his arts degree within the next six months, said, 'I don't think my arts degree is going to be much good for any job. Unemployment here is almost ten per cent. I have also come to realise now that although I love arts, I am not an artist.'

Rajesh asked Amrit, 'Do you think we can employ him to run our business?'

Amrit replied, 'The business is now well-established. It only needs someone hardworking to run it day to day. I am here to guide him and I am sure Mr Prakash will also help with advice as needed.'

It was agreed that until Milan's exam in a few months' time, the business would be run by Amrit with help from Prakash. Rajesh and Milan would also try to help out by coming over to Ealing on as many weekends as possible. Most of the events were over the weekends anyway.

After a sumptuous dinner, when they were leaving, Devi showed her mother the brightly lit shops on the street which were still open late in the evening.

'We'd better get back home now. It's getting late. Did you know that in Uganda it is past midnight?' asked her father.

The next morning, Rajesh telephoned the company in Birmingham accepting the offer and was asked to join in two weeks. Two days later, Devi got a letter by first-class post saying that she had been accepted for the locum job in Leicester and to telephone the personnel department immediately. On the telephone, she was asked if she could start from the next day, which was a Friday, as she would have to cover on-call for the weekend.

'I will be happy to start from tomorrow. I can come over by the first train from London tomorrow. But where will I stay?' asked Devi.

'We will arrange accommodation for you, no problem. Make sure to bring all your original certificates and references. Come and meet me in the personnel office as soon as you arrive tomorrow.'

After Devi had left in the morning, as it was a sunny day, Rajesh and Milan took the rest of the family to London for sightseeing. Their mother and Nana were wearing colourful saris with long overcoats and Prakash was wearing an Indian-style suit and warm jacket. At the end of the day, Rajesh took them to see the famous Oxford Street.

As they were slowly walking, dazzled by the big shops with their showcase windows, a group of white youths coming from the opposite direction whistled and shouted, 'Here comes the tribe.'

Nana asked in Gujarati, 'What did they say?'

Milan turned around and wanted to confront the group but Rajesh stopped him by saying, 'You have to learn to ignore these ignorant people, Milan.'

In Leicester Hospital, another SHO, who was from Madras, introduced Devi to the children's ward where she met the consultant on call for the weekend.

'I will be here to do a ward round at eight thirty tomorrow morning. If you have any problems, do not hesitate to call me at home in the night,' the consultant said.

Then the SHO showed her the dining room and her residence.

'My room is only three doors down. I am not on call this weekend luckily, but I am not going anywhere. I will be either in my room or in the doctor's mess TV room if you want to find me.'

'Thank you. Where can I find some tea, coffee, and snacks in the hospital for my room?'

'In the doctor's mess there is always tea, coffee, and toast. If you are busy and hungry, you can also get a free meal after midnight in the canteen. Otherwise, in the front entrance of the hospital there is a shop run by the volunteers during the visiting hours.'

After sorting out her room, Devi went back to the ward where the staff nurses welcomed her with a cup of coffee and some chocolates.

'We are never short of chocolates in this ward, you know. Boxes and boxes from parents to say thank you, which is always welcome,' said one of the nurses who was from Jamaica.

'Which hospital have you been working in before?' asked another nurse from Kerala.

'This is my first job in this country,' replied Devi.

'Really? Where are you from?'

'I grew up in Uganda.'

'Don't worry. You will be fine here. Sister is on tonight. She will look after you.'

Devi went around the ward with one of the nurses after their coffee break. She was surprised to find most of the children were relatively well compared to what she had been used to in Kampala. There was one child who was recovering well from sepsis and most of the others were almost ready to be discharged. It was nothing like in Kampala, where the ward was always full of seriously ill children. She loved the playroom in the ward where a few of the children were playing.

Devi joined the children in the play area for a few minutes before saying to the nurse in charge, 'I think I will go back to my room and get myself sorted. Please call me if you need me.'

'Don't worry. We will,' said the nurse to her as she was leaving, and then said to another nurse next to her, 'She seems nice.'

In the next few weeks, during coffee breaks at the end of ward rounds, Devi was encouraged by the consultants to apply for the regular job from February when the post in the hospital was due to be advertised around Christmas. Devi enjoyed the Christmas in the children's ward with the showering of gifts for the children from the local charities, carol singing, and even Santa visiting the very few remaining patients. There were always boxes of chocolates everywhere, of course. Being on call for Christmas and Boxing Day, she could not go back to meet her parents. But she was happy to be allowed to leave on the afternoon of New Year's Eve and spend the New Year with her family in their new country.

In the meantime, Rajesh had joined the Birmingham Farm, which turned out to be a company dealing with electrical goods. Their business had been doing well until a year back but now was stalling. He dived into the job with full vigour. He visited the local factory where the productivity was falling below standard with recurring strikes. He discussed this with his manager and found him less than enthusiastic to tackle the issue head on.

He got the opportunity to put forward his views during a presentation at the directors meeting. He also put forward the idea of exploring the opportunities of purchasing components from non-

European markets and assembling them in the UK with a streamlined workforce. Conscious of the shareholders meeting in a few months and profit for the last three quarters being down, he was given the job to visit other countries with cheaper production costs to explore his idea.

He travelled to Turkey, South Korea, and India and was soon able to negotiate cheaper contracts for the components. He then suggested to the board that rather than cutting the workforce at home, they could use them to increase assembly and explore exports to the European market.

Within three years, the company was making forty per cent more profit. As well as his bonus, Rajesh was promoted to being a manager with a place on the board. After successfully working there for another few years, in 1981 he left the company to start his own management consultancy firm.

By 1981, Devi had already got her MRCP in paediatrics and a few years later was appointed as consultant in the same hospital where she started her career in the UK ten years back.

Milan and Amrit expanded their event organiser business outside west London to Leicester, Nottingham, and Birmingham with minimal help from Prakash. Soon Milan sold their house in Ealing and moved up north to live with his parents and Nana to Leicester where the business was now blossoming. Amrit continued to look after the business in Southall. A year later following discussion with their father, Rajesh and Milan sold their business in Southall to Amrit. Apart from their event organiser business, Milan started another business of providing catering supplies for the airlines in the Midlands area.

Prakash and his wife were happy to see their children doing so well and remained only nominally involved in the businesses. Nana, apart from complaining about the cold from time to time, was quite happy as she was now able to meet with more families from Gujrat and visit the temple in Leicester. She died peacefully three years later. Since moving to Leicester, both Prakash and his wife had met up with Madhunath and his wife and became regular attendees at the Navnit Banik Association.

Madhunath's family had needed longer to make their arrangements before finally leaving Uganda. In the last week of September 1972, the family of six packed their valuable items as best they could. They hid all their jewellery inside the clothing of the women and children who were wearing winter clothes on top of their shalwar kameez, pretending that they needed all the warm clothes when arriving in England.

On the way to the airport they were stopped four times at the military checkpoints. Most of the valuables in their cars were taken away, as well as their expensive wristwatches, which they regretted wearing. In one of the final checkpoints, just outside Entebbe Airport, the mother and their daughters shuddered at the leering comments made by two of the sergeants towards Neela.

They were truly relieved when they were finally allowed to go through, albeit being looted some more of their possessions. After spending more than ten hours at the airport, they finally boarded the last of the four chartered flights leaving that day for the UK, all of them with only the allowed fifty pounds in their possession.

On arrival at Stanstead Airport they were met at the immigration checkpoint by officials from the resettlement board and scores of volunteers from WRVS, the British Red Cross, St John's Ambulance, and the Variety Club of Great Britain. The family accepted temporary settlement at the newly opened Stradishall, an unused RAF air base.

As soon as their bus, arranged by the volunteers, was slowing down outside the reception centre at Stradishall, men and women with cameras and notebooks appeared from all directions. The press and TV crew were there in droves to interview the first batch of Ugandan Asians at this resettlement centre. Bewildered families clutching their meagre belongings walked into the large reception centre. Each family was welcomed with broad smiles on the faces of volunteers, who were allocated to act as their escorts, and were shown to comfortable armchairs while awaiting the formal reception procedure.

Adults were served tea or orange juice and biscuits. Milk and some toys and storybooks were laid on for the babies and children. The families, who had already been shivering on the journey from the airport in late September, were grateful for the coats, sweaters, and knitted shawls distributed to them. Apparently these were all donated by the local volunteers. Some toys and storybooks were also found for Sumit and Kalpana. Then, family by family, they were escorted by one of the volunteers to be taken to the documentation room.

As head of the family, Madhunath was called to produce their passports and details of their family. Then the number of their allocated accommodation and name of the road was written on a badge and pinned onto the lapel of his coat. The family was now taken for chest x-rays, vaccinations, and medical checks. They were taken in a minibus to their allocated house where the welcoming heating was already on. Finally they were offered to be taken for a meal in the canteen at the centre.

Madhunath, already absolutely exhausted, said, 'Thank you very much, but I think I will just rest now.'

His wife said, 'Me too. Thank you.'

Sanjay and Neela, with their brother and sister, followed the volunteer to the canteen for a meal but more for a chance to explore the place. The English meal provided at the canteen was bland for the tastebuds of the siblings used to spicy foods, but they were hungry and were really happy to have some chocolate dessert at the end of their meal. Sanjay stayed around to speak to some of the volunteers. Neela decided to go back to their room with Sumit and Kalpana. On the way back, walking in the large, open area without any signposting, they got lost. Luckily, they found one of the volunteers who was going back home. She took them to the reception office and soon they were taken to their accommodation.

In the next few days, the families were really grateful to find out that not only were the volunteers coming early every morning and leaving late in the evening, but also that before the settlement centre opened, they had been responsible for cleaning up all the buildings and rooms in this disused air base. Genuinely taken by the volunteers' generosity, Madhunath and Sanjay discussed with other families and arranged a day at the reception centre to show them the gratitude of the Ugandan Asians. They organised an informal lunch with the Asian women cooking Indian meals and making some Indian snacks. Many addressed the volunteers, thanking the hundreds of people who had freely given so much of their time and effort to make them welcome.

Madhunath said, 'We say among ourselves that you have given us so much, if possible you would have given us your heart. We dread to think what would have happened if we were still in Uganda today. Through the generosity of British people, we are now safe and free. We can look forward to a bright future here.'

Afterwards, the volunteers were entertained with some traditional Indian singing and dancing organised by Neela.

Amongst almost 2,000 settlers in the centre there were many children. Soon, a school was set up in the centre. Local communities donated books, teaching materials, and toys. The children, who were very quiet in the beginning, soon became more relaxed. The teenage boys and girls came to the reception asking for jobs they could do at the centre. Soon Neela and Sumit and many other teenagers were proudly wearing 'On WRVS work' badges on their coats, doing jobs as messengers and helping to keep the place clean of litter. They were given a bar of chocolate each day for their work. Kalpana was really jealous of them, especially of her brother Sumit. Sanjay, like many other young adults, was already helping at the reception centre, welcoming and reassuring new families coming from Uganda.

Like many at the centre, although thankful for the generosity shown on their arrival, Madhunath's family were keen to move out to start their new lives in the country as soon as possible. Following discussion at the enquiry office, Madhunath agreed with his wife to try to find somewhere to move in around Leicester where some of their relatives already lived. They were told that according to the resettlement scheme the local authority would support them for the first year, if they needed, in finding housing or securing mortgages from the local building societies.

Madhunath and Sanjay travelled to Leicester for a few days and managed to meet up with several of their countrymen from Uganda as well as from India. Within a few weeks, they were allocated a two-bedroomed council house in Leicester by the council. Used to a luxurious lifestyle in Kampala, in the beginning they found this place cramped for the six of them, but they soon got used to it. Sanjay went out every day to find some contacts to start any new business idea. Soon he found that a childless elderly Gujarati couple, owners of a local Asian grocery shop and newsagent, were thinking of selling their business and retiring back in India. Back at home, Sanjay discussed with his family about how to raise the money to buy this small business.

His mother immediately said, 'We have been lucky to hide and bring our gold and jewellery from Uganda. We could have easily lost them to those dreadful soldiers in Kampala. Why not sell them for us to have a fresh start here?'

After some discussion, it was agreed that they would take some of the jewellery to the local bank and try to raise the money against a gold bond.

The next day, Madhunath and Sanjay went to one of the local banks and opened a joint account with a total of the 150 pounds the whole family still had since moving to Leicester. They also asked about a loan against a gold bond and were happy to find that the bank would definitely consider this. The next day they brought some of their jewellery and were glad to find that the family's twenty-four-carat gold ornaments were worth enough to get the required loan to buy the business they had in mind.

Within two weeks they bought the shop, which was luckily only fifteen minutes' walk from their house. Madhunath ran the shop daily from early in the morning and it stayed open until late in the night, and Sanjay went around to negotiate cheaper prices for the supplies from the local wholesale depots. While most of the shops in the street opened at 9 a.m. and closed at 5 p.m. sharp, their shop opened at seven thirty in the morning and stayed open until ten in the evening. This gave them the edge, with the customers coming to the shop before going to work or after finishing their work. Madhunath's wife brought him lunch and ran the shop while her husband was having his break in the back. Luckily, many of the customers were Asians and her scant English with a thick accent did not matter.

In the first few weeks, while walking on the street, they often heard comments such as, 'Can you see? It is turning out to be like a plague here now. Coloured people everywhere in our street.' Soon they learnt to ignore these and other racist remarks.

For Madhunath, having a shop gave him very close contact and friendships with everyone, including the English customers who often came to the shop and shared their gossip, sorrows, and joys. This in turn helped him to learn about English society very quickly. Soon, he knew almost everyone in the street and everyone knew of his shop.

Within a few months, Sanjay suggested to his father that they could extend the business by bringing deliveries to the families, mainly to those who were working every day and only had weekends to come to the shop. In the beginning, he made several trips daily on his bike loaded with goods, but within a few months he was able to hire an old van to collect and distribute his merchandise.

In the meantime, Neela, while helping out at their store from time to time, went around the town to meet people in the local law firms. She still had one more year of her law degree to finish when she had to leave Kampala. She now went to some of the Indian-run law firms in the town trying to find the opportunity to do an apprenticeship for free over the next few months before she could resume her law degree at the end of the summer.

Luckily for her, in the second place she visited one of the solicitors turned out to be from the same town she had visited in India a few years back. During further conversation, she also found out that they were actually related, although distantly. She was offered an unpaid apprenticeship from the following week. Her whole family were also invited for dinner a few days later at her mentor's house. During an elaborate dinner, the two families recounted memories of their family connections in India. Neela was advised to try to get entry to the famous Birmingham Law School to finish her degree.

'Of course, Coventry Law School is nearer and she might even be able to commute. But I will advise Birmingham. It is more prestigious and she will come out from there with better opportunities. Yes, she will have to go away and live there, but it's not too far and she should be able come back over the weekends and holidays,' said Neela's mentor.

Sumit and Kalpana were admitted to the local comprehensive school.

After the second day at school, Sumit came home from school and asked Neela, 'Can I tell you something secret? But you must promise not to tell anyone.'

Neela said, 'Okay. Go ahead.'

Sumit said in a muted voice, 'For lunch today they had something called sausage and mashed potato. I tried to tell one of the teachers that we were vegetarians. But she asked me to hush and just finish my lunch. It tasted not bad though, only a bit weird.'

Trying to suppress laughter, Neela replied, 'Don't worry, I won't tell anyone. Try not to make any fuss at school.'

Both the children settled down easily in their school and were able to make many friends, some of whom were Asian. Both Sumit and Kalpana found the school atmosphere here less strict than in Kampala with more time for playing and being involved in small projects. Sumit loved his football and, although not quite sure of what to make of the new game of rugby which he came across, he enjoyed the rough and tumble of it and soon became quite good at it. Kalpana joined the local swimming pool and every Saturday she was taken there by her mother, who regretted that she never learnt to swim when she was young.

Neela, while doing her apprenticeship at the law firm during the weekdays, also took over managing the accounts of their family shop and helping there whenever possible, as well as taking a part-time job as a shop assistant at a superstore over the weekend. Working hard every day since moving to Leicester, the family barely noticed the cold winter. Within six months, their shop was making enough profit for Sanjay to suggest to his father about making an offer on another newsagent-cum-grocery shop in other part of the town.

'But how will we run the two shops between us?' asked Madhunath.

'We will employ someone. I have already spoken to another family from Uganda who have an eighteen-year-old son who is trying to find a job for now.'

By now the family had bought a television set and the Sunday morning programme of *Nai Zindagi Nai Jeevan*, shown on BBC One, was everyone's favourite. All the family sat together to watch while Sanjay went on to open their shop so that Madhunath did not have to miss the programme. The programme, broadcast in Hindi and Urdu and aimed at non-native English speakers, included domestic and international news, mostly from the Indian subcontinent. The children's favourite were the cultural and music performances. Whoever missed the programme on Sundays tried to make sure to catch up on the repeat shown on BBC Two later in the week.

By the time Neela went to Birmingham in September 1973 to complete her law degree, the family were the owners of three shops in the town with six employees in total. Madhunath went to the bank to release their bonded family gold. Three months later, he managed to secure a loan from the same bank to further expand their business.

During the Diwali celebration in 1974 with several other Indian families in the town, Madhunath proposed his idea to some of his friends, saying, 'I think we should seriously consider setting up a formal association of us entrepreneurs to support each other in our community.'

'That way we can support each other in our business ventures and ideas,' agreed one of his friends.

His wife said, 'It could also become the hub of cultural life here for us, the Asians who still find the English way very foreign.'

'True. It is easier to make friends with other internationals, Africans, Caribbeans, Malaysians, Ceylonese, and even Pakistanis than with the native English, because most of them have gone through the trauma of getting here and trying to be someone in this country,' replied Madhunath.

By 1975, just over two years since their arrival in UK, Madhunath and his wife became the founding members of Navnit Banik Association, where many Asian families joined to support each other. Families came together through many traditional cultural celebrations where members of the city council and other organisations were also invited. By this time, Madhunath's family had already moved from their council house flat to a five-bedroom property in Milton Road, and were owners of a chain of newsagents and Asian grocery shops in Leicester as well as in Nottingham. Apart from two delivery vans, they now had two family cars, one almost exclusively for Sanjay for his business travel.

After completing her law degree from Birmingham Law School, Neela finished her well-paid two-year legal apprenticeship in a prestigious law firm in the same city. She was offered a more permanent position as a junior partner in the same firm in the near future. However, she chose to move back to Leicester and join the firm of her first mentor in the town. In the law school in Kampala, Neela was fascinated by the dramatic roles barristers played in the courtroom, but during her later years she had come to realise that the role of a solicitor was more suitable and enjoyable for her personally with its more intimate and direct contact with people and their daily needs.

Her daily work now ranged across the whole spectrum of legal areas, from high value commercial work to personal injury cases, family law issues such as children's law and divorce, criminal law, immigration, wills probate, and the general administration of estates. Although she represented clients in disputes in the court occasionally, more often she had to instruct barristers or specialist advocates to appear in the court on behalf of her clients. Within a couple of years, she also drifted towards specialising in disputes in company law, although she also did the other general duties of a solicitor. She also soon became a notary public, the only one in her firm and in the nearby locality.

By now, Sanjay was running several newsagent-cum-grocery shops in Leicester, Nottingham, Coventry, and Birmingham, employing over fifty people in his business, a significant number of them displaced Indians. Madhunath was these days only nominally looking after the businesses but was busier with his wife with the Navnit Banik Association activities.

Sumit passed his O-level exam with decent marks but decided against further studies. He was enjoying his football too much and was playing for a local club in the lower division. At the age of seventeen, he decided to join the police training school.

By 1982, only ten years since their arrival empty-handed from Uganda, Neela was already a senior partner in a law firm. Their family business, run by Sanjay, was employing over 150 people and worth over two million pounds. Madhunath had been elected as a local councillor for the last few years running and next year was seeking election for the deputy mayor's post. Sumit, as a police constable, had done night classes to qualify for officer training and was now a police superintendent. Kalpana, after finishing her A-level exams with good grades, was due to start a business studies course in Leicester.

Chapter Thirteen

1987: Geeta's charity

With Raju now in school and Ashok in a permanent job, Geeta engaged in the disabled charity with even more energy. Apart from pushing for improving the educational opportunities for the disabled children in the school, the charity soon set up a volunteer group to offer those children's parents respite by offering childcare services. It took them longer to organise for the group of disabled children to go on holiday with their parents and the volunteers from the charity, but it was so much fun that they agreed to make it an annual event. They were lucky that from the local hospital, where their activities were regularly advertised, speech therapists and behavioural therapists offered their services as volunteers on a regular basis for those who needed them.

Emotional support, not only for the parents but also for the siblings of the disabled children, was another area which the charity started to address by organising after school clubs. Sundays and school holidays were the normal times for these clubs and they became very popular.

The children were eased back into these clubs gently, usually for one or two hours initially as in the beginning they were easily exhausted, but when it was gradually stepped up for them they started enjoying it more. The principle for the club was always 'no one-size-fits-all solution' for the disabled children, their parents, and siblings.

One of the most significant outcome of these clubs was that the disabled children, as well as their parents, were able to form new friendships. Flexibility, celebrating any improvements, however small, continually monitoring progress, and communicating with the family about progress in turn improved their self-esteem. The charity's regular connection with the schools ensured the school's strict policy against bullying of the vulnerable disabled children.

216

Following the publication in 1981 of the Jay Report, promoting a 'Care in the Community' programme for people with learning disabilities, the charity's goal of supporting disabled children in their homes rather than in residential institutions was given added support. Soon, the Warnock Report and legislation also came up supporting the charity's aims. Geeta had always been known in the charity for her gift of advocacy for its cause to the wider audience. She herself, however, loved spending as much time as possible with the disabled children and their families.

One afternoon, she came across a newly arriving ten-year-old boy named Adam with cerebral palsy and severe visual impairment.

As she was trying to get to know him and his parents, Adam said to her, 'Can you let me feel your hand?'

Geeta looked towards his mother, who just smiled. Geeta put her hand out for the boy to touch.

After gently touching Geeta's hand for a few seconds, the boy said, 'You are okay. I think I can trust you.'

Tears started rolling around Geeta's eyes and Jaya's face came returning back to her again and again.

Geeta was totally unprepared when the local radio station called her for an interview in one of their early evening broadcasts.

'How am I going to speak in a radio interview? I know I will be nervous and mix up my words. I am so nervous already. And I have got an Indian accent; no one will understand a word I say.'

Ashok, holding her hands, said, 'I am so proud of you. I know you are nervous now. I cannot tell you how to get prepared as I have never had the opportunity myself to go on the air. But I know that you strongly believe in the charity, and why not just tell them what you understand from our personal experiences? And regarding our Indian accent, just remember to speak slowly.'

Ashok accompanied Geeta to the radio station and sat in the office outside. Geeta surprisingly found the allotted fifteen minutes of the interview went surprisingly well.

Geeta said, 'Until now, only tests by doctors, psychologists, and teachers were designed to try and pinpoint the nature of the learning difficulty within the child. Trying to explain why children with disabilities were "slow learners", the society was still holding onto medical or biological causes rather than socio-educational factors.' She then talked about needing to pay attention to the shortage of textbooks pitched at the right reading level and specially trained teachers to teach this group.

'Do you think a child with disabilities should be taught in a regular school?' asked the interviewer.

'Most of them, if we can make special provisions for them,' replied Geeta. She then said, 'Rather than labelling the disabled child as faulty, we need to identify barriers to their development and find solutions.'

'We now, of course, have for the first time a government minister appointed for disabled people,' agreed the interviewer.

'We need to see more resources available, not only for the schools but also for the training of parents and other professionals. Diversity needs to be welcomed, not only in the schools but also by the society,' concluded Geeta.

On the way home, Ashok said, 'We were listening to you on the radio in the office room there. You were fantastic.'

'You think it went all right then? I am still shaking.'

'Absolutely.'

In the next few days, many people from the charity congratulated her on her radio interview. Geeta had known some of the children supported by their charity for several years now and was happy to see their progress in education. A girl called Gemma with severe cerebral palsy, whom she had known from the second year of their charity, had always reminded her of Jaya. Geeta's proudest moment was when Gemma passed her A-level exams and then got admission to the university in her preferred subject of economics. The charity had to provide her with a volunteer personal assistant to attend her degree course in the beginning, but soon funding was found in the university for a PA.

Geeta, along with the board of their charity in their annual general meeting, agreed that the charity had achieved as best it could locally but that there were many other issues which needed national campaigning and support. It was agreed unanimously to merge with a well-known national charity who did not have any local branch in the community.

Chapter Fourteen

1990: Jiten and Mita

In 1990, Geeta got her master's from the Open University. After doing her BA several years back, she had already done an honours degree from OU. It had taken a lot of courage from her and encouragement from Ashok before she finally undertook the master's course. She telephoned Ashok in his surgery as soon as she opened the letter from OU confirming her success. Ashok came home for lunch after buying a big bouquet of flowers from the florist.

He said, 'You know what? We must celebrate this properly. This is such a wonderful achievement. How do you want to celebrate?'

'Maybe we can go out somewhere nice this evening after Raju is back home from his school and sports,' she said. Then she added, 'Do you know what would be really nice? The graduation ceremony is still a few months away. It would be fantastic if Dada and his new wife could come over for this. I could request to attend the graduation ceremony in any city. I will ask for London.'

Ashok said, 'That's a great idea. I will telegram home tomorrow with your news and try to call Jiten in his office in the next couple of days so that we can talk to him about this.'

They were all excited, especially Raju, when they heard that Jiten was trying to come over with his wife, Mita, and their just under two-year-old daughter, Kabita, for Geeta's postgraduate ceremony and for a short holiday with them. Geeta had been really upset that they could not go to her brother's wedding a few years back. They had to cancel their trip to Calcutta for the wedding only the week before their flight. Like many of his friends at school, Raju had got chicken pox.

Jiten was now working as a lecturer in political studies in Maulana Azad College. Mita was a nurse in the NRS Medical College Hospital but had not gone back to work since she had the baby. Their letter said that Jiten could only manage a maximum of four weeks leave in June and July and that they would love to attend Geeta's ceremony. Although it was only early February, Geeta started planning the holiday with her brother's family in earnest. Ashok sent the sponsorship and invitation letter they would need for their visa to them by urgent registered post. He clearly mentioned in his letter to Jiten that he would be happy to pay for their return flights as well as all their expenses in the UK. Jiten replied thanking Ashok and saying that he would be paying for the tickets himself in Calcutta.

Getting passports for himself and Mita was reasonably straightforward as Jiten had already learned the tricks of this while getting passports for his parents a few years back. Kabita's name was endorsed in Jiten's passport. Armed with the invitation and sponsorship letter from Ashok, Jiten went to the British High Commission in 1 Ho Chi Min Sarani in Calcutta. After filling out some forms and having a brief meeting with a Bengali employee at the High Commission, he was given an appointment with the entry clearance officer, the ECO, a week later with his family. He was asked to bring along his employment certificate, any bank statements, and the birth certificates of all three of them. The Bengali officer explained that the ECO had the sole power to grant or refuse visas for them.

The interview a week later was with a British officer named Mr Cruickshank. Although Jiten and Mita could speak English well, both found it difficult to understand the thick Northern Irish accent of the ECO.

After saying, 'Could you please repeat that?' several times within the first five minutes of the interview, they were relieved to be offered a Bengali translator. The interpreter was the same Mr Das whom they had met the week before. The interview began with Jiten and Mita answering back in English with Mita also trying to keep Kabita quiet.

Mr Das interpreted, 'How long do you want to go to the UK for?'

Jiten replied, 'Between three and four weeks.'

'What is the purpose of this visit?'

'It's a social visit to meet my sister so we can attend her postgraduate degree ceremony and spend time with her family.'

'When did you last see her?'

'When they all came over a few years back during our youngest sister's wedding.'

'So you are going to spend all the time on your holiday in the UK with your sister's family?'

By this time, Kabita was getting more restless and the ECO, after looking at his watch, indicated for Mita to take her outside. Then he looked at Jiten for an answer.

'We would also like to visit some places in the UK.'

'What places?'

'London and other places.'

'What places other than London?'

Jiten could not immediately think of other places and said, 'Whatever places they can arrange for us to visit.'

'Do you have any other relatives in the UK?'

'No.'

'What is your sister working as in the UK?'

'She is now a full-time housewife and also runs a charity. Her husband, my brother-in-law, is a GP there.'

'How long has he been a GP?'

'I think for about fifteen years.'

'What is your job?'

'I am a lecturer in a college here.'

'How much is your annual income?'

'Nine thousand five hundred rupees.'

'So just over five hundred pounds? Is your wife working?'

Jiten replied that Mita was a nurse but had not gone back to work since their daughter was born. Then Jiten was asked about his savings, to which he replied that he had a total of over 25,000 rupees in the bank and the post office. The ECO asked Jiten where they

222

lived in Calcutta, to which he replied that he lived in the joint family home with his parents. He was then asked about how many rooms there were in their house. He counted on his hand before saying seven bedrooms, a sitting room, a kitchen, and two bathrooms. The ECO asked about his father's business income and savings. Jiten answered that he did not know about the savings but the annual income from the business was over 50,000 rupees.

'Does your family have any other property?'

'Only the business office and the showroom there.'

Then he was asked about how much the return tickets for this trip would cost and who would pay. Jiten replied that for the three of them it would cost about 13,000 rupees and he would pay.

Slightly agitated, Mr Cruickshank asked, 'Are you telling me that you are going to spend more than your annual income just for a social visit?'

'We have been saving for this visit as we want to see England.'

'How much do you know about England?'

Jiten was going to reply that he was a lecturer in political studies and had a master's degree in history, but just then Mita came back with Kabita who was now crying to go home.

The ECO looked at the wall clock in the room as it struck twelve noon. He called the interview to an end by saying, 'We will notify you of our decision within two weeks by post.'

Jiten was at his college when the post arrived in their house exactly two weeks later. Mita already had a handful with her daughter and looking after her mother-in-law, who was not feeling so well today. She decided to wait until Jiten came home before opening the envelope. By the time everything had quietened down a bit, it was almost three in the afternoon. She looked at the post but as it was only around a couple of hours before her husband was due back home, she decided to take a nap herself next to her daughter.

As soon as Jiten was back home, Kabita jumped on his lap and started singing a few words of a Bengali nursery rhyme she had learnt. 'Tai tai tai. Mamabari jai. Mama dilo dudhbhat ghare bose khai.'

'Yes, yes, we are going to your uncle and aunty soon,' Jiten happily clapped with the song and then gave her a big kiss on her forehead. Mita arrived with a cup of tea and a couple of thin arrowroot biscuits. She then brought out the post to him with a big smile on her face. Jiten opened the envelope and read through the letter as his face turned gloomy.

'What does it say?' asked Mita.

'They have refused our visa, saying our intentions are not genuine as tourists.'

'What does it mean by "not genuine"? Let me have a look.'

While she read the letter, Jiten went with Kabita to read her more nursery rhymes in another room.

Geeta opened the large envelope with an airmail sticker from Jiten eagerly and her face dropped when she read through the copy of the refusal letter from the British High Commission in Calcutta. She showed the letter to Ashok as soon as he was back from surgery.

After reading the letter, he said angrily, 'They can't do this. It's blatant discrimination. Any Australian or Canadian can come over here for a holiday whenever they wish but Indians are not genuine tourists! And all of us are in the same Commonwealth!'

'But what can we do?' asked Geeta.

'We will appeal. Definitely. It says at the end of the High Commission letter that we can appeal.'

The next day he sent a telegram to Jiten saying, 'We are going to appeal here against their decision.' Then he made an appointment to see the local advocate, who also happened to be one of his patients.

The advocate looked at the refusal letter carefully and then suggested, 'There are a few charities with the law society who specialise in these situations with visas. Let me find their contact number, Dr Basu.'

He called his secretary. After asking her to get the telephone number, he said, 'Also two cups of coffee here for us, please.'

As they waited for the secretary to come back, the advocate said, 'I have not had the chance to properly thank you since my operation.

If you did not come over to my house that night and send me urgently to the hospital, I don't know where I would be today.'

'You are back to normal now, aren't you?'

'Yes, it took three months or so getting over my ruptured ulcer but I am back to better than I was before. And the good news is I have also given up smoking. They said it might have caused the ulcer.'

The secretary connected to the telephone of the charity and the advocate spoke to them for a few minutes. Then he said to Ashok, 'We need to send them a copy of the refusal letter with your personal details here as you were the sponsor. They think it shouldn't be a problem.'

At home, when he talked to Geeta, she said, 'Why not give Neela Patel also a call in Leicester? Didn't she say that she specialised in visa cases?'

Neela assured them that their case should have a very good chance in appeal. As she herself was also involved with the law society charity, she offered to speak to them.

A date was set for the adjudication five weeks later. Ashok met with the lawyer from the law society charity an hour before the meeting over a cup of coffee outside.

He said, 'Your case is simple. It's just some low-ranking British officer in a foreign country feeling too powerful, using refusal as the default position and making this kind of decision knowing that most people will not consider appealing.'

A retired air vice-marshal was the adjudicator. The Home Office read out the determination letter from the High Commission. Then Ashok was asked to give his evidence. Apart from giving his personal details, he explained, as his lawyer from the charity had suggested, that a few years back both his wife's parents had come over for a few weeks to them for a holiday and went back within a few weeks.

The adjudicator looked at Ashok with a pleasant smile on his face and soon gave his decision, saying, 'I am satisfied on the balance of probability that what is intended is indeed a family visit and I therefore direct that the appellants be granted entry clearance as visitors.'

The whole hearing process took less than twenty minutes.

Ashok sent a telegram to Calcutta from the nearest post office and then had a telephone chat with Jiten in their house. As it was already June, the question was whether Jiten could take leave from his college before the end of the summer season in England. Fortunately, he managed to get three weeks' leave in early September and went to purchase their tickets. However, Jiten could not be present at Geeta's postgraduate ceremony in London in July and as Kabita was now over two years old, the price of the tickets for them was going to be higher.

Chapter Fifteen

1992: Raju and Tina

Raju had always enjoyed their yearly family trip to different seashores in the south of England. This summer, they were going to spend a few days near Bournemouth. Now a teenager, Raju was a strapping lad and definitely big for his years. After their leisurely breakfast in the hotel, they all headed for the beach. Ashok was in his t-shirt and shorts. Geeta was wearing light-coloured trousers and a t-shirt over her bikini. All of them were wearing their sandals. Neither Geeta nor Ashok was keen on sunbathing, but both of them enjoyed walking around the beach, watching the gentle waves crashing onto the shore and the children playing in the sand. Ashok helped Raju to make a really large sandcastle with a deep moat all around.

'You are getting too old to make sandcastles,' mocked Ashok.

'You are never too old to make sandcastles,' Raju replied, and then after a while said, 'I am going for a swim in the sea.'

'Wait, I will come with you too!' shouted Geeta as she took off her outer clothes.

Ashok watched them with intense pride.

Soon they came back and after Geeta had dried herself, she asked Ashok, 'Why don't you go for a swim yourself?'

'Maybe a bit later,' he replied.

After playing in the sand for a while and some more swimming in the sea, Raju was getting hungry. 'When are we having our lunch, Baba?' he asked.

'Whenever you want. What do you want?' replied Ashok.

'Can I have a chicken burger and chips, please? And no lettuce and all that.'

Ashok smiled and then asked Geeta, 'And for you?'

'I will come with you and see what they have got,' she replied. Gathering their towels in a bag, Raju decided to follow them slowly as well. Two clearly drunken men covered in tattoos with sunburn all over their bare upper bodies were coming out from the shops. One of them looked at Ashok and Geeta after coming almost in touching distance and said, 'Hey, Paki. What are you lot doing here? You don't need a tan.'

The other guy joined in, laughing with him and sniggering at Ashok and Geeta.

From behind them, Raju now came in front. 'Why don't you leave us alone and go back to your drinking?' he said to them.

The two of them now turned on Raju, but before a fight could break out a few other people from inside the shop came out and separated them quickly.

During their lunch, Geeta said, 'You have to learn to ignore these remarks, Raju.'

'Why should I let anyone get away with insulting us? And they were making racist remarks,' Raju replied.

'I think you are both right to some extent,' replied Ashok, and then added, 'There is no reason to get into unnecessary trouble. And there is a law in this country against racism.'

'But the police and the law are not everywhere to check on us, Baba. I have not told you how many times I have been sniggered at because of my colour by not only the boys in the school but also people in the street. Both of you tell me to always stand up for what is right.'

'You need to stand up against injustice but that does not mean getting into a fight each time with ignorant people,' replied Ashok

'Let's finish our lunch. I want to go back to swimming. We can talk later,' said Geeta.

In his comprehensive school, Raju was popular as a keen sportsman. Ashok was proud when, at the age of fifteen, Raju was selected for the local club's under-seventeen cricket team. Raju, however, enjoyed rugby more than cricket. Ashok enjoyed watching him train at the cricket nets in the club. The usual club members all knew him as a local GP. Occasionally he would put on pads and gloves and let his son and other bowlers bowl at him.

'You should play for our Sunday team, doc. We have three divisions. You will easily fit in the third division, or even in the second,' the club coach said to him.

'Thanks. I would have loved that, but Sunday is the only free day after my work that I have got with my family. I won't be popular at home if I spend all day outside playing cricket,' replied Ashok.

When it came to choosing subjects for his O-level Raju chose English literature, economics, history, geography, and Spanish, along with his core subjects.

'You need to spend more time with your studies now that your exams are getting nearer,' Geeta said to him.

'But Ma, the exam is not until the end of May. This is the rugby season, and also time for indoor cricket net practice,' replied Raju, and looked for support towards Ashok, who was trying to make himself look busy reading his newspaper.

'Well you have to work harder to get everything in, I suppose,' Ashok replied.

Raju thought his O-level exams had gone quite well. The evening after his last exam, he went out with some of his friends, three boys and four girls, to the town. Apart from his all-round qualities, Raju's

228

skin colour was another thing that always attracted the girls. He did not have a regular girlfriend but several of them fancied him.

'Even after a week in the sun, I will never get tan anywhere like you,' he was often told by the girls.

After getting some ice cream from the local shop, Raju's group went to the park. Sitting on a bench, the boys and girls were chatting happily at the end of their exams. One of the boys had started kissing his girlfriend while others were teasing them. Raju was sitting next to one of the girls who held his hand.

While passing by them, a family of two women in their fifties commented loudly enough for everyone to hear, 'I don't think that sort of thing should be allowed, especially between the races. No wonder the country is going downhill these days.'

The girl who was holding Raju's hand got up and wanted to confront the women, but Raju stopped her.

'Some people are so bigoted. I am ashamed of my country,' said the girl.

Others agreed with her, but Raju replied, 'Don't worry about some stupid remarks. I hear them so often that not only is my skin dark, but it has also got thicker.' Then, to lighten the situation, he put his arm out near the girl, saying, 'I mean it, honestly. Feel it.'

Everyone laughed.

After getting A's in all his subjects, Raju decided to take history, economics, and English literature for his A-levels. Although he managed to carry on with his sports, he needed to spend more time now with his studies. A year later, his school advised him to apply for Oxford or Cambridge. Raju chose to apply to both places, as well as to Manchester as a back-up. After his interview in Cambridge, he was coming back by train. The train was almost empty in the mid-afternoon. He was sitting in a coupe by himself. In one of the stations, a family with two young children got on the train. As the train was starting to move, the children rushed to take a seat opposite the window by Raju.

The father sternly told the children, 'Come out of this compartment. We are going to the next one.' Then, as they were going, he said to his wife, 'I am not going to be sitting next to a brownie for the next hour on the train.'

After his interviews, a few weeks later he got offers from both Cambridge and Oxford, subject to grades. He did not need an interview for Manchester.

Before his A-level exams, Raju had stopped playing sports for a few weeks. He thought his exams had gone reasonably well and was glad to be able to start playing cricket and rugby again.

One evening during dinner, after coming back from a game of cricket, he said, 'Baba, today I got five wickets and scored fifty not out. We won.'

Ashok said, 'Wow! Five wickets and fifty runs in the same match—that was always my fantasy. Never happened, of course. India won the world cup beating the mighty West Indies in England a few years back. Both my dreams have come true now. '

While they were talking afterwards about the chances of the visiting Indian cricket team and about a young prodigy named Sachin Tendulkar, Geeta smiled tenderly at both of them before saying, 'Do either of you pass the Norman Tebbit test now that India is playing England here?'

They just laughed.

Raju got an A* in all three of his subjects and took entry in Cambridge. Ashok and Geeta wrote to their families in Calcutta with the news. They replied saying that he was fulfilling their families' dreams.

In the next three years, Raju thrived in his college, especially loving the atmosphere of freedom living away from his parents. He became a member of the debating club, as well as being a regular member of the college cricket team. He had tried rowing a couple of times because some his friends were doing it, but soon realised it was not the sport for him. He passed his BA with Honours before taking a master's in Political Studies. His parents had already been to his graduation ceremony but were almost in tears when they attended his master's ceremony in the grand hall. Raju was offered PhD studies in political science in the same college and finished his thesis within two years. By this time, he had an English girlfriend named Tina from Sussex who was also studying politics in the same college.

He wanted to do his second PhD in the States and was offered a place in Harvard University. It was the year after the 9/11 Twin Towers bombing when he was travelling to USA. He was by now sporting a beard and a moustache. With his coloured skin and current look, it took him considerable time to get through the US immigration with his papers being examined repeatedly.

Raju thrived in the atmosphere of Harvard. Being a keen cricketer, he had a go with the baseball team. He found the game too lame compared to cricket but his big hitting earned him a place in the college team. He could never stop giggling to himself when the pompom girls were coming alive with their routine as soon as someone hit a homerun.

Tina came over for a holiday in the summer and they travelled in the States for a few weeks. For both, their special favourite was Yellowstone National Park.

Raju had been offered another fellowship in Harvard, but he told Tina, to her relief, that he wanted to go back to England as soon as possible.

Back in Cambridge, he got a lecturer post in his old college in Cambridge. By now Tina was completing her master's. Soon Raju proposed to Tina and was engaged. Together they had visited Ashok and Geeta a few times over the last three years and had only twice been to Tina's family.

Tina's family took them out to a restaurant in the town to celebrate. They had a table in the corner of the restaurant.

As Raju was returning from the toilet at the other end of the place, someone from a table nearby shouted, 'Hey, waiter! Can I have a drink? We are waiting a long time here.'

'Sure. Get one, because we have already got ours,' replied Raju, before joining his English girlfriend at the table nearby.

'What were they saying to you?' asked Tina.

'The usual thing. Never mind. I am starving,' replied Raju.

Tina's parents were shocked to hear from Tina that both she and Raju were often taunted by people in public because of their different racial backgrounds.

Raju and Tina got married in a registry office. This was the best day in Geeta and Ashok's lives in the country. When Tina first had a son, and a couple of years later a daughter, they were over the moon. Without seeming to be too intrusive, they visited their grandchildren as often as they could and wished Raju and Tina could visit with them in their house more often.

Chapter Sixteen

2000: The RAF pilot

'Mr Rawat?' called Ashok, opening his cubicle door. An eighty-year-old turbaned Sikh gentleman came through, walking ramrod-straight and wearing a RAF tie. After he sat down, Ashok asked about his problem.

'The last couple of weeks I have been feeling dizzy when I get up and sometimes I also feel quite lightheaded. So I thought I'd better get it checked out.'

After asking a few more questions, Ashok checked his blood pressure and said, 'Your blood pressure is quite high, Mr Rawat. When was the last time you saw anyone?'

'I don't think I have seen a doctor since I broke my leg during the war,' he replied.

'Well, your pressure is quite high. I am going to start you on some medicine and we will check you again in two weeks.'

Before leaving, Mr Rawat asked, 'Doctor, you look like an Indian. I was born in India too. Where are you from?'

'I was born in Nairobi but I am from Calcutta,' replied Ashok.

'My uncle was in Calcutta. He was stationed in Fort William.'

'Was he in the army then?'

'Yes. Listen, doctor, I can see the surgery is teeming with people at the moment. I will see you in two weeks and maybe then we will have more time to talk,' said Mr Rawat as he walked towards the receptionist.

Ashok learned more about Mr Rawat during his next few visits to his surgery. Anil Rawat was born in 1919 near Dehradun in North India. His father served in the district magistrate's office in the town as a clerk. The only son of his parents, Anil, after finishing school, went to college in Delhi. His father, a loyal servant of the British, wanted him to become a lawyer and go to England to train as barrister. However, in Delhi, Anil got the taste of flying and joined the local flying club. After six months he got his Indian commercial pilot's licence and found a job as a pilot with a local airline.

Only six months later, the war broke out in Europe. Anil was immediately interested when he found an advertisement asking for pilots to join the Royal Air Force. He went to his father in Dehradun on the same day and asked his permission.

'This is an opportunity for me serve the Raj in their time of need, and also I can fly to many places in the world.'

While his mother cried, his father, always a faithful servant of the Raj, agreed with his son.

Anil and only twenty or so other Indians were accepted and started their training as commissioned officers of the Royal Air Force. He felt proud to be amongst the elite band of pilots in India. Chacha Singh, older than him by only eleven years, was already known worldwide for his solo flight from England to India and narrowly missing out on the Aga Khan Prize. He was his hero in the group. After a short training period in India, the group travelled by boat for England. As officers of the Royal Air Force, all were eligible to travel first-class with individual cabins.

A Sikh RAF officer in wartime England was a rare sight. People were always respectful of an RAF officer. In the evenings, cinema halls and restaurants did not want money from them.

Often people saluted Mr Rawat and called him 'sir'.

'You know what impressed me most? In spite of all the carnage going on during the Blitz, the German bombings in the country, British people showed no panic. They were really courageous.'

Stationed near Croydon, Anil was chosen to fly fighter aircraft in the Royal Air Force.

'Within the first year, a quarter of our Indian pilots were killed.'

After flying several sorties during the war, on his way back from France after escorting a bomber, Anil's plane was hit by enemy fire. He just about managed to fly his damaged plane to the English shore but broke his left leg after jumping off with a parachute. By the time he was discharged from the hospital, the war was over.

By this time, his father had retired and his mother was very ill with kala-azar in India. He returned back to India and after India became independent he joined the Indian Air Force. His father unfortunately soon passed away from a stroke. His mother also died within a year. Anil got married three years later. His wife, Kapila, was sadly diagnosed with blood cancer only a year after their marriage. In spite of the best treatment, she died four years later.

'When I retired in 1975, I wanted to settle down somewhere I could be comfortable. To me, in India, even if you have servants, everyday life is struggle. Nothing goes smoothly. There is no discipline or order. I had fond memories of England during the war. I had no one close in India. I decided to come to live in Great Britain.'

Anil was allowed to enter the UK in the same year as the Government's 'honoured guest'.

'When I first arrived, the local people generally didn't like us coloured people. Once, I remember being confronted by a white neighbour living in the same street as me.

He was telling me, "You coloured lots are good for nothing. You come over here and take our jobs, and we don't like you."

I told him that it was my country too. I had fought for it and if we had been late in getting to the battlefront, this country would have been in the hands of the Germans. I told him not to give me any trouble as I had sacrificed a lot for this country. The man apologised to me in the end, saying he didn't know.'

'These days, many people here see an Indian with a turban and assume he does not understand or speak English. So many times I had to ignore rude comments behind me from people who thought I did not understand what they were saying.'

'This is modern England. They are supposed to pretend that they don't notice certain things, such as whites and Asians or blacks,' replied Ashok.

Mr Rawat added, with some sadness, 'Do you know, people in public duty like bus drivers or even police constables in the street will be rude to me or almost ignore me, and then be so polite and

235

helpful to white old people much younger than me? During the war I would have been called "sir" by their grandfathers!'

His blood pressure was now under better control. Ashok advised him to continue with the medicines and to make an appointment to be seen again in six months unless there was any problem before that.

Ashok saw Mr Rawat again about five months later. He was going back to his car after a house call in the neighbourhood in the afternoon. As he was walking on the pavement, he noticed Mr Rawat was attending to his small flower bed in the front of his house.
'Hello, Mr Rawat. I did not know this was your house,' said Ashok, standing by the fence.
'Hello, doctor. So nice to see you. Please come in for a cup of tea,' said Mr Rawat, opening the front gate.
As Ashok had no more house calls to make that afternoon and his surgery was not due to start for another hour and a half, he said, 'Thank you, that will be nice,' before following him into the house.

The small living room was neat and tidy. There was a framed picture of the Queen over the fireplace, as well as a picture of Mr Rawat with his wife at an earlier age and a couple of pictures of himself with his squadron in front of a Spitfire fighter on the other walls. After bringing both of them a pot of tea, milk, sugar, two cups, and some plain biscuits on a plate, Mr Rawat sat next to Ashok.
'You must have enjoyed the fiftieth anniversary celebration of VE day at the cenotaph, and surely you're now looking forward to the sixtieth anniversary in a few years?' asked Ashok, sipping his tea.
Not looking directly towards Ashok, Mr Rawat replied in a forlorn voice, 'I have never been invited to any of these official celebrations.' Then he added, 'I have privately gone to the cenotaph many times and laid flowers in the memory of my fallen comrades. I wrote to the Ministry of Defence asking why I was not invited to the fiftieth anniversary celebration. No one has replied—so far.'
Ashok looked at him, genuinely shocked, and said, 'Are you serious?'

Mr Rawat nodded sadly.

After few more minutes of conversation, Ashok said, 'It was great talking to you. I learned a lot. But I have to go now, Mr Rawat. Thank you very much for inviting me. We will see each other again soon.'

In the next few months, Ashok had a few more visits at Mr Rawat's house and many interesting chats with him.

Mr Rawat said one day, 'Did you know that in the Second World War, the British Indian Army, which was a volunteer army anyway, was the largest volunteer army in the history? Two and a half million fought in the war for the British, fighting on three continents in Africa, Europe, and Asia. Eighty-seven thousand Indian servicemen lost their lives, while another thirty-five thousand were wounded, and over sixty-seven thousand became prisoners of war.'

Then he added, 'They were awarded about four thousand decorations, including thirty-one getting either the Victoria Cross or the George Cross. Field Marshal Claude Auchinleck, the commander-in-chief of the Indian Army, said at the time that the British "couldn't have come through both wars if they hadn't had the Indian Army." Even the British prime minister, Winston Churchill, paid tribute to "the unsurpassed bravery of Indian soldiers and officers."'

Ashok replied, 'I also know from the history that up to two and a half million died in India due to the war-related famine and diseases at the time. In 1943, there was this major famine in Bengal that led to millions of deaths by starvation. Churchill declined to provide emergency food relief.'

Mr Rawat said, 'All the cotton parachutes used for dropping supplies in the Eastern Front in Burma, over four million of them, were produced in India.'

Ashok said, 'This is when the Indian National Congress demanded independence before it would help Britain and London refused. During the "Quit India" campaign in August 1942, tens of thousands of its leaders were imprisoned by the British for the duration of the war.'

As Mr Rawat poured him more tea in his cup, he said with sadness, 'This country has changed so much now. Do you think it is getting worse, doctor? In the last few weeks, I had rubbish pushed through my letter box. And once someone threw a brick at the window. You can see it's still cracked. I hope you don't face this kind of racial prejudice in your work.'

He went on to say, 'The BNP are now using the Spitfire as a symbol of their party. They forget that people from different backgrounds helped in the Second World War. I am proof of this—I was flying a Spitfire!'

The next time Ashok saw Mr Rawat was in his surgery three months later. It turned out that he had had to attend the A&E a week earlier with an injury to his face and needed his stitches to be removed and to be checked over in the GP surgery after.

Apparently, he was out for his usual evening walk across the park from his house. He did not know it, but only an hour or so earlier a BNP rally had finished in the town. A small group of the supporters were going back home through the park when they found this elderly man with a turban taking a stroll. After throwing verbal abuse, one of them had pushed him to the ground before the rest started kicking him. Fortunately, people in the park had come to his rescue and called for an ambulance. Ashok found Mr Rawat still shaken from the incident.

'This is not the England I knew,' he said, before leaving.

Ashok came across Mr Rawat for the very last time when he had to attend his house on an out-of-hours call. Apparently, he had been having mild pain in his chest since lunchtime. He did not feel well enough to come to the surgery and definitely was not keen to call for an ambulance unnecessarily. When Ashok arrived at his house he called for an ambulance immediately as Mr Rawat was barely conscious and appeared to have had a massive heart attack. Before the ambulance arrived, he passed away in front of Ashok in his beloved England.

Chapter Seventeen

2013: A Fijian - Indian British Soldier

Tina had been slightly curious about this young woman who had been bringing her one-year-old daughter to the same nursery where her own son of the same age had been going three times a week. She found her always withdrawn, but after a few weeks of exchanging smiles, the opportunity came for Tina to talk to this woman named Kyla. After dropping off her son at the nursery with a hug and kiss, Tina had decided to go to the coffee shop opposite. As she had settled down with her coffee and the newspaper, Kyla came in through the door. Tina indicated the empty chair opposite her to Kyla.

After ordering her coffee, Kyla said, 'It breaks your heart to leave them there, even for a few hours.'

'But have you noticed that although sometimes they cry a bit going in, as soon as you turn your back they are happy playing with each other?'

'That's true,' replied Kyla.

During their talk, it turned out that Kyla's husband has been posted in Afghanistan only last month. She was desperately worried about him, especially with all the news coverage around.

'Do you get a chance to speak to him from time to time?' asked Tina.

'Only for a few minutes on video call once a week at the most.'

Tina and Kyla were soon spending more time together, sometimes even going shopping with their children. Almost a year later, when the news of a British soldier being refused citizenship became a national headline, Tina realised that he was Kyla's husband and heard his story of immigration from Fiji in detail from her.

In 1913, in one of the tea gardens of north Bengal, the British owner called all his estate workers outside his bungalow.

He talked enthusiastically to them, saying, 'We need some healthy working families to work in this sunny island far away in the sea in our new sugar plantations. In a way, this could be the dream life for you, compared to the miserable weather up here in the foothills of the mountains.'

The workers, all bonded labourers, listened with some interest.

'Your pay will be better and you will be bringing up your families on a warm, wonderful island.'

There was no real protest when twenty recently bonded young families were selected by the sahib with the help of his diwan.

At the end of his day's work, thirty-year-old Satish went to his hut, which was leaking from its thatched roof after heavy rain. He broke the news to his wife, Deepa, who was feeding their two-year-old son, Kumar.

'We will soon be moving to a better place. Nice and warm, not like this,' he said.

'Are we going back to our village in Birbhum? But we have still four years of bond to work for,' said Deepa, glad to be moving close to their families.

'No, we are going to a new place for sugar farming. It is an island far from here but it's nice and sunny and the work will be easier,' replied Satish.

It turned out that from the surrounding fifteen tea estates, a total of 300 families had been selected for their new life. Following a long journey by foot of nearly forty days being herded like cattle by the agents, they arrived at the Calcutta port. Five children and three adults were very sick from the journey and their families were refused by the agents to take any further part of the journey. Sick and far from home, they were told that they were free to go back to their own villages or to the tea estates if they wanted. Only healthy labourers and their families were loaded into the two relatively new steamships sailing for Fiji. These ships already had nearly a hundred

241

labourers from Madras onboard who were also making the same journey.

Life on these steamships for the labourers, although crowded, was not too bad. A medical supervisor ensured that their health was attended to. The journey in the calm waters of the Indian Ocean and then on the South Pacific to the small island of Fiji was long but not too arduous. Satish and Deepa enjoyed being on the deck with their son Kumar, occasionally being lucky enough to watch sea creatures like dolphins swimming by their boats.

All the labourers were pleased to have been brought to a sunny island where there were many people of Indian origin. The contracts of the indentured labourers, also called 'girmits', required them to work in Fiji for a minimum period of five years. After a further five years of work as girmitya, they would have the choice of returning to India at their own expense or remaining in Fiji. The great majority opted to stay because they could not afford the fare to return with their low pay, or sometimes received no pay at all with a number of excuses by the British. Sometimes they were just flatly refused to be sent back.

After the expiry of their girmits, Satish and Deepa, like a few others, leased a small plot of land from the local Fijians and developed their own sugarcane fields and a small cattle farmlet.

'If this goes well, we should be able to make enough money to buy a small business in the next town in a couple of years,' said Satish during his dinner.

'We can then send Kumar to a good school there as well,' replied Deepa.

In the next few years, the family made enough money and one day Satish asked Deepa, 'Do you think we should go back to India? We can just about afford it now.'

'I will do whatever you decide, but we are well settled here now. The neighbors are mostly Indian. And most of all, Kumar is enjoying his school here and doing well,' replied Deepa.

'True. And we have to start all over again there anyway, and neither of us is getting any younger,' agreed Satish.

Kumar, after finishing his schooling with good marks, wanted to join the new and only medical school in the capital, Suva. But the competition for just forty places was tough and he missed out narrowly. Still interested to continue with medical practice, he joined the Native Medical Practitioners programme and his parents were extremely proud when he got his certificate from the missionary doctors. He soon started his own practice. With his earnings, he persuaded his parents to give up their cattle farming and to continue with only their steady business in the town.

During the war Kumar joined the Fiji Defence Force as a medical orderly in 1940, initially under the command of the New Zealand Defence Force. The main purpose of this unit at the time was to protect vulnerable points such as fuel dumps and important government buildings in the Suva area. Fiji was not affected much in the early days of the Second World War but it all changed with the Japanese attack on Pearl Harbor. During his assignment in a neighbouring Pacific island, despite twisting his ankle during landing, Kumar gallantly continued to attend to the injured allied soldiers and was later awarded a service medal in recognition.

Fiji-born Indian Balaram had grown up looking up at the proudly displayed service medal and photo of his grandfather, Kumar, in military uniform in their house. Both Balaram's grandparents had died when he was only a child. After finishing school, he trained for four years at the Fiji Institute of Technology before qualifying in 1997 at the age of twenty-three. As a skilled engineer, he had no problem finding a decent job in Fiji, but worried about increasing political tension in the country between indigenous Fijians and those of Indian origin, he started looking for options abroad. While he was considering an offer from South Africa to work as a mine engineer, he found with interest a recruitment drive in the British army from Commonwealth citizens.

One afternoon, he was sitting in a coffee shop waiting for some of his friends to join him when a young girl with a backpack came in. As there was no other empty table in the shop, Balaram indicated to the girl that she could take the empty chair at his table.

'Thank you. I am dying for a drink. It's so hot outside,' she said as she put down her rucksack.

'I am Balaram. My friends call me Ballu,' he replied.

'I am Kyla. I am going to get a drink. Do you want one?'

'No, please, let me get you one. What do you want? A coffee or a beer?'

'Oh, thanks so much. May I just have one of those cold green coconut waters, please?'

Balaram returned with another cup of coffee for himself and a green coconut with a straw for Kyla.

'It's so refreshing,' said Kyla after a few sips.

'Have you tried kava, our national drink, yet?'

'No, what is it?'

'Kava is a beverage which will numb your mouth and throat and calm you. After few drinks, you'll feel a buzz.'

'Is it alcohol?'

'No, it is made from the powdered root of a pepper tree. You drink it in a ceremony where people gather around and drink from coconut shells among friends with guitar playing and singing. You clap once before and three times after each drink.'

'Sounds wonderful. Now you have to help me find a place where I can join a ceremony like that,' said Kyla.

'I would be happy to take you to one this Saturday, if you want.'

The kava ceremony by the beach with Balaram's friends was one of the highlights of Kyla's trip to Fiji. Balaram found that Kyla had been on a working holiday picking fruit in Australia and was in Fiji for only a week's holiday before she returned home to England.

'What do you do in England?' asked Balaram.

'I trained as a hairdresser. I always wanted to travel. Once my parents finally divorced, I just wanted to get away for a while and my father was kind enough to lend me money for my fare. What do you do, Ballu?'

244

'I am an engineer.'

Before Kyla left at the airport, she kissed Balaram in the mouth for long time and said, 'I genuinely hope to see you again soon.'

A week after Kyla left, Balaram went to the British overseas army recruitment office and joined. He e-mailed Kyla with the news, and she was thrilled to bits.

'If I join the British army and serve for four years, I am going to be allowed to have British citizenship,' Balaram explained to his parents, and then added, 'And it's also something Granddad would have been proud of.'

'But I will be scared of you fighting in the battle zone,' replied his mother.

'I am a mechanical engineer and will not be fighting in the front line,' Balaram tried to convince her.

Balaram came to the UK for orientation training for a few months before being posted to Afghanistan. While in the UK, Kyla and Balaram saw each other regularly. After fighting for more than six months in Afghanistan, both of them were relieved when he was sent to the Falklands. Although it was thousands of miles away, it was not a war zone. On his return to the UK, he proposed to Kyla and a few months later, before his next posting to Iraq, they decided to get married.

While he was posted in Iraq, he received a video telephone message from Kyla asking, 'When are you coming back? I am pregnant.'

This message from Kyla kept him going during his posting in Iraq, as although not physically injured, he was severely mentally traumatised by the events unfolding in front of his eyes close to the battlefield.

Within three months of his return to the UK, Kyla gave birth to a baby girl they named Annie.

'She looks so beautiful, much like you, except her colour is going to be more like mine,' said Balaram, holding Annie.

Soon he was sent away for another posting for six months, this time to Cyprus.

He was besotted with their young daughter after returning from his posting and was extremely upset at being told, after only a few months, that he would soon be posted back in Afghanistan for another six months.

While driving his wife and their baby girl back to the barracks one afternoon, he was stopped by the police and was charged for dangerous driving when his car lightly bumped into the back of another vehicle. The driver had stopped suddenly to ask directions from a pedestrian and claimed whiplash injury.

'I am going to fight this in the court. There was no accident and no one was hurt,' said Balaram stubbornly.

Before the case came to the court, Balaram had already been sent on his way to the fighting zone in Afghanistan and he was convicted in his absence. In Afghanistan, he was recommended for promotion by his officer for exceptional diligence under difficulty.

Following his return to the UK, he applied for British citizenship for himself, now that he had served in the British army for almost five years. But for the UK Border Agency, when it came to assessing his application for citizenship, his criminal conviction for dangerous driving was reason enough to refuse him British citizenship.

Balaram was already offered a job as an engineer in the railways soon after he had left his army post. But now, without his British citizenship, he was not considered British enough for the job. Without any job, he was not British enough to claim benefits for himself, although he had been British enough to pay thousands in taxes and National Insurance in the last few years. He was also given a deadline for deportation by the Home Office within three months.

Fortunately for himself and Kyla, a few national newspapers and a charity for veterans took up their case. Following a few weeks of national outcry, including from the service groups, their community, and his local MP, the Home Office agreed to introduce a new rule allowing Commonwealth soldiers with relatively minor convictions to be allowed to live and work in the UK.

Later, Balaram contested his driving charge in higher court and the decision against him was quashed.

'Thank God that we still have free press and enough decent people in this country to stand up against this kind of discrimination, although I am sure these mental scars of ours, especially for Balaram, will take a long time to heal,' said Kyla. She then added to Tina, 'We sincerely hope that our Annie will grow up in a world better than this.'

Chapter Eighteen

May 2016: The award

After the last week's May bank holiday washout, with wind and rain, it was very sunny today. In the garden, both the cherry trees were already in full bloom in early May. The tulips were still holding up.

'Must do the lawn after I come back from the meeting,' thought Geeta as she gathered her post from the post box by the gate. She was thinking about how to approach this afternoon's meeting with the local mayor, which was going to be about asking for further support for resources to raise awareness for the disabled children in local schools.

There was a large white envelope along with a few other pieces of post, plus the usual ads about pizza shops, cheaper TV and broadband packages, and a leaflet from the Britain for British party. She put them on the coffee table before carrying on with hoovering the living room. Then, once settled on the sofa with a cup of tea, she started checking her post. The telephone rang in the hall.

'Hello?'

'Is this Mrs Geeta Basu?'

'Yes. What can I do for you?'

'This is the mayor's office. I am just confirming that the mayor will be happy to meet you at three thirty this afternoon.'

'Thank you. We will be there. You know that there will be three of us?'

'That is fine. See you later. Bye for now.'

At last, she sat down with her cup of tea and opened the letters. She put aside the ads. The letter from the county council was asking them to confirm their electoral register status. The letter from the bank stated that their five-year savings deposit was coming to its end and the future rates may be different. The white envelope was stamped 'ER' with a crown on top, and instead of a postal stamp, there was a red ink stamp from Buckingham Palace.

She had received a similar envelope almost two years back inviting her to a special reception given by the Queen at Buckingham Palace for the charity care workers from all parts of the UK. It was one of the best moments of her life and she would never forget the thrill of going through the gates of Buckingham Palace while hundreds of tourists were outside the rails excitedly taking photographs of the palace.

After she had walked past the gate and through the side of the front part of the palace building, which all those visitors to London take photographs of, there was a large courtyard. Then, through a beautiful staircase, she had entered the stunning main palace hall. She had wandered around the royal rooms and their treasures with fellow charity workers from all around the country, none of whom she had known before. Ladies-in-waiting and other officers of the royal household had mingled with them.

Then there was a hush in the big hall and someone came around to arrange them in groups of about ten, asking them to wait for Her Majesty. The Queen came across the room, stopping in front of the small groups and actually talking to them. Geeta's heart was fluttering when Her Majesty stopped in front of their group and asked her about her work. Geeta mentioned her work with the disabled group.

'Very important work. We are glad to have people like you in our country,' said Her Majesty, before moving on to the next group of people.

The lasting memory of that day for Geeta was how small the Queen was, yet how regal she was in her appearance.

The envelope today was marked 'IMMEDIATE' and the instruction was to return it if not delivered to the Central Chancery of the Orders of Knighthood, St James's Palace in London. Trying to clear the coffee table in front of her before opening this with trembling hands, Geeta spilt some tea on the county council letter. She quickly got up to get rid of the tea mug and clear the table. The letter inside the white envelope was from the ceremonial officer at the Cabinet Office. It said, in strict confidence, that the prime minister was recommending that Her Majesty may graciously approve her to be appointed a member of the Most Excellent Order of the British Empire in the 2016 Queen's Birthday Honours List. With shaking hands, she tried to read the rest of the letter but everything was hazy.

She dialled Ashok in the surgery immediately but he was with a patient. A few minutes later, when he called back, Geeta tried to explain that she had received a letter from Buckingham Palace and could he come home immediately.

'Sounds really interesting! I have two more patients waiting to be seen. I will be home within an hour.'

During a hurriedly put together lunch, they looked at each other in stunned silence for a while.

'Wow! You are going to be an MBE! I am so very proud of you. You are going to meet the Queen again!'

'We are not supposed to tell anybody until the list is officially published. I still cannot believe it. We must call Raju immediately though. Do you think he is taking a class now?'

The call to Raju went straight to voicemail.

After leaving a text message for him to call back as soon as possible, Ashok said, 'You'd better send the acceptance form as soon as possible. I know we cannot tell anyone but we must celebrate this evening. Where do you want to go? I must go back to the surgery now. I will try to get away early this evening if I can. I am so proud of you.'

After he kissed Geeta, Ashok said, 'In fact, I am going to text Raju to come home this evening with Tina and the grandchildren. Cambridge is only just over an hour and a half's drive anyway. Today is Friday and they can spend the weekend here with us.'

'By all means, ask them to come tonight if they can. It would be lovely to see Garry and young Sonia. We can go out somewhere nice tomorrow. I have a meeting late this afternoon anyhow.'

She dropped her acceptance letter in the prepaid envelope in the post box outside the mayor's office.

The newly elected mayor listened to the three of them with interest and promised to do his best to support them, and then added, 'You know that our budget is being cut to the bone every year by the government. But this is an important project and should not really cost much in the way of money. The education department should be able to help you to liaise better with the schools in our county.'

His secretary arranged for them to have a meeting the following week with the officer responsible for the education and learning department of the county council. After their meeting was over, the other two suggested that they stop for coffee in the nearby shop.

'I'd better get going. My grandchildren are coming over this evening,' said Geeta.

'Have a great weekend with them, Geeta. We will catch up next week before our meeting with the education guy,' said one of them as the two went into the coffee shop.

It was now too late to mow the lawn, so Geeta just watered the plants before going inside to tidy up the house. Ashok texted to say not to bother with cooking for tonight and that he would order some takeaway when Raju and Tina were home.

Ashok came home early with a big bouquet of flowers. Later in the evening, Raju and Tina arrived with their children. Sonia was fast asleep in her car seat and Ashok took her straight to her bed. Garry woke up and once out of the car straight came running to Geeta with a card he had made for her.

It said, in multi-coloured pencil writing, 'MY DIDA. QUEENS FABARIT' with a picture of a crown inside. After his dinner, he soon went to bed too. Raju ordered a Chinese takeaway, Geeta's favourite, for the four of them.

The next morning after breakfast, Tina and Geeta were sipping coffee on the couches on their decking by the garden. Sonia and Garry were being chased around by Ashok. Raju had started mowing the lawn.

Tina asked, 'How do you feel about the award, Ma?'

Geeta liked that Tina called her 'Ma' like Raju, which was unlike the usual practice here of calling mothers–in-law by their names.

'Excited and very honoured, of course. But look at them running around there. What could ever be a better award for anybody than those two?'

'I can't wait to tell my parents. They will be so happy.'

'We are not officially supposed to tell anyone until the Queen's birthday.'

'I will ask them to keep it secret.'

Later, they went to a countryside restaurant for their lunch where there was a children's play area outside. They chose to have a table outside near the play area.

The waiter came over as they were all congratulating Geeta. 'Is it someone's birthday today? We can bring some birthday cake with candles later if you want?' he offered, looking at them.

'No, thank you. We will just have the menu,' replied Ashok, looking at Geeta and trying to hide his proud smile.

In the afternoon at home, they sat relaxing in their sitting room while Geeta was playing inside with the grandchildren. Tina brought some coffee for Ashok and Raju and sat by them. The news on the television was about the staffing crisis in NHS hospitals.

Raju said, 'Baba, did you see in the newspaper recently that the NHS is sending managers to India looking to find trained doctors to make up for the shortages here?'

'It's going full circle, like when I came over here,' replied Ashok.

Tina said, 'I also recently saw a link saying that a few years back someone sent two applications to different hospitals in the country with the same CV, but one had an Indian surname and the other a British surname. The ones with Indian surnames did not get shortlisted in most places, whereas the ones with British surnames did. I think they published this as a paper in the BMJ.'

'At least I am not looking for a job in the hospital now,' laughed Ashok, and then said, 'I am going inside to see what Sonya and Garry are up to.'

'I understand that although only two per cent of the population in the UK is Indian, almost ten per cent of doctors are from India,' Raju added.

The next day, when it was it was time for Raju and Tina to go back with their children, Sonia, who was on Geeta's lap, held on to her tightly and said, 'I am going to stay with Dida.'

A week before the Queen's official birthday, the local TV station telephoned Geeta to congratulate her and asked if they could set up an interview with her before the official announcement. It was agreed that she would be interviewed in the local community hall with the disabled groups and a few other members of her charity, with comments from the group on the charity's work, although the MBE would not be mentioned to them at that time. The documentary would go out on the eve of the official announcement of the Queen's Birthday Honours List.

Geeta did not expect that her TV appearance this evening would have gone like this. She had dressed in a simple but elegant blue sari and blouse and had the thin necklace Ashok had bought for her on their last anniversary around her neck. With a small bindi on her forehead and with only a touch of sindur between the partings of her hair, she was ready. Ashok had put on a dark suit and a smart tie.
After giving a quick polish to his shoes, he asked, 'Is it okay, you think? Of course, it's not about me this evening, I know.'
'Wait, a text from Raju. "Ma, very proud of you. Go and stun them." Let me send a quick reply.'
'Shall I get the car?'
'No. It's only a ten-minute walk and it's a lovely evening,' replied Geeta.

On their way to the hall, Geeta, holding hands with Ashok, noticed that about twenty metres away a few young men and a woman were drinking on the footpath and shouting abuse at the passing cars. All but one were no older than their early twenties. The other man was probably in his forties.

'Shall we cross over to the other side of the road?' asked Ashok.

'No, just ignore them.'

As they came near the group, they were stopped by two of them standing right in front of them.

'You Paki. Fucking Paki, go back to your home!' they were shouting.

In the beginning, Geeta and Ashok were annoyed rather than worried and tried to walk around them. But very soon they were surrounded by this group.

'Are you not a Paki then? So are you one of those Indian cow kissers?' said one as he pushed Ashok.

'Fucking bastards, what are you doing in our country?' said another.

'Wasting the money of our NHS by having everything for free. How many children did you have for free in our hospital then, you bitch? I know you bitches produce large litters.'

'What do you do then? You fucking curry muncher. Sponging money off our country. Are you one of those gas pumpers?' another poked Ashok on his chest.

'I am a doctor,' Ashok tried to murmur before he was pushed to the ground by a couple of them. One kicked him on his back.

'Please let us go,' Geeta tried to say.

The hefty woman, both of her forearms covered in tattoos, came over to her and put her hand over Geeta's forehead, rubbing the sindur and saying, 'You dot-dot bitch. Why are you here in our England? Go back home to your napkin niggers. Why are you wearing a curtain cloth anyway, you fucking cunt?'

As Ashok tried to get up, one of them started punching him. The woman confronting Geeta was joined by a man and they tried to pull off Geeta's sari.

Geeta started screaming out as loudly as she could, 'Help us! Help us, please!'

Two young Polish men were already running towards them from the corner shop opposite and started to fend off these attackers. They were soon joined by two dog walkers, one of whom recognised

Geeta. Soon, more people started arriving and the attackers took off. One of them tried to snatch Geeta's handbag before running off but he was stopped by the people around them.

They ran away to the next lane, shouting, 'Fucking cow kissers, go back home!'

Geeta was shaking like a leaf.

Ashok, who was bruised from the attack, holding Geeta's hand, asked, 'Do you want to go back home?'

Geeta's eyes filled up with tears. She could not say anything.

'I know we are both in a bad state after this. But I think we should let the community and the local media see how we have been treated just because of our colour.'

Geeta looked towards him for few seconds and then said, 'Let's go there.'

The community hall was packed with disabled people of all ages and their carers. The local charities had not yet been told about Geeta's award but only knew that the local TV wanted to do a programme about the valuable work being done by their charity for the vulnerable people in the society. The TV cameras were already set up and the place was buzzing when Geeta and Ashok walked in looking completely shaken and dishevelled. People in wheelchairs and their carers gathered around them, shocked and concerned to find out what had happened. There was genuine anger from all of them towards the assailants.

One teenage boy with cerebral palsy said, 'I am ashamed of my country.'

Everyone present agreed.

That evening, in their news, the local TV channel featured the earlier attack briefly, which they said was probably racially motivated. Of course, they could not be seen to be taking sides so close to the Brexit referendum. They also kept safe the official secret of Geeta's MBE award for that evening's broadcast.

A few days later, on the Queen's official birthday, the local chronicle published the news of the attack, categorising it as racial, as well as the news of Geeta's award.

Acknowledgements

For the historical evidence in writing this book, leafing through many acclaimed books on Indian immigration to Britain has been extremely valuable. Books such as R Visram: Asians in Britain 400 Years of History, R Ranasinha et al: South Asian's and the shaping of Britain, 1870-1950, M Fischer / S Lahiri and S Thandi: A South Asian History of Britain, R Desai: Indian Immigrants in Britain, R Visram: Ayahs Lascars and Princess, M Fischer: Contraflows to Colonialism, S Lahiri: Indians in Britain. Anglo-Indian encounters and M R Anand: Across the Black Waters are worth mentioning amongst many others.

Personal stories and reflections from friends and families have also helped tremendously in writing the second part of this book.

I am grateful for Peter O'Connor of BespokeBookcovers with the cover design.
Finally, I would like to acknowledge Amazon with their help in publishing this book and open to the public for reading my first fiction.

Printed in Great Britain
by Amazon